SO-BBF-123

DEATH

AMONG THE

ANGELS

JOHN WALTER PUTRE

CHARLES SCRIBNER'S SONS • NEW YORK

COLLIER MACMILLAN CANADA   TORONTO
MAXWELL MACMILLAN INTERNATIONAL
NEW YORK   OXFORD   SINGAPORE   SYDNEY

This is a work of fiction. Names, characters, places, and incidents either are the product of the author's imagination or are used fictitiously. Any resemblance to events or persons, living or dead, is entirely coincidental.

Copyright © 1991 by John Walter Putre

All rights reserved. No part of this book may be reproduced or transmitted in any form or by any means, electronic or mechanical, including photocopying, recording, or by any information storage and retrieval system, without permission in writing from the Publisher.

Charles Scribner's Sons
Macmillan Publishing Company
866 Third Avenue, New York, NY 10022

Collier Macmillan Canada, Inc.
1200 Eglinton Avenue East, Suite 200
Don Mills, Ontario M3C 3N1

Library of Congress Cataloging-in-Publication Data
Putre, John Walter.
Death among the angels / John Walter Putre.
   p.   cm.
ISBN 0-684-19238-1
I. Title.
PS3566.U86D4 1991
813'.54—dc20   90-42242   CIP

10 9 8 7 6 5 4 3 2 1

Printed in the United States of America

DEATH AMONG THE ANGELS

1

The light rain, which had been falling since daybreak, gave the concrete a dark and shiny look. From his table in the Salisbury airport's snack bar, Doll watched as the wheels of the small commuter plane first brushed, then settled onto, the runway.

The plane had touched down right to left. It needed only a quarter of the runway's length to brake to its taxiing speed. Doll watched the water spray up from the pavement as the twin propellers powered up again just enough to keep the aircraft moving forward at a jogger's pace.

Opposite the small terminal, the pilot executed a sharp left turn onto a perpendicular taxi lane. Only then could Doll hear the first buzz of the motors and the fanlike whoosh of the propeller blades. But as the plane drew closer, the sound deepened and intensified until it grew into a throaty, echoing roar.

A final turn—this one to the right—brought the airplane abreast of the only passenger gate. There the hammering exhaust from the engines abruptly ceased and the propellers spun down in a whisper. A door opened in the side of the fuselage. A short flight of steps folded down, and a trickle of passengers began to disembark.

Doll picked her out from the others before she'd crossed half the distance between the plane and the glass-enclosed arrival-departure vestibule.

But then, he had to admit to himself, picking her out wasn't all that impressive a feat.

Ann Raney was slender, fresh despite her journey, and apparently untroubled by the precipitation that greeted her arrival. Her age was somewhere in her early to mid twenties. Time folded back upon itself in a disorienting sense of déjà vu. Doll had to remind himself of the place and the year. She might have been the twin of her older sister—at least as Doll remembered Diana Raney from more than a decade before.

She saw him from the opposite side of the glass at almost the same instant he saw her, and, although she gave no sign of greeting, there was no mistaking the look of recognition in her eyes.

Seconds later, she came through the door of the snack bar and proceeded directly toward Doll's table. Her approach showed not the smallest trace of hesitation.

Doll stood.

She stopped before him and extended her hand.

"Mr. Doll?" The words had the sound of a question, but weren't. "Good morning," she said. She smiled, Doll sensed, more as a matter of form than of pleasure. "I'm Ann Raney, Diana's sister. Thanks for agreeing to meet me."

She was neatly and comfortably dressed in a pair of slip-on canvas shoes, white slacks, and a pink oxford cloth shirt with long sleeves rolled up two cuff lengths at the ends. Her forearms and face were deeply tanned. She carried a dark blue nylon tote bag with the woven strap slung over her shoulder.

Her handshake was firm, as Doll had guessed from her directness that it would be. She met his eyes with the kind of confidence that flows from being attractive and capable, a self-assurance that so easily arises from having met the world in the first round and subdued it—without quite appreciating how many more contended rounds there are to come.

Doll asked if she'd had a good flight.

"From Orlando to Philadelphia," she answered. Her tone and her choice of words cleared the way for qualification. "This last part, in that"—she glanced back over her shoulder toward the turbo-prop commuter—"you can just as well keep."

Ann turned her head and looked around at what she could see of the airport.

"My God, this is a one-horse operation," she said. "I tried to find Salisbury on a map, and I couldn't. I knew you said you lived in Delaware and that the airport was in Maryland. I didn't realize this was Maryland over here, too."

"It's the closest airport with regular commercial connections," Doll explained. "It's just an accident of boundary lines that puts it in the next state."

For a second or two Ann studied Doll while she seemed to grant his answer at least a provisional level of acceptance; then her smile broadened.

"You know, I recognized you as soon as I saw you," she said, insuring that Doll hadn't missed the achievement. "Diana has a picture. Of the both of you. Maybe you remember. You're on a dock somewhere. She's in shorts and a blouse. You've got on swim trunks and a pullover shirt—the kind that has alligators or something on the pocket?"

"There are probably a couple of dozen photographs like that," Doll replied. "I couldn't even guess at where they all are."

All the while her eyes went on with their inspection.

"What's amazing, though, is that, twelve years later, you look so much the same." But then, having made the point, Ann Raney didn't pursue it.

Doll was just as happy with that—letting the past return to the past. The answer he'd given her about the photograph, while not a lie, had certainly skirted the truth. He remembered the dock and what Diana was wearing and even the day that the picture was taken. There were more memories in all of this than he wanted to acknowledge. He nodded toward the chair at the opposite side of the table.

"It's after eleven. There's coffee," he said, "or we could get an early lunch if you like."

"Coffee. But why don't you order it for me?" Ann proposed, putting her stock smile back in place. "I need a minute or two to myself—to comb my hair and wash some of the trip off my face."

By the time she got back to the table, the coffee Doll had ordered for her was getting cool.

"I hope that wasn't too long," she said, taking the seat across from Doll. She didn't wait for him to answer, nor did she seem to expect him to. Her hair was brushed and soft. Her eyes seemed larger. Doll guessed that a reapplication of mascara accounted for the latter change.

She began, keeping her manner businesslike.

"I'll come right to the point so as not to waste your time, Mr. Doll. As I said on the phone, Diana's in trouble." She looked up from her coffee and met Doll's eyes. "Very serious trouble, and I don't know how to help her. She's in jail now. They won't let her make bond. The prosecution made a big deal out of her not having ties to the jurisdiction and not enough assets to hold her there. No ties to anywhere, really. She's being held on a charge of murder."

"Then I take it she already has a lawyer," Doll said. "If she can't pay herself, they've got to give her one. But it's better if she gets her own—and the best she can afford. It's one of the few things that it's smart to mortgage the family farm for."

"It's not that. I know that much myself." Ann glared at Doll; then she sighed and shook her head. "I'm sorry. I didn't mean to be short. Not with you. It's just a habit I've had to get into lately. It's only that I wish it was that simple—as the lawyer, I mean."

She added a half teaspoon of sugar to her coffee, stirred it in,

and tried a sip. She didn't actually grimace, but then neither
was there anything in her expression that implied the slightest
enjoyment.

"Yes, Diana has a lawyer," she explained, this time with
forbearance. "Someone who someone she knows recommended.
She has friends. She's always had those. Somebody talked him
into taking the case on a kind of 'pay what you can now, and
we'll work the rest out later' basis. From what I can tell, he
may even be good—smart enough to know his job and not
somebody who's trying to make points with the system. But he
could be Clarence Darrow reincarnated for all the good it would
do. He can't defend Diana without her help, and she only
barely talks to him."

The obvious question was why. Doll didn't ask it. The best
that he could do now was to let Ann talk at whatever pace she
wanted to set. He took a swallow of his own coffee and waited,
watching her as she gazed through the restaurant windows at the
airfield, staring out across the wet, gray emptiness into space
where there was nothing to see.

"I don't understand her," Ann finally said. Her voice was
quieter, her manner less efficient, more rambling and open
now. "She doesn't deny anything. She doesn't say anything to
help herself. It's like she's given up, Mr. Doll. I don't know
how else to describe what she's like these days. She's given up
on herself and on everything else—even before it's gotten started.
If she keeps it up, God knows what they'll do to her. She'll
spend the rest of her life in jail."

"There's a lot that has to happen before it comes to that,"
Doll replied, which was a true enough statement as it stood but
not nearly so reassuring as the words made it seem—like saying
there were a lot of steps, but once you started climbing them,
unless something happened to stop you, eventually you wound
up at the top.

"Is there all that much? I wonder," Ann said distantly. "She's got to decide to stand up for herself. I know that. But nothing I've said seems to make her understand it. You've got to help her, Mr. Doll. I came to you because . . . because of what she's said about you—and because you're the only person I could think of she might listen to. I would have gone to anyone else if I'd thought they'd have a better chance.

"She wrote some letters to you back when you first went North. Envelopes and all. You wouldn't know that because she never mailed them. I took the chance you'd be at the same address and asked the operator to find me a number. That's the only way I knew how to find you."

"You said on the phone," Doll recalled aloud, "that you've stayed as close as you could to her since the arrest?"

"I've been staying at her place." Ann nodded. "That's why I was able to come up with the letters. I got down there as soon as I heard what'd happened. I've gone to see her whenever they have hours, not that the visits have done any visible good. I've still got my apartment up in Atlanta, but I chucked my job when they wouldn't give me leave. I can always get another job. I'm a graphic artist, and I've got the credits to prove I'm a good one. But I've only got the one sister."

"What about Diana? Does she want me to help? Does she even want to see me?" Doll asked.

"She knows I called you," Ann said and hesitated. "And she knows that I was coming up here to see you."

"And?"

"She didn't like it. She didn't like it one bit. She pulled every trick she knew to make me promise that I wouldn't do it. She cried. She swore. She shouted. None of it worked. Because I didn't let it work, Mr. Doll. When a child needs a doctor, you don't let it scream its way out of going. Diana doesn't know what's good for her now. I'm her sister, and even if she doesn't want my help . . . she's going to have to get used to having it."

Ann Raney's face was pure defiance—with just a trace of tears in her eyes.

She'd made the decision to help her sister whether Diana wanted the help or not. "Her sister"—those were the important words. Doll, on the other hand, had no bond of kinship to evoke. Moreover, he had a rule of his own, a variation of "Do unto others . . ." which, in his interpretation, meant that you respected people and their wishes enough to leave them alone. You didn't intrude yourself into other people's lives—especially when they'd made it clear they didn't want you. Except that, as with all such rules, there were times when you said to hell with the rule.

Doll's decision was made the only way it could be made, but still a recalcitrant corner of his mind persisted in asserting its resistance.

"I don't know," he said. "I don't even know if there's anything I could do. Besides that, I gave Diana some pretty bad memories. I won't push the point. I assume that you already know about those. But I can see her side—why she wouldn't want me involved."

"The past is past. That's all it is. That's all we can let it be," Ann Raney insisted. "I don't know what you can do, or can't. I know nobody else can do anything. Diana needs you. Do you think I'd be here if she didn't? She needs you very badly. *Now.* Damn it, you know what went on between the two of you. Don't you see that, however much she might want to, she can't ask?

"But all right, Mr. Doll," Ann went on, suddenly lowering her voice to a level only fractionally louder than a whisper. "I should have been ready for you. Diana warned me. She said there were times when nothing she said seemed able to reach you—times when she wanted to use a two-by-four as a club just to get your attention."

Doll sat deliberately back in his chair, letting the emotions cool before he replied. Like a duelist who had fired first, Ann had no choice but to stand—or in this case to sit—her ground and wait for his answering shot.

"Do you remember what you said before about Diana?" Doll asked at last. "About her trying everything she could to get you not to come up here. If you think back, you'll maybe recall that you went on from there to give a few examples."

"And you think, now," Ann replied, "that I've turned the scene around—that now I'm using the same tricks on you with the opposite purpose. A little hysteria, a little guilt—go on about how bad things are for Diana now, about how it was between you and her back in the past. Okay," she acknowledged indifferently, "it's another version of what Diana tried to do to me. No apologies. This time I got caught; next time maybe I won't. The fact is, if I thought it would work, I'd try bringing you back at the point of a gun."

"That sounds honest, at least. It's a start," Doll replied. "Suppose we just leave it for now that I'll listen. I want to hear what happened with Diana—as much as you can tell me. Not here, though. To talk a thing through takes time. Here it's like trying to talk in a fishbowl."

"I've got a motel room booked," Ann Raney said. "It's supposed to be about ten minutes from here. My flight back to Orlando's not until tomorrow morning." A corner of her mouth curved up roguishly. "Don't look so scandalized, Mr. Doll. I don't think you're a danger to my virtue. Besides Diana saying you could be cast-iron stubborn, she also said that you could be absolutely trusted. She doesn't say that about very many men."

"Naturally, I grew up thoroughly liberated," Ann said with no particular enthusiasm. "That was the contemporary, 'in' thing to do at the time. All the girls in my generation did."

She had the drapes of the window drawn back and stood

staring out at the motel's nearly empty parking lot. The rain beaded up on the few cars. The sullen day continued into early afternoon.

"It was kind of like thinking the millennium had come—that everything that happened from here on out was going to be good. I don't think we ever quite saw that the only thing we really got was the right to make our own choices. What we missed was that the choices we made could turn out to be fully as bad as the choices that we used to let the men make for us. I'm not saying I want to go back to the way it was. I don't want that at all. But it's not the automatic paradise that some of us thought it would be."

Ann moved from the window, pacing off a few feet.

"Wrong presents. Wrong futures. Wrong people," she went on. "I wasn't really making generalizations or talking about me. I was talking about Diana—getting at it politely from the edges. Sean Dabney. Maybe he was one of Diana's wrong choices. He was her latest. He's the man they say Diana killed."

Doll asked what Diana had said about the murder.

"That's part of the problem." Ann frowned and walked to the window again. Her faint reflection peered back at her from the glass. Her voice stayed gentle, but took on a cynical edge. "I'm afraid Diana's not too helpful on the point. The only thing she's said so far is that she doesn't know if she killed Sean or not."

"Doesn't remember," Doll suggested.

"I suppose that's a kind of refinement. It gets us back to bad choices again."

"Rum?" Doll remembered from the earlier years. Handling it hadn't been a problem for her then, but Diana hadn't exactly been a prospect for the temperance movement either.

"And some grass. There was always that," Ann said. "And maybe something harder now and then—though she never admitted that to me. I'm not saying a habit. Diana couldn't have afforded that. I know it sounds like I'm down on her. I'm not. It's just that when I decided to come to you, I also decided that you'd better have it all."

"What does she remember?" Doll asked.

"About the night of the murder?"

Doll nodded.

"She says that she went out drinking with Sean. Out on the town. That was the usual thing for most any night they got together. Diana half remembers getting back to Sean's apartment. He's got this place—it's a kind of Shangri-la condo overlooking the beach."

"Big money?"

"Big enough," Ann answered. "I suppose 'big' depends on how much you've got yourself. By my standards or Diana's, very big. Country club rich. Not Rockefeller rich. He owned a couple of package stores. Two of the big ones in town. Little bars attached—that's how they do it in Florida. How rich does somebody get doing that?"

"Rich enough. I define it the same way as you and Diana."

Ann smiled, but Doll read into it some of the strain that he knew she must be feeling by now. He let her pick her own time to go on.

"Anyway, they got back to the condo," she said when she was ready. "After that, things start to get fuzzy pretty fast. She remembers being in the bedroom. She was on the bed and arguing with Sean about something. I'm sorry, but she has no idea about what. Not sex. As I said, Sean was only Diana's latest. I don't mean that to be catty. I'd say the same thing about myself. There aren't many Victorians left these days."

"After they argued . . . ?" Doll said.

"Nothing," Ann answered. "That's it. That's all there is. She either passed out and that was the end of it, or else she just doesn't remember any more. Or else she's not telling the truth, but I don't think it's that. If she'd done it and she remembered, she's so down on herself these days that she'd have confessed it all long before now."

"So we're stuck there. She and Sean go out. They come back to his place. And the next thing we know, Diana crashes. Sometime later she comes around and, when she does, she finds out Dabney's dead."

"The next thing she claims she remembers is early the next morning," Ann said. "She heard somebody shouting and banging on the door. She got up to answer it—she was still dressed as she had been the night before. She got to the living room and saw the body on the floor. It was a bad scene just about every way you could think of. He was facedown with the back of his head smashed in. There was blood on him and on the carpet all around where he was. She screamed. The police—who it turns out were the yahoos doing all the banging—broke the door in, and there she was. Just her all alone with dear, dead Sean."

"And that was enough for them to arrest her?"

"I don't understand the technicalities of the law," Ann answered. "I leave it to the experts to draw their clever lines. But in practice that's what it amounted to. That was a week ago last Saturday night—or I guess Sunday morning's more accurate. They haven't let her out of jail since."

They talked through the rest of the afternoon and, after a break for dinner, on into the evening. But by nine o'clock, Doll could see the pattern of yawns and clipped responses that told him Ann was rapidly losing the battle with fatigue. Doll said it was time for him to leave.

Ann asked the question with her eyes.

"You want it in writing?" Doll said, looking at her with a mildly amused, sardonic stare. "We both knew what the answer was before we left the airport this morning."

"So maybe, after all my trouble, the guilt and hysteria worked," Ann Raney said, smiling.

              *   *   *

And maybe it had worked—at least to some degree, Doll admitted to himself.

It had been a long day for Ann Raney. It had started early, and, Doll understood, a very large portion of it had been hard. Hard for Doll, too, a little, he allowed. Driving home toward Lewes through the rural Delaware darkness, he watched the road as the headlights of the occasional oncoming cars streaked up and across the VW's windshield.

In his thoughts, he found himself drawn back in time, remembering Diana Raney as she'd been when he'd met her in Florida years before.

She'd come to the party in a long pink and orange dress that set off the dark brown hair that fell to a length just short of her shoulders.

Tampa days. Doll had been diving salvage for Stathe Vicarias then. He remembered what he'd nearly forgotten: that, somewhere in the years between then and now, Stathe Vicarias had died. Part truth, part cliché—but death comes to everything in its time. It had come to Doll's first and only marriage eleven months into that first year in Tampa. If there was any irony to be found in the night of the party, as Doll recalled it, it was that he'd been on the rebound then for almost exactly as long as his marriage had lasted.

The pairing of Doll and Diana Raney had occurred through no element of chance. The match had been the very deliberate work of Stathe's sister-in-law, Penelope, who, besides being the party's hostess, was also the salvage firm's bookkeeper and its self-appointed matriarch. Steering Doll by the arm, she'd hustled him along beside her, then brusquely hauled Diana free from the conversation in which she'd been involved.

"Diana, I want you to listen to Pope." She'd used her nickname, pronounced Po'-pee. *"I have someone it will do you so much good to meet." The poor girl.* The song went on. *The terrible divorce that she'd only just come through. Doll would understand. Hadn't he been through the same thing, too?*

And then she'd left them alone, just the two of them, to start by laughing their awkwardness away. Part of the plan was to bar all the polite doors of disengagement. Penelope Vicarias—Doll gave her credit—was an artful social tactician. She'd left no graceful way for either Diana or Doll to get out.

On the other hand, Doll admitted with a half smile at the onyx night beyond the windshield, Vicarias's sister-in-law hadn't done all that badly by him either.

Diana Raney, that night that Pope had introduced them, was a woman of twenty-two who'd had her bubble burst. She was beautiful, with a kind of regal quality about her—and yet, simultaneously, tremendously fragile. Smiles, gaiety, laughter— all the up emotions—came out badly timed, just an almost undetectable instant too quickly.

She was trying too hard, Doll had sensed. The pain from the divorce was there and real, but greater than she was ready then to comprehend. It went beyond rejection. More than just the other person had been lost. What was lost as well was something that Diana Raney had grown up to believe would last for at least an earthly forever.

And there, again, Doll thought, maybe Pope had been right. Hadn't Doll been through the same thing, too? Maybe he really could understand.

2

The tourist map on the right hand seat described the particular stretch of Florida shore as the Treasure Coast. In fact, Doll saw, the whole Atlantic side of the peninsula had names that sounded much like that: the Palm Coast in the north, then farther south near Cape Canaveral, the inevitable Space Coast. And then the Treasure Coast, between the Space Coast and Palm Beach, which served as the current line of demarcation against Miami's urban sprawl.

The hot, humid gusts that swept through the VW's open window beat an irregular pulse against Doll's cheek. He could barely hear the music from the car's radio over the buffeting rush of the wind. From the western side of the interstate, the too sweet scent of orange trees added to the heaviness, until the air became something a man might almost drown in.

A highway sign set against the green vista of the open land and groves announced that Doll's exit was now just two miles ahead. From there, the town where Diana Raney had chosen to reestablish her life in the wake of the unsettled Tampa years was almost exactly an equal distance to the east.

Doll's first impression on leaving the interstate was that he'd somehow crossed a line in time and, absurdly, left the present he'd been in behind him.

Low, separated, white-shingled houses hid behind yards dense with foliage. Pine mixed with palm. Overgrown bushes and runaway shrubs filled in the spaces between. Other houses were veteran masonry structures from a time when concrete was sculpted with hand trowels. Their facades and the columns of their porches crawled with thick, verdant, climbing vines.

Nineteen thirty-five? Doll picked the year, though he might have done as well to pick any other from the decade. Doll hadn't been born in nineteen thirty-five. More than ten years would pass before that was to come. But his overriding impression was that, had he been born and had he been here then, what he saw would have looked very nearly the same as it did now.

He drove on toward the town, keeping his pace deliberately slow. Acutely aware he was following footsteps, he tried to see—or, more honestly, to guess at—what it was that Diana saw in the countless times she must have come this way before.

Four, perhaps five minutes passed—by Doll's guess the town's municipal limit had to be near—when the yards and trees came abruptly to an end.

Replacing them were clusters of close-quartered buildings succumbing to various stages of disrepair. Two men and a woman sat, along with a handful of children, beside a rusting and apparently broken refrigerator on one of the half-collapsed porches. The voices that Doll overheard spoke in Spanish. Two houses farther along the language was English. But the too familiar trappings of poverty were, for any purpose of argument, identical, except that, this time, the faces that Doll saw were black.

The town's size was modest, and distances within it relatively short. The ghetto ran on only a small number of blocks, though Doll, of course, had no way of telling how deeply it spread out to either side.

A church appeared, white and clean and well kept, too much like a mocking pot of gold set out at the end of a rainbow of impoverishment. Beyond it, a stone's throw away, the one- and two-story orange brick buildings of the downtown business district emerged.

The road on which Doll had come into the town ended in a T where it abutted US Route 1. At the intersection, Doll turned right, then quite soon left onto the southernmost of the two causeways that spanned the river.

The elongated barrier island he found on the opposite side had the effect of completing the cycle of Doll's excursion in time and returning him fully to the present. Sand and beach grass and coconut palms—all of it looked exactly as it ought to. The island was the Florida that people from the northern states have, over the span of years, been trained to regard as the norm, the picture from the television ads that northern stations are well paid to air, especially during the middle weeks of January. It was an island of beachfront motels and high-rise condominiums and, across the road, quiet streets lined with jalousie-windowed retirement homes.

And, like the ghetto and the downtown business district, and like the bush-hidden houses beyond the town line, the island gave Doll a sense of yet another entity standing alone—a part of a conglomerate by virtue of proximity, but lacking any greater sentiment of common union.

Doll stopped long enough on the island to check his single piece of baggage and complete the registration routine at his motel. After that, he was back on the road again.

Following the instructions he'd been given, he retraced his path and drove back toward the interstate but, a mile before it, turned off on a small street to his left. Two more turns and another quarter mile brought him to a horseshoe-shaped driveway surrounding a swimming pool.

Around the outside of the horseshoe were eight identical cottages—small boxlike cabins, white trimmed with blue—three along both of the vertical sides and two more across the base. Each had a screened-in porch that ran the width of the front.

Doll parked beside the polished red Camaro convertible that Ann had told him to expect. The letters on the vanity plate, in Florida green and orange on white, spelled out the name DIANA R.

The unit nearest the car was number six. Doll knocked at the porch door and took the chance to look around while he waited.

What, at first view, seemed like a 1950's edition of a family motor court, on closer inspection showed traces of accumulation around the cabins that implied a more permanent pattern of residence. Yard swings, charcoal grills, an outboard motor mounted for repair on a water-filled oil barrel—all gave evidence that the people in the cabins, for at least some undetermined, intermediate time, were there to stay.

"C'mon in. It's not hooked."

Ann Raney stood looking out from the inside doorway that led from the porch into the cottage. She was barefoot, dressed in a pair of shorts with a sleeveless blouse, the tails of which were tied at her waist.

Inside, despite the noontime sun, the cabin was in twilight— deep twilight before Doll's eyes had adjusted from the white-hot brilliance from which he'd just come. The curtains were drawn. No lights were on. The effect, Doll supposed, was worth the darkness. Certainly it kept the cottage cooler. A single large room incorporated a living, dining, and kitchen area. Two doors opened off it, one to a small bedroom and the second to a bath.

Ann pointed to a bamboo chair and took one nearby for herself. She leaned back and stretched her legs out before her, tensing the muscles, then relaxing them.

"Diana tells me I got it wrong," she said. "Never *Mr.* Doll; only Doll. That's what she says people call you."

"I answer to both, depending on the occasion." Doll sat. "Just the 'Doll' alone is shorter."

"Don't you have a first name?"

Doll shook his head. "Not anymore. It's been so long since anyone used it, I've forgotten what it is." He asked how Diana was doing.

"She's managing." Ann looked down at her toes. "At least she's come around to a point where she understands she has to accept you being here. When you left me at the motel, you said you'd come. You never said what it was that made up your mind."

"Pope Vicarias—a long time ago." Doll knew the reply would have no meaning.

"Po-pee? Is that somebody's name?"

"It's not important," Doll said. "What we probably ought to talk about is where we're going to go from here."

"You don't like that, do you—explaining yourself to anybody else?"

"I guess I'm just not used to doing it," Doll answered with a measure of diplomacy.

"Diana said that about you, too. That was the other thing about you that used to get her angry. It's probably the eighth wonder of the world that the two of you lasted as long as you did."

Doll wondered if Diana had said that or thought it, or if it was only Ann's way of seeking to provoke a reaction.

"I guess it's a wonder that we did," he said. "You said that you've been seeing Diana since they've had her in jail. How are the visits restricted? What arrangements have to be made?"

"Three times a week there are open visiting hours. You can go anytime during those. You just sign in and follow the rules. Willard Giesler—he's Diana's lawyer, the one I told you about— he can make arrangements for other times. I have his phone number. I can give you that. He wants you to call him anyway."

Doll asked where the jail was.

Ann pointed in a vaguely westerly direction. "They're holding her in someplace called 'the Pods.' It's less strict than a prison. She's being detained. She hasn't been convicted. She's still presumed to be innocent—one of those nice little legal distinctions—which does nothing to get her out of jail. It's a hell of a system."

"All right. I can get the rest of the local ground rules from Giesler. I want to see him anyway before I talk with Diana. Right now, I want to move on to something else. I want to go back to something that you said the other day."

"What? What did I say?" Ann asked.

Her manner seemed to Doll to mix equal parts curiosity and caution. The curiosity was innocent, the caution that of a witness who'd given her testimony and now had to face up to cross-examination.

"You told me that Diana woke up when she heard noise at the door. And the noise turned out to be the police? Something's missing. What were the police doing there? Why were they at Sean Dabney's condo at some ungodly hour on a Sunday morning?"

"I don't know. What *were* they doing there?" Ann's eyes widened at the implication of Doll's question.

"It's an interesting thought, isn't it?" Doll said. "What do you know about how the police are set up around here? How do responsibilities get divided up between the local police and the county and the state?"

Ann Raney shook her head.

"Then that's one of the first things we'll have to get at," Doll said. "Who was it who arrested Diana?"

"Do you mean which policeman?"

"I mean the office. Who the boss is."

"The county sheriff. His name is Eldwin something—Eldwin Rush. But I don't know if he's the one who arrested Diana."

"It doesn't matter. He's the one we'll have to start with. Let's try one more topic. There's another name I want to bring up—maybe the most important name."

"Who?"

Doll sensed the cautious half of the mix return to Ann's voice. "I want you to tell me," he said, "all you know about Sean Dabney."

"How should I know anything about him?" Ann looked away from Doll, out through the open door and across the porch beyond. "He wasn't anything to me."

"You met him, though? You knew him that much, at least."

Ann nodded.

"Then let's start with that—just the basics. How old was he? What did he look like?"

"Well, there's a choice on that second part." Ann seemed to find the topic of Dabney unpleasant. "Do you want to know what he thought he looked like, or do you have the stomach to face the real thing?"

"Any way you want to tell it."

"He was past it, all right?" Ann shifted in her chair, glancing first at Doll, then down at the floor. "Does that tell you what you want to know? He was pushing forty, but he tried to play it like he was still twenty-five. I don't know how to tell you what he looked like. It wouldn't have hurt him to drop twenty pounds. His hair was black, but I always thought that he dyed it. Diana said he went to a hair stylist so he could get it cut to look like Robert Redford's, only dark."

If "pushing forty" was what Ann defined as "past it" . . . Doll abandoned that dispiriting line of contemplation in favor of proceeding with his inquiry.

"What about his personality? What can you tell me?"

"Obnoxious." Ann clipped the sentence short. "I didn't like him, Doll. I guess you figured that out by now. I didn't like him before this happened, and—as dumb as this is going to sound to you—I like him less now for getting himself killed in a way that made things bad for Diana."

"That's a good enough reason for you not to like him," Doll replied. "There are probably some, but not too many, better."

Ann frowned, then pushed herself out of the chair and onto her feet.

"I'm going to get something to drink," she said. "I can offer you beer or a frozen mix lemonade. Mine's lemonade and vodka, if that's something you like. If you want something else, you can ask and take your chances."

While she talked, she walked across the room to the corner where the refrigerator, sink, and stovetop constituted a kitchen.

"He was a loudmouth—egotistical, self-serving, sometimes maybe paranoid," she said. "Everybody saw it, not just me. He knew all of the people around here—like he must've lived here for all of his life. And for all that, I'm not sure that he ever had any real friends."

"And enemies?"

"Well, he had at least one, didn't he?" Ann Raney flashed a sharklike smile. "Did you say," she asked—her expression benign again—"if yours was the lemonade or beer?"

"Hold the vodka. Keep it to just the lemonade for now." Doll looked across the room at Ann's back. "One last question— though maybe it's more of an observation. If you knew of any reason Diana might have had to want Sean Dabney dead, I don't suppose there's any chance you'd tell me."

From her place at the sink, Ann stared coolly at Doll. She added a moderate quantity of vodka to her own glass and drank a small swallow from it.

"I don't know of any reason like that," she replied evenly. "But then, it doesn't mean a whole lot for me to say that. Because you're right, Doll—at least for now. As far as knowing anything like that—unless you could show me exactly how it would help Diana—I wouldn't tell you if I did."

The answer, Doll thought, was candid, if nothing else, and, as such, was as much as he could reasonably have expected.

*   *   *

Willard Giesler, according to his secretary, would be in court for the rest of the day. She could take a message or a number where Doll could be reached, or else Doll might wish to call back the next morning. Doll thanked her and said that the morning would be fine.

That left the afternoon for Sheriff Eldwin Rush. They took Diana's Camaro for the drive into town, a choice necessitated by Ann's insistence on more than the windows-down air-conditioning of Doll's VW bug.

The county sheriff's office was just beyond the limits of the town in a gray stone building with a closely shaved lawn and a flagpole in front, a nearly perfect clone, Doll thought, for any of a couple of thousand municipal buildings scattered like hand-thrown seed across the country. A receptionist, who spoke to them through a microphone connection from behind a thick glass window, took down their names and business and pointed toward a short and empty row of egg-shaped fiberglass chairs.

"I'm not sure I know what we're supposed to be doing here," Ann whispered almost as soon as they'd sat.

Her change of clothes to a white oxford cloth shirt and a full-cut denim skirt produced a transition from the morning that, to Doll's mind, touched on the edge of credibility. Ann Raney looked, in that particular moment, like the image of what every father prayed to God that his daughter would turn out to be.

She leaned closer to Doll to satisfy herself that she wouldn't be overheard. "If it was someone from here who arrested Diana, why is the sheriff even going talk to us? Why should he change his mind? What makes you think he'd want to do anything to help us out now?"

"Only an enduring faith in the system and human nature," Doll answered. He turned his head to meet Ann's gaze and smiled. "It's an adversary system, the way it's set up. The reasons that Rush'll talk to us are exactly the same as the reasons we want to talk to him. He wants to pick our brains—yours especially—for anything that will strengthen his case. He isn't going to talk to us because he has any thought of wanting to help us."

"You mean he wants to use me to make his case against Diana? Who does the son of a bitch think he is?"

"Exactly that, a son of a bitch. Just like we want to use him to pick the case that he's trying to build. It makes him a son of a bitch, just like us."

Ann stared at Doll as she seemed to take the meaning of it in.

"It's all a little hypocritical, isn't it?" she said faintly.

Half her question, as Doll interpreted it, was rhetorical and meant as a protest, but an equal part seemed heartfelt, the quite reasonable response to yet a further step on the lifelong path to disillusionment.

"About as hypocritical as it gets," he agreed.

Twenty minutes passed, then half an hour. It could have been that Eldwin Rush had more demanding business. They'd come with no appointment, a breach in protocol that commonly got one placed at the end of the line. But Doll thought that the motive for the delay was more probably tactical, a deliberate lesson meant to induce humility in the face of the sheriff's authority.

Another ten minutes slid by before the receptionist called their names and led them back through a catacomb of corridors.

"Miss Raney. I'm Eldwin Rush." Rush offered his hand, stepping out for a moment from behind the cluttered desk in his office. "And you're Mr. . . . eh, Doll—unusual name if I've got it right. Please come in." He offered chairs. "This other gentleman is Detective Sergeant Vrane."

"Now we all have our witnesses," Rush added and smiled in what, to Doll's mind, was a wholly unsuccessful attempt to toss a precisely accurate observation off as humor.

Rush sat. Vrane, without comment, followed the unspoken directive. Doll and Ann did the same.

From his swivel chair, Rush did a quick inspection of Ann and looked pleased, then a much longer and more critical one of Doll.

"Well, now, it's good to meet you, Miss Raney," he said, returning his attention and his service-to-the-public smile to Ann. "Though I surely wish the circumstances were other than they are. How is it I can help you all out this afternoon?"

"You could start off by letting my sister out of jail," Ann suggested.

"Yes, well, I only wish that I could." Rush put his palms flat on his desk and stared with a saddened expression down at the accumulation of paper. "But I think we both know that the process has gone forward and that any decision along those lines is a long way outside my power."

Doll asked if Rush was familiar with the police reports from the night Diana was arrested.

"Well, yes, I guess you could say that I am." Rush stared back at Doll, but added nothing more.

"We were wondering what you might be able to tell us," Doll said, "about the night of the murder—especially about the circumstances that led you to charge Miss Raney's sister."

"I can tell you they were carefully considered," Rush answered. "The fact is, Mr. Doll, that anything I could say is already contained in the reports. Miss Raney's lawyer, of course, has all of those. It wouldn't be appropriate at all for me to go beyond what's in them."

"I only thought," Doll said, "there might be something you could add. Something that would make it all a little easier for Miss Raney's sister here to understand. Like how it just happened to be that the sheriff's department came to be knocking down that particular apartment door at that hour of the morning."

"There's no secret on that." Eldwin Rush made a show of

turning his attention to give his answer to Doll's question to Ann. "It's all in the reports that Willard Giesler has. I'm sure he'd be only too happy to let you read them. It was a standard response to a domestic disturbance call. One officer in a cruiser, with a backup as soon as the second can get there. Calls like that are the most common we have. This one, like a lot of the others, was anonymous." He turned up his palms. "But, as I say, there's nothing there that's not in the reports."

Ann glanced across at Doll.

"I see Miss Raney looks to you, Mr. Doll," Rush observed aloud, "which, for me at least, raises certain procedural problems. You'll excuse me, but I feel the need to be blunt here. You'll have to agree, I think, that Miss Raney's case for being here is one thing, she being next of kin. Yours is quite another. Just exactly what capacity is it that you're here in, Mr. Doll? If memory serves me right, I don't recall your having said."

"A friend of Diana," Doll replied.

"May I take it, a good friend?" Rush leaned back in his chair.

"You can take it as good as you want." Doll met the sheriff's eyes. "You can put the motive down to jealousy and charge me with Dabney's murder, if you want. But then you'd have to let Diana out of jail."

Eldwin Rush smiled, but the smile held no humor.

"Not an entirely unappealing offer," he said. "But I think now we know where both of us stand. I've been in the business far too long to be pumped. I know what game you're playing, and I don't intend to play it with you. The fact is, Mr. Doll, that Ms. Raney—that is to say Ms. Diana Raney—happened, at one point, to mention your name and your intentions in the presence of the state's attorney. Naturally, we did some checking. We already know a great deal more about you than you might think."

"I hope that whatever you found was up to your expectations," Doll replied in a voice intended to imply his indifference.

Rush shrugged. "Four years in the military. Navy special forces. 'Nam. Far as I'm concerned, that's about two centuries ago. You hold—or used to hold—a couple security clearances. That's how you got an FBI file. Used to live in Florida—for three years in the seventies, as near as I can tell. Smart enough to keep your nose clean back then. Not so, lately, I understand. Nothing official, but cops talk to cops. A couple years ago you killed a man up in Delaware. The man was a hood, and the decision was it was self-defense. Unofficially, the verdict is you were interfering in matters that you should've left to the police."

Doll added nothing to Rush's synopsis; neither did he say anything to refute it. At the same time, he felt Ann's hot but uncertain stare of reappraisal.

"I've seen it happen before, you know, Mr. Doll," Rush continued. "People come down here from out of state. They like to poke around and stick their noses in places where they don't belong. Maybe nobody minds that back up in Delaware. Just so you know, down here we do."

Doll started to push himself up from the chair, but before he could move Rush was talking again.

"Now Miss Raney . . ." In the intervening second, he'd switched his attention back from Doll to Ann. "Miss Raney, you're, of course, another matter altogether. I might be willing to continue this conversation with you—without the presence of either Mr. Doll or Sergeant Vrane. I might even go to the point of saying things that I wouldn't want to say in front of someone else."

"And you'd have no other motive in talking to me—just your natural sympathies and inclination to be helpful?" Ann said.

"No, that's not the case. Actually, I do have motives of my own," Rush admitted without the slightest trace of embarrassment. "What I was hoping for is that, in exchange for what I might tell you, you might be prepared to tell me some other things as well. I was thinking particularly, Miss Raney, of what you might know about why your sister might have had her differences with Mr. Dabney. I understand, of course, that what passes between sisters can be very personal things. That may be a reason that you'd also prefer that no one else but the two of us be around."

"I don't know anything about any differences," Ann said. "For as much as I know, they were Barbie and Ken."

"Well, it's nothing that needs an answer now. Think about it, though," Eldwin Rush suggested. "If there's anything you come up with—even if it's only a thought—it might be smart to give me a call. You know that if the state's attorney decides to subpoena you for a statement, he can do so. On the other hand, whatever you may choose to say to me is voluntary. Just something else for you to consider. All I ask is you keep it in the back of your mind."

"And I guess that makes it pretty clear where we *all* stand," Doll said, getting up from his chair as he glanced across the desk at Eldwin Rush. "Sean Dabney's apartment, by the way, I assume that's not still under police lock?"

"The lock's off. We've got all we need out of there," Rush replied calmly, leaning back in his chair with his eyes fixed on Doll. "Just remember later on when the time comes: as of this conversation, you've been warned."

3

The property was on the south island just over four miles beyond Doll's motel. It was shaped like a baseball field with the Atlantic Ocean as its outfield. If Doll pressed the analogy, the six-story condominium building became the infield diamond, with Sean Dabney's apartment on the top floor in that most highly prized position, corresponding in the baseball metaphor to second base.

Doll parked along the third base line, in the section of the lot reserved for visitors. Outside, the readjustment from the Camaro's air-conditioning only made the temperature and humidity seem worse. Standing by the right-hand door, Ann Raney looked at him across the waves of heat that hovered above the canvas roof. With a nod of her head she gestured toward the structure across the broad strip of lush grass and coconut palms.

"You'd have to say that it pays to be a bastard," she said, "if all you got to look at was the way some people live." The words Doll heard had a sour edge as anger and envy mixed in her voice.

He followed her gaze. The building's design was sleek and modern, all tinted glass and shiny metal. The view, for aficionados of beachscapes, was probably as good as you could find. The money it took to keep a place here would be big—big on even a far less modest scale than Doll's.

"Now what?" Ann glanced back at Doll. "Unless somebody lets you in, you can't get past the lobby."

"Then we'd better find somebody to let us in," Doll replied and started toward the building.

The lobby wasn't large, not much more than a square, fifteen feet to the side. It was also, Doll noticed, austere to the point of being indestructible, except for the parts of the intercom and video security systems which function required be exposed.

He surveyed the options presented by the intercom panel: four rows of six buttons each, one connecting to each of the twenty-four apartments, plus one more, centered at the bottom, which bore the label SUPERINTENDENT'S BELL.

The name below the last button was barely legible, penned in dark ink in short, jagged strokes. Doll made it out as "Emilio Secassa." He pressed the button for the bell, waited in the silence, then pressed it again. The voice that answered was mechanical, a man's voice with a strong Hispanic accent. It demanded, with very little embellishment, to know who Doll was and what he wanted.

Doll answered not in English, but in a fluent, colloquial Spanish. He asked first if he was speaking to Señor Secassa, then gave his name and said that he was there as a friend of Diana Raney. Would Señor Secassa, as a personal favor, grant a few moments of his time?

"And the woman with you?" Secassa's voice from the intercom speaker asked, returning the question now in Spanish.

"Señorita Raney's sister," Doll said.

Emilio Secassa was short, with narrow hips and shoulders. The straightness of his body reminded Doll of a length of pipe. He was, Doll guessed, no older than his early to middle fifties, but already his black hair had thinned to the point where the top of his head was bald. He wore a loosely fitting muslin shirt and a pair of khaki trousers.

He looked from Doll to Ann, then back at Doll again. The expression on his face seemed to Doll to convey something less than unbridled trust.

"You speak very well," Secassa said, following Doll's lead, in Spanish. He didn't need to add "for a gringo." The qualification was implicit. Without it the compliment meant nothing.

"When I was in the Navy," Doll answered, also in Spanish, "I was stationed in Puerto Rico and later in the Philippines." As though to excuse his proficiency, Doll added that he seemed to have an unaccountable ear for the language.

"Then God has given you a gift."

"The only way to explain it," Doll said and nodded. Or as good as any other, he thought to himself. But the acceptance of Secassa's interpretation was mostly a part of Doll's deliberate effort to draw the superintendent out. Doll wondered for an instant if Secassa understood the stratagem, then decided, in a glance at the Latin's eyes, that he did.

"Did you know Señorita Raney?" he asked.

"Not really. She would say hello," Secassa answered, "if we passed when she came to see Señor Dabney. I would nod and say 'Señorita.' I never presumed to speak more than that. That was as much as I knew her."

"You make it sound almost like a point of honor."

"Not to speak beyond that? And so it is in its own way," Secassa replied.

Doll waited.

Secassa met his eyes with a stare that seemed distinctly inappropriate in a man making an argument in favor of servility.

"America has many fine things to say for itself, Señor Doll. But respect for social station, I must tell you, isn't one of them. I know what it is to have station—and what it is not to have it. I had it once; I do not have it now. I suppose you can say it's a part of my honor to know that and not to pretend that I do."

"No contest. Not from me." Doll held up his hand as a

gesture of capitulation. "All I know about social philosophy is
that, when the subject comes up, I'm already out of my depth."

Emilio Secassa shook his head. "I must tell you that I doubt
that," he replied with a thin smile. "Years ago—many now—I
completed the university in Havana. Before the Communists
came to power, of course. But I was trained in the management
of agricultural estates, not in philosophy. And you, Señor Doll,
are anything besides the innocent you would like to make
yourself appear. You are, at the very least, as skilled in your
reading and handling of people as you've shown yourself to be
in the mastery of language. I prefer the game with the cards
dealt open. You have come to me today because there's something you want."

"We'd like to see Sean Dabney's apartment," Doll said.

"I don't understand what your reason is," Secassa went on,
still talking in Spanish. He withheld any commitment stronger
than continuing to listen. "How would seeing the apartment
serve to help this lady's sister?"

"To see if what the police say holds together, maybe." Doll
shook his head to acknowledge that he realized the answer was
weak. He, too, felt easier with the artifice behind him. "I can't
answer your question any better than that. Until you see a place
yourself, you can't know."

"Yes." Secassa scratched his chin and nodded. "I see, perhaps, how a thing like that could be."

"Is it still the same as it was the night that Dabney died?"
Doll asked.

"Naturally, it's been cleaned," Secassa replied. "Señor Dabney
left no will. Apparently he hadn't planned on dying. The
probate court has named an executor who, in his own time, no
doubt will dispose of the estate. Meanwhile, the maintenance
costs, including the housekeeping service, get paid. The apartment is kept just as it would have been. You'll see that yourself.
The blood—except for a trace, maybe—isn't there anymore.

The furniture's been straightened. Everything else is as it was. I can't account, of course, for anything that the police might have taken."

Doll asked what Secassa remembered of that night.

"Of the night, nothing. Of the morning . . ." Emilio Secassa cast a rueful eye upward at the ceiling. "I woke up to the flashing of the lights from the police car—or else it was from the ringing of my bell. I let the officer in. And, in a second, another car and officer came. They were in a great hurry. They asked how to get to the apartment."

"Dabney's?"

"Yes. They asked for Señor Dabney by name. I told them I would have to get my keys to operate the elevator. They said that was too long. I said there are stairs to be used in case of fire that come out on the same hall as my quarters. They told me those would have to do. I was to get my keys and meet them at the apartment."

"And in the meantime," Doll filled in, "they went up by the stairs."

Secassa nodded again. "It took me time—five minutes, maybe more, to get up there—when you think that I had to go back to my apartment—get the keys—then ride the elevator up. By that time, they had already broken the door in. I asked what had happened. They told me there was trouble, that they'd used the phone to call for an ambulance and that more police were coming. I should go downstairs again and wait to let the others in, they told me. This was what I did. They came perhaps ten or fifteen minutes later."

"But before all that—during the night," Doll said, "you didn't see anything else that might be important? I'm thinking of Dabney—when he came home with Diana. Or anyone else who might have gone up to his apartment before or after that. Or anyone who might have left."

"The police asked this too," Secassa replied. He said that he'd seen nothing before he'd gone to bed, and, before the police had come, nothing had happened to awaken him.

"As for someone who might have come?" He rubbed at his chin again as he thought. "That's always possible. Any tenant could be called on the intercom. Anyone could open the door to the elevator from his apartment. It would have been no surprise." He glanced toward Ann, Doll guessed from his manner, for some special purpose—perhaps to estimate how much of the Spanish she understood. Apparently the vacant and sullen expression on her face conveyed the obvious impression.

"This sister, I think," he said to confirm his appraisal, "doesn't understand what it is we've been saying?"

Doll replied he had no way of being certain, but that, like Secassa, he didn't think from her attitude that Ann understood.

"It's only that I wouldn't be at ease," Secassa explained, "saying this in front of her. It's the sister, señor, the sister of this woman. She wasn't the only woman that Señor Dabney brought here. He was always with others. Even when he seemed to be with one, he was with others at the same time. A man with so many women . . ." Secassa shook his head. "A man with so many women is always asking for trouble."

Doll asked who the others were.

Secassa shook his head and said it wasn't any of his business to know names. "I would never have known your friend's name," he added, "but for the fact that what happened was naturally all over the local news."

"What about the other visitors?" Doll asked.

"No one I know," Secassa replied. "You didn't know Señor Dabney, am I right? The women weren't friends. For anyone who brings them in, in strings like that, they never can be. And yet, I think sometimes that they were the closest things to friends that Señor Dabney had."

Doll remembered that Ann had said very nearly the same thing and asked why Secassa thought that was so.

"Sad to say." Emilio Secassa sighed. "Señor Dabney was a man alone, a man who had no genuine feeling for other people. A man who is like that with people gets his own feelings returned in kind."

A small red light caught Doll's eye. Toward a corner near the ceiling of the lobby, the lens of an unblinking video camera stared down.

"What about tapes?" he asked.

"They used to keep them," Secassa said, "but then the tenants' board decided to stop. The recorder was a special kind and very expensive to maintain. And with monitors in all the apartments, they thought that was enough." He smiled as though to say that the question was a wise one. "The police, they also asked if there were tapes."

"How about the apartment?" Doll reached for his wallet. "Do you think there's any chance we could see it?"

Secassa glanced at Doll, then took the offered twenty and fingered it reflectively.

"What's the harm?" he replied as he finally slid it into his pocket. "Fair pay for the story and the extra few minutes of my time. I don't see where there will be any complaints. Whoever goes to see it now, I don't think that Señor Dabney is going to mind."

The elevator Secassa led them to was a hypermodern affair. The experience was like stepping into a deep letter "U." The floor curved up into the walls. The same wheat-colored carpet covered the floor and the sides to where they curved again into the translucent fluorescent fixture that constituted the ceiling. At both the front and back of the car were polished aluminum doors.

The floor selection console differed from the normal variety in that, instead of the usual single button, there were two keyed cylinders for each of the six floors. The first row of six had the letters "A–B" above them. The second were designated "C–D." In addition, there was an intercom board—smaller, but essentially a copy of the one Doll had used in the lobby.

All more security, Secassa explained. Each tenant's elevator key gave access to a hall from which only two apartments could be entered. The front elevator door opened to the "A" and "B" units, the rear door to apartments "C" and "D." Guests whom a tenant had buzzed past the lobby could call again when they'd reached the elevator. From the apartment, the tenant could then activate the elevator, which would bring the guest directly and only to that apartment's side of the floor. Finally Secassa pointed to a corner of the car where another of the ubiquitous video cameras looked down.

At the sixth floor, Secassa held the door while Doll and Ann got out. Nodding toward the right as he fumbled through his keys, he directed them to the door of the apartment designated with a modest aluminum plaque as "6A." The lock, above the doorknob, made a sharp snap as it opened. Standing aside again, Secassa let Doll and Ann go ahead.

The architect's attempt at drama became evident at the moment one stepped through the doorway. Immediately, one saw the ocean—just a tantalizing bit of it from there at the entrance—through a window in a room at the end of a white, picture-lined hall.

Doll stopped to inspect the locking mechanism, but when he looked, he found not one lock, but two. The first, the one Secassa had used, was a formidable intergrip ring lock, with twin bolts that converged from top and bottom into the ring holes of a powerfully seated steel strike. The second—if it could be called a lock at all—was the standard, spring-loaded, in-the-doorknob model, the kind that any high school sophomore with street smarts and a plastic card could open.

Neither lock, to Doll's eye, showed any evidence of damage. He pointed to them both. Secassa understood immediately.

"Policemen," he said, "are not always known to be respecters of other people's property. The strong lock was not on. Had it been, they probably would have ruined both it and the jamb, and still broken their shoulders before it gave way. As for the other, I replaced both the doorknob and plate. It gave way so easily that the damage was almost nothing at all."

Doll stared again down the hallway. Ann was looking back from perhaps a dozen feet ahead of him. He followed after her, taking his time, trying to get a sense of the place and its owner. The pictures he passed were mildly abstract seascapes and sailboats—neutral, unobtrusive things, meant only for casual observation, the kind of art that interior decorators always seem to love.

Halfway along, a second hallway, shadowy and more narrow than the first, opened to his left.

"To the back—by that I mean the side toward where we came in—" Secassa explained, "are a den and after that the master bedroom. To the front are the kitchen and, further along, one of the two baths. Down the end, where you can't see from here, the hall turns toward the front of the apartment again. There's a second bedroom along that wall. The hall ends in the living/ dining area that runs across the whole front of the apartment. It's that same place you see up ahead there where the window is."

Secassa's description gave Doll the general idea, enough anyway so that he felt able to fill in the details as he made the circuit.

He followed Ann to the end of the entry hall.

His first and strongest impression was that of sheer size—so much so that he needed a moment to set it in perspective. Even then, the combined living and dining room looked large, but at least the dimensions became a little more believable. The windows provoked the illusion—uninterrupted floor-to-ceiling glass along the entire front of the apartment, then wrapping around to become the opposite wall of the dining area as well. And in every direction Doll looked there was the sea.

Second base, with the ocean as the outfield, he reminded himself. That was how the apartment was positioned. The space seemed to go on forever.

"It's like one of those top floor, city restaurants," Ann said, "where the windows look out over everything." Her voice seemed to carry an edge of awe, in spite of her effort to suppress it.

Doll turned toward Secassa. "Do you know where they found Dabney's body?" he asked.

In answer, Secassa pointed toward a furniture arrangement, a beige and off-white sofa set to face out toward the water, flanked farther toward the window by two chairs facing one another. The coffee table in front of the sofa was placed within reach of the side chairs as well.

"I never saw the body myself, you understand," Secassa admitted. "But if you look good, you can still see where the blood was, though."

Doll could see it, or perhaps only imagined that he could—a dark ring in an irregular oval, fifteen, maybe eighteen inches long and only slightly less wide.

He asked what the weapon was.

"Something to hit a man on the head with. More than that . . . ?" Secassa shrugged and said he didn't know.

And then, quite suddenly, it seemed there wasn't that much more to see. Doll walked the length of the living room, past a line of stools along the countertop shelf that opened into the kitchen. He came to the edge of the dining area and, to his left, the section of hall he hadn't been able to see before. At its end, where Secassa had said that it would be, he came to the door of the master bedroom—the room where Diana, by Ann's report, had said she'd slept on the night of the murder. Doll went inside, and a new ocean-fronting wall of windows greeted him.

The king-sized bed was made and waiting. Doll could only wonder for how long and for whom. He looked to Secassa, who replied that he'd had one of the maids go through the whole place.

Doll took less than a minute to give himself a tour of the closets: sports jackets, pastel shirts, and an eclectic collection of slacks that ran the gamut from somber dark to plaid. Unless he kept it in moth balls somewhere, it appeared that Sean Dabney didn't own even so much as one suit.

Nodding his satisfaction to Secassa, Doll brought his inspection of Sean Dabney's apartment to an end.

From the beach out front, the glass windows six floors above danced and blazed like crystal in the late afternoon, near-solstice sun.

Ann asked why they were walking there. Doll replied that he wanted the time for them to talk a little and to think.

"There's a problem you get into with murders," he said. "They tend to become very personal things. That's not quite the cliché that it sounds like. It means that, at some point, sooner or later, you come down to asking personal questions. I'm telling you because this is one of those times."

"What are you telling—or asking me, exactly?" Ann looked doubtfully across at Doll. "Because I certainly don't know what it is from what you just said."

"I take it," Doll continued, "from your reaction back there, that you don't speak or understand Spanish."

"But you do. You speak it like you were raised on it. That's something Diana didn't tell me. I admit it, Doll, I was a little past miffed for a while. What you did in there—cutting me out of everything—was rude as hell. Then I calmed myself down by telling myself what you had to be doing—and what you were doing it for."

"Then I hope you won't mind the next question." Doll paused until Ann looked up at him. "It goes back to something Secassa said but wouldn't have admitted in front of you in English. I'm asking you not because you're the best source, but because I'd rather ask you than to have to ask Diana. Dabney, if Secassa is right, made something of a habit of women."

"A habit? What does 'a habit' mean, Doll?"

"If you want to help Diana," Doll replied, "you could pick a better time to play it coy."

Ann turned sharply on Doll, then stared up the beach.

"A habit! God, Doll, what a way to say it." She smiled at him and shook her head as though confronting a hopeless case. "All right, he chased women. Maybe like a hound dog chases rabbits. So what? Diana knew that. She told me about it before she ever got involved with him. Probably everybody else around here knew it too."

"What women besides Diana?" Doll asked.

"Did he chase? Sylvia Guillette." The name came out, but not at once. "Before Diana. It wasn't pretty. She had a husband. Then Dabney went and dropped her when Diana came along."

"Others?" Doll prompted.

Ann shook her head. "He could have had others, I suppose. I don't know. If he did, I don't know who they were."

Doll thought for a second and let it stand at that. "The other thing that I was thinking about . . . ," he continued. "It's something you said—two things really—going back to that first day when we talked at the motel. I didn't put them together right away."

"What two things?"

"That they'd been out drinking." Doll ticked off the first item on his finger and then the second. "And that they'd argued when they'd gotten back to Dabney's place. You told me you wouldn't tell me about any motive Diana might have had and maybe this comes too close to the same thing. But it occurred to me, if we knew where they'd been, we might nose around and see if the fight got started there."

"Why does it matter? What does it matter what they were fighting about?"

Doll answered that he didn't know if what they'd argued over mattered or not. Neither, he added, was it any particular problem if Ann didn't know where Sean and Diana had been. Diana would know—whatever else she'd forgotten. And even if she didn't, the possibilities were limited. It only took leg work. There simply weren't that many cocktail bars around.

"Mickey Zale's place, the Piña Colada."

"Do you know that for sure, or are you guessing?" Doll asked.

"I don't know. I suppose somewhere in between. That was where they always went and where they were supposed to go. Look, what I haven't told you before . . . is that I wasn't absolutely honest with you that first day when we met at the airport. I didn't come down here when I told you I did, which I said was after I'd heard what had happened. I was already here. I was staying with Diana that weekend. That's how I know where they said they were going, but I can't tell you I know that they wound up there. I didn't ask Diana. I never thought it was important."

"Okay," Doll said. He nodded mechanically as he ran his hand back through his hair, then stopped his walk and stared out at the water. The small waves rolled in, one after the other, and lapped at the shore near his feet.

4

The next morning was pleasantly warm. The day, as it progressed, would succumb to the heat again, but the dawn had brought with it a respite of rain that the new sun had yet to convert into steam. Doll's run along the beach turned out to be an unexpected pleasure.

He showered and dressed with no particular hurry. Outside the motel, the island was quiet. At eight o'clock, it seemed it was hardly awake. Across the causeway, though, the town held to a different standard of time. Businesses were open or in the advanced stages of preparation for the day. Trucks with the names and logos of groves stenciled on their sides carried oranges in wooden box-shaped containers the size of dumpster trash bins.

By the time Doll parked the VW beside Diana's Camaro, his watch gave the time as a quarter past the hour.

His lateness was deliberate. If kinship counted for anything, Doll reasoned, the odds were good that Diana Raney's sister would need the minutes of grace. He stood at the screen door and knocked with his free hand. With the other, he balanced a honeydew melon in his palm.

"Doll? It's open. You can c'mon in," a voice that Doll assumed was Ann's called from somewhere inside.

Her contempt for caution, it seemed to Doll, was such that, one day, with a little bad luck, it could get her into serious trouble.

In place of the shorts and sleeveless blouse that she'd worn the day before for Doll's arrival, Ann had substituted a far tamer pair of cutoff jeans, tennis shoes, and a white, satiny, long-sleeved shirt.

Today, too, there was light. The glow from two incandescent lamps dispelled the semidarkness. A coffee pot perked on the small table set against the wall near the short row of appliances that passed for a kitchen. The rich aroma of brewing coffee filled the room.

Doll presented the melon.

Ann looked down at the fruit, then back up at Doll before she smiled. "I always like a man who comes equipped with his own breakfast," she said. "How much of it do you want? A quarter slice? Will that do?"

"Half of that." Doll added that the coffee smelled good.

"I hope you'll think it tastes good when you've had the chance to try it," Ann said. "You can take the attempt as a partial apology. I was in one of my bitchy moods yesterday—especially in the morning when you asked about Sean. I gave you a hard time, and I shouldn't have."

Doll brushed the need for any apology aside, not out of any particular effort at gallantry. Ann's reaction to Sean Dabney's name had been hostile, and openly so. If what she'd said on the beach outside the condo was true—that she'd known of his meanderings outside his relationship with Diana—it was also true that there were lots of people who took a dislike to others with far less reason than Ann's.

"What I ought to do is the honest thing and tell you about the coffee," Ann warned as she poured. "I've never used anything but instant before. But Diana says you always made your coffee fresh, so I gave it a try."

Ann's use of Diana's name in the context brought on a twinge—more an attack—of memory. There were mornings

Doll recalled with the same odor of coffee—like this, right down even to the replica of the girl.

Ann asked what plans he had for the day.

"To see Diana," Doll answered almost too quickly, silently grateful for the interruption of his unintended attack of nostalgia. "If it works out with the visiting schedule or if Giesler can arrange it. And then Giesler if he can find the time to fit me in."

Ann cut the melon and put the slices onto plates. She set the table with the cups of the coffee and glasses of orange juice.

"If I *can* get in to see Diana," Doll said, "it may go better if I see her alone."

Taking the melon plates from the countertop, Ann set them down on the table.

"I ought to resent that," she answered. "I might still if I didn't agree with you. I know I haven't got the words exactly right, but there's a saying with the idea that sisters are sisters until there's a man. When the two of you see each other, a lot of the past is going to get stirred up. It's a past that I can't and shouldn't ever be a part of."

It was a graceful admission, Doll acknowledged to himself. He even felt a little humbled by it. He moved to the table at Ann's invitation. It would have been nice to relax and let a quiet morning's meal be no more than that, except there was more that he needed from Ann—more details, more observations and ideas, more of nearly everything before he had his talk with Diana.

"I doubt it had anything to do with what happened here," he said, "but do you know the reason why your sister left Tampa?"

Ann took a swallow of her juice, then shrugged, leaving Doll to put an interpretation on her body language. The gesture seemed, on the one hand, to ask if anyone's reasons for doing anything were ever really knowable. At the same time, the smallness of it suggested that one was always free to guess.

"Did you ever see one of those pain-avoidance experiments?" Ann held her juice glass in both her hands and stared into it, as though her mind was absorbed in the pulp that floated on the surface. "Psychologists like to use them a lot. They show you some bugs spread all over a screen; then they put an electric current through one side, and, like magic, all the bugs that were there go over to the other.

"Maybe Tampa was a little like that for Diana. Her first husband. Then you—I'm not saying you did anything wrong. It just didn't work, and it was bad. Then Walter, her second husband. You didn't know about him. Diana says she never told you. Anyway, he was worse than the first, or maybe only as bad in different ways. It just went on. Not all the bugs move when they first throw the switch. Some take it and take it—until finally enough is enough and they move."

"Why here? Did she have any friends here?"

"Not that I know of." Ann raked one of her hands back through her hair, working out a knot along one side. "So far as I know, the only ones she has from here are ones she made here since she came. That was true of Sean Dabney—or at least that's what Diana told me. I only met two others, and I got the impression it was the same with them."

She shrugged again when Doll asked who the other friends were.

"We went to the Colada—just Diana and me—one night when I was down a few months ago. My memory's not very good about people. One was an older man—fifty?—more than that, if I had to guess. He had a last name that meant something. That's the only reason I remembered it. I think it was 'Tack'! The other was a woman called Valerie something. She was a lot younger. Diana's age, I'd say. I'm sorry. I really can't do better than that."

"It's enough. It's not that big a place down here. It's enough even if Diana decides not to be helpful." Doll took a taste of the coffee and nodded, honestly, to say that it wasn't bad.

"First Tampa. Now here." He put the cup down on the table again. "No matter where she goes, it just doesn't seem to work for her, does it?"

"Maybe she doesn't expect it to. Maybe that's her trouble."

Doll looked up.

"Oh, it's nothing clever. You knew her after she moved to Florida. That was a second edition Diana. How much did she tell you about the one who came before that?"

"She kept things in the present," Doll said. "I put that down to the marriage and the divorce. It could have been more."

"It could've been more," Ann agreed. "I don't want to make it a hardship case. Not her. Not me. Neither of us. But there were reasons why it was harder on her than on me. I don't remember my parents, Doll. Diana does. She was fourteen when we got farmed out. I was only two. I'm not saying abuse. Not even a lack of interest. Simple economics, that's all it was. No money at home. We got sent to live with our mother's brother's family in Georgia. That's a longer way from Louisiana than it looks. There's more than just Mississippi and Alabama in between."

Doll wasn't sure what it all meant and so didn't know what Ann might be expecting him to say.

"Not that Georgia was that bad. It just wasn't good. Uncle Hewlett's family favored the male side—three boys, no girls. The boys were Diana's age and a little older. They were just big, oafish brothers to me. By the time I got to a point where I would have been of any interest, they were long since gone from the house."

"Diana never told me any of that," Doll replied.

"Then I didn't either," Ann said. "And don't misunderstand me. I'm not saying any of the three of them ever got near her. I'm only saying that the fact that they didn't can't be put down to any shortage of trying on their part. And after all, why not? We were free-loading kin, and isn't that the worst kind? What was Diana supposed to say? Who was she going to complain to?"

Ann tried a taste of the coffee before she went on. "You're right. It's not that bad," she said, and allowed herself a smile at the achievement. "Anyway, Diana did the smart thing and got out of there—the week after she graduated from high school. She had something lined up in Tampa-St. Pete. I don't know how she managed it. She was eighteen by then; I was only six. She wrote and sent money for me whenever she could. I still hated her for leaving me. It took me a few years and a lot of reading between the lines of the questions she asked in her letters before I even started to understand. After that, we got to a point where we could talk."

"I didn't know any of that," Doll repeated.

"I don't even know if any of it means anything." Ann stared distantly out a nearby window. "Maybe it all comes down to nothing. Maybe, though, when you put it together, it explains why Diana's gotten so that she doesn't expect a lot of favors out of life."

Doll offered his help with the breakfast dishes, but Ann declined it. Two glasses, two cups, two plates, and the utensils. She only intended to rinse them, she said, and then they could dry in the air in the rack beside the sink.

Doll, in the meantime, tried Willard Giesler. The secretary was pleasant, as she'd been the day before, and after a short wait on hold Doll heard the connection click live again.

"Good morning, Mr. Doll. This is Willard Giesler." Giesler's voice had a hearty, fraternal ring.

"Mr. Giesler, I'm a friend of Diana Raney—" Doll began.

"Know who you are, son," Giesler interrupted him. "M' secretary said that you'd called yesterday afternoon. Diana told me you'd be coming down. She puts a lot of faith in you, though I understand that the two of you haven't seen one another for some time."

"More than ten years," Doll said.

"So I understand, so I understand. And after all that, you still take the trouble. She says you want to try to help her and that talking to you is the same as talking to her. So I'll tell you right off, I'll be honest with you, Mr. Doll. I want to help her too. I don't know that either of us can."

"You could help me if you could arrange for me to see her. If I could, I'd like to do that sometime today."

"Now that I think I can do," Giesler replied. "Let's see, today's Tuesday? Yeah, it is. You don't need me, really. It's an open day. You could just go by yourself. But I'll give a call over ahead and grease the way."

"How about this morning, if that's not pushing the limits?" Doll asked.

"That's what limits are for. They're there to be pushed." Giesler laughed. "I don't see why that should be any problem. Look, I'll tell you what I'll do. I'll get you something a little better than one of those out-in-the-open partitioned deals like maybe you've seen if you've visited someone in the lockup before. This'll be in one of the counseling rooms—which means it's a small room and there has to be a guard in there with you all the while. But after the time you haven't seen each other and the circumstances and all, it might just suit you both a little better."

"That'd be fine. I'd appreciate it," Doll said.

"Good, then. It's done. One word of warning, though. I told you about the guard. What I'm saying is that nothing that passes between you is going to be what you'd call confidential. The guard will see everything you do and hear every word that either of you says. I expect you see the implications in that."

"Nothing incriminating gets said," Doll replied.

'You're a quick study, m'boy,' Giesler said and laughed again. Then the laughter stopped. "Not that I think that girl could do herself much more damage than she's already done."

"That's the same thing her sister told me. I'd like to talk more with you about that—that and a few other things, too."

"No problem with that," Giesler answered. "Like I told you before, Diana gave you a clean bill of health. There's no confidentiality problem as far as talking with you is concerned."

Doll asked about an appointment, then waited on hold for a second time while the lawyer consulted his secretary.

"How's four-thirty this afternoon?" Giesler said when he came back on the line.

"That'd be fine."

"Good. Then we'll put it down for that," Giesler agreed. "And in the meantime, you'll have a chance to see Diana and have a little talk. I'll make those arrangements as soon as we're off the phone. Give me the number where you are, and if there are problems—which I doubt—I'll call you back within the next fifteen or twenty minutes."

"One more thing, first, if I could." Doll remembered what Giesler had said about limits and took the chance of doing a little pushing on his own. "I have two names—or half names— that Ann gave me. I wanted to see, if I ran them by you, if you could fill in the rest."

"So try me," Willard Giesler invited.

"A man. Something Tack," Doll said. "And a woman. Valerie Something."

"Tack'd be Calvin. Calvin Tack. He's hard to miss." Apparently there was something funny in that as well, because, for yet a third time, Giesler laughed. "You know him yourself if you've been down along Route One. Southern States Auto. Great big franchise on your left going south. Got a plywood cutout of a man in a Confederate hat. It's supposed to be Calvin, but it doesn't look a thing like him. Calvin Tack's the man who owns the place."

"And the other one—just the Valerie?" Doll asked.

"Sounds harder unless you know your way around here,"

Giesler acknowledged. "But there's a kind of a common denominator at work here. A club called the Piña Colada. Tack hangs out there some. So did Diana. And so did Sean Dabney. So does Valerie Albrecht. That's the other name you want. In the daylight, she's an independent accountant. But a lot of nights you can find her at the Colada, too."

The counseling room the guard showed Doll to was small, smaller even than Doll had expected from Giesler's description. Moreover, it was further cramped by a table and three wooden spindle-back chairs that nearly filled it.

Doll checked his watch for yet another time and realized to his recurring astonishment that scarcely more than a minute had passed since the last time he'd looked. The Hundred Years' War, it seemed, might have come and gone in the time he'd spent in that little room. A noise and sense of movement somewhere beyond the door alerted him.

The knob turned. Diana Raney stood in the open doorway. The guard who loomed behind her watched with a mute, implacable stare.

Doll stood.

And, for a moment, neither of them moved. Doll wanted to say something, knew that he should, but he couldn't find the words. Finally, it was Diana who broke the silence.

"You look great, Doll," she whispered and smiled a little. "Just great."

He held her in a quick embrace that Doll was certain the guard wouldn't let last. But the guard only stared at the two of them. Doll guessed from her disapproving expression that the bent rule was another of the products of Willard Giesler's grease.

Time, twelve years, collapsed—almost. Twelve years ago there had been no uniformed matron to look on.

They sat, at last, across the table from one another.

She wore jeans and a work shirt. Doll guessed it was the standard issue. Her deep brown hair was combed and shiny. The time in jail hadn't yet taken the tan from her face. Her eyes were a cool blue and quiet.

Doll realized he hadn't known what to expect, which was just as well, for whatever he'd have expected, it wouldn't have been this. If Tampa had been the second edition Diana, the woman he saw before him now was the third. She was still beautiful, her skin smooth, her figure superbly maintained. Her face showed no lines, her hair no gray, from the intervening years. And yet, Doll sensed, Diana Raney was older—older in the only real way that there is to get old. The spark of the future was gone from her eyes. The only world this new Diana recognized was now.

"Are you all right?" Doll asked. "You look fine—a lot more than that—but *are* you?"

Diana nodded. "It's not even as bad in here as I thought. In some ways, it's almost easy. The hours and meals are regular. There haven't been any hassles. There's almost nothing you have to decide. Maybe it's tougher in serious time. Right now it's probably the best thing for me. Sometimes my life seems to need a little controlling."

"We'll get you out," Doll promised.

But Diana seemed hardly to notice the pledge.

"These last few days I've been wondering how it would be seeing you again. I've been up and down, and, now that you're here, you'd think I'd know. But I don't. I'm very sad, and then, at the same time, I'm very happy."

"We don't have a whole lot of time," Doll said, "but in the time we do have, there are a couple of things I'd like to go through. What I want you to do is answer some questions for me. But only the ones that I ask you. For now, at least, I don't want you to talk about anything else."

"You sound just like Willard." Diana sighed. "Always careful. Always a purpose. Always something you want to get done. He can't help me, Doll. What makes you think that you can? Sometimes things happen that you just can't put back. Like diseases—sometimes there isn't any cure."

"Do you trust me?"

"Of course." She smiled lightly as though the answer was part of a geometrician's given. "But that's not the problem, is it?"

"Enough to answer my questions?"

Another smile was as close as Diana got to saying that she'd try.

"You had an argument with Sean Dabney the night that he died," Doll began. "Ann says you told the police that you didn't remember what it was about."

"What Sean and I fight . . ." Her initial impulse toward anger folded back on itself, and her voice fell away. "Or fought about," she went on, listlessly now, "isn't anybody's business but our own. Not even yours."

"You went to the usual place that night, the Piña Colada?"

"Well, you have been busy." Diana accorded Doll a tiny half nod of respect, but then, in nearly the same instant, she withdrew it. "Oh, but that wasn't such an achievement, was it? My baby sister knew all that, and she's the one who decided she had to get you down here in the first place."

Doll kept on with the questions. "There were other people there. Do you remember who else was there that night?"

"People, just people," Diana answered vaguely. "It's a popular place. There are always a lot of people there."

"Valerie Albrecht? Calvin Tack?"

The pair of names, if nothing else, produced a more animated reaction. Diana stared wide-eyed at Doll. Her mouth opened. The words came out almost despite herself.

"How do you know about them—Valerie and Calvin? What have you been doing? Who have you been talking to? Can't I have any privacy left to call my own?"

"Were they there that night?" Doll asked again.

"And if they were? So what? And anyway, why ask me? I told the police. I was drunk. Stinking drunk! I passed out when we got back to Sean's. You can't expect me to remember."

"Do you remember Sylvia Guillette?" From what Ann had said on the beach, Doll guessed the effect that the name would produce. The tactic was born of desperation. But he was willing to let the rush of anger bring the answers if that was the only way he could get them.

"Oh, God." Diana glared hotly at Doll from across the narrow table. "Is there any limit to what you won't drag up? Let the woman alone, Doll. She lost her husband; then she lost Sean when I came along. I didn't take Sean away from her. I wouldn't have done that. But, if you knew Sean at all, you'd understand. Sylvia's big mistake was not giving up Sean after her husband found out. Sean doesn't stay with women. He isn't made that way. He'd have left me when the mood finally struck him. It was there all along. I knew that, and I was ready for it. With Sean, it was just a matter of time."

"Nice guy," Doll said.

"Not so different from some others." Diana's eyes flashed. "The difference with Sean was that you knew it all along. You never expected more than what you were getting."

Doll said nothing.

Diana covered her face with her hands and exhaled into her open palms.

"Look, I'm sorry for that." She looked up at him. The surface of her eyes showed a film of moisture. "It wasn't fair. You never led me on, and I don't have any right to make it sound as though I thought you did. I told you before I didn't know how I felt about seeing you again. That's changed, Doll. I'm sorry. Now I do."

"Not happy," Doll anticipated.

Diana tried a small, dark smile, but even that effort didn't succeed.

"Go home, Doll," she whispered. "Wipe today out of your mind and just remember the good times from the days in Tampa. There's nothing you can do here. They say I killed Sean. I don't remember. For all I know, I probably did."

"I don't believe that. Not for less time than it takes to say it," Doll answered.

"Then don't. It's something else that's not important. Let's go. Get me out of here," Diana Raney said as she stood and turned toward the guard. "No matter how bad it gets in here, it can't be worse than this."

She turned her head, but not her body, to face Doll again.

"Good-bye, Doll," she said softly. "Thanks for coming and trying. But give it up. There's nothing you can do, and nothing I want you to do. Go back home. Live your own life, and for God's sake, let whatever's done be done."

5

"I'll be straight with you, Doll. I'll tell you I've got mixed feelings about it." Ann took a long swallow of beer from the can. "As much as I want to help Diana—as much as I want her out of that damn jail—it would've been hard for me to take it if she'd opened up with you when she wouldn't to me."

Ann sat in one of the two bamboo chairs with one knee up and a foot on the edge of the seat and the other leg stretched out before her, still wearing the cutoff jeans, shirt, and tennis shoes she'd had on since the morning. "If I've seemed a little crazy since you got here, it's because I've been up and down on that roller coaster—hoping she'd come around for you, and then feeling jealous and hoping that she wouldn't. It's been like that since I came back from Maryland, and when you got down here, it only got worse."

"Well, you can relax." Doll took a taste of his own beer and then put the can on the floor. He felt tired, though not from any need for sleep. Doll recognized the symptoms. It was only his mind's way of trying to find an escape from the morning's grand disaster.

"She was glad to see you—I mean at first?"

"I thought so." Doll massaged his eyes. "I thought she was going to be fine. Then I started asking questions about what happened, and she backed off. I dug in my heels. Hard near the end." He shook his head. "Maybe I should've backed off too."

"You just hit the same wall that her lawyer and I hit."

"But why is it there?" Doll searched Ann's face as though he might find the answer there, yet knowing at the same time that he wouldn't.

"I don't know why. I'm no psychiatrist," Ann said. "Why does anybody do what they do?"

"I don't know. I don't want to." Doll frowned at the floor. "I don't like trying to climb inside people's heads. Short of murder and rape, it's probably the most indecent invasion there is."

He picked up his nearly full can of beer, rotated it with his fingers, then put it back on the floor. "Guilt. Self-destruction. Those are the only explanations I can see."

"Then maybe you ought to look some other way." Ann stared sharply across at Doll. "I hope you're not saying what that sounds like you are. I hope you're not saying you think Diana killed Dabney."

"What I was really beginning to wonder was if you think she did," Doll replied.

Ann continued to stare at Doll, then drained some more of the beer in what seemed another way to postpone having to answer him.

"I guess I blew the time limit, didn't I?" she said sourly after still more seconds had passed. "I was thinking about trying a bout of hysterics. Too bad. I waited too long for that now. It's a lousy question, Doll. If it matters, I think you're a son of a bitch for asking it."

"You don't know, yourself, do you?"

"Worse than that. I don't care." Ann stared indifferently at Doll, seeming to anticipate his condemnation, then going on when the expected didn't come. "You're right. I don't know if she murdered Dabney or not. I told you before that I thought she would have confessed if she had, but I've never been really sure of that. I'm not in this for justice. It's not impossible that I'm here for something like the very opposite of that."

"You might as well be honest about it," Doll said. "Nobody in his right mind is going to believe anything else."

"And you?" Ann asked. "Do you think she killed him? Are you telling me you want to quit? Is that what all this buildup is about?"

"Diana didn't murder Dabney." Doll's reply came without hesitation. "She probably even knows that herself, at some level—even though she says she doesn't."

"How can you possibly know that? I've been over it a hundred times myself. To say something like that you'd have to have been there that night in Dabney's apartment to see it."

"I only have to ask myself why," Doll answered, shaking his head. "There are people who can kill just for the violence of the act. Not Diana. Maybe least of all Diana. Then provocation? Where is it? Not sex. You said that much yourself. She and Dabney weren't strangers. They weren't Platonic lovers either. Whether it was wanted or not on that particular night, she wouldn't have gone so far as to kill him to avoid it.

"Not jealousy. She said—and you said—that she never expected the relationship to last, and I believe her. She knew what had happened with Sylvia Guillette. Diana, as you also said, can make bad choices, but she doesn't make them bad because she's dumb."

"There are other reasons besides sex and jealousy," Ann said, "other reasons why people kill."

"There are, but they don't fit Diana either. Greed? Blackmail?" He shook his head. "To protect herself from physical harm? Maybe I could see that. But nothing in the evidence implies she was threatened. Sean Dabney was a bum where women were concerned, but we've never even heard any suggestion he was violent."

"But you talked about guilt," Ann remembered. "If it's not Dabney's murder, what does Diana feel guilty about?"

"Everything. Her whole world." Doll leaned back in the

chair. "All the things you said this morning, plus some more you said back up in Maryland. She didn't kill Dabney, but a part of her thinks she deserves to be punished. She's using the chance that she might get tagged with Dabney's murder to make that judgment come true."

The first seconds of silence drew out into minutes. Ann worked mechanically at what remained of her beer, giving no clue to what she was thinking. Doll, meanwhile, stared blankly out at a wall he didn't see.

All the reasons that he'd given for believing in Diana's innocence were, from his perspective, true—which was to say they were grounded in the facts that Doll knew, but facts reflected through the prism of Doll's interpretation of the woman whom he believed that he knew. In other words, while the facts worked perfectly well for Doll, there wasn't any inherent logic in them that would automatically make them work for anybody else.

Doll was thinking about how they might work for Willard Giesler in the context of their four-thirty meeting. But that, he realized, still left the biggest part of the afternoon as open time in which he could try to eclipse the debacle of the morning.

Doll waited in the hypercooled showroom. To pass the time, he began an inventory of the cars outside on the Southern States lot. After a first attempt during which he lost count, he abandoned the precision of a car-by-car tally and settled instead for a column and row approximation. It came out to two hundred cars, give or take.

Allowing an average price of fifteen thousand apiece, he estimated the value of the stock at three million dollars, a lot of money to keep tied up—money that, by the inflexible dictates of capitalism, would have found somewhere else to go if the business wasn't yielding a competitive return.

It all went a long way toward explaining Willard Giesler's instant recognition when Doll had been able to offer him only Calvin Tack's last name.

The man who came through the door was tall, but he carried with him a sufficient paunch so that the overall impression he left was one of midterm pregnancy. Doll put his age in the middle fifties, which meant that Ann's guess had been about right. His hair was white, but with patches of blond at the sides that still remained from an earlier day.

He wore a gray-striped seersucker jacket, a white shirt, gray slacks, and a blue tie with a pattern of white images that, from across the room, appeared to be polka dots, but on closer inspection turned out to be tiny vintage automobiles. He offered his hand and introduced himself, then led Doll to a corner of the showroom, as far away from the receptionist and secretaries as he could get without actually going out into the yard.

"That's quite a fleet you've got out there," Doll began.

"It is." Tack allowed himself a grin to convey his sense of pride, which, Doll felt certain, Tack had to work to keep within the bounds of acceptable moderation. "We like to call it the biggest on the beach. We think it is. We get some minor arguments. It depends on how you count trucks and vans and how many franchises you represent. But the volume's enough so we're able to offer our customers prices as good as anyplace outside of Miami. And, if you had a car that needed service—" Tack smiled. "Would you rather go here or have to go in there?"

Doll nodded just enough to say he understood the point.

"To be frank, I've been expecting you," Tack said, without pushing the sales pitch any further. "Diana's sister told someone you'd be coming. Under the circumstances, word like that gets around."

Doll read two messages into that. The first was resignation—someone was coming to stir up the cauldron, and there was nothing Tack could do to stop it or to get himself out of the pot. The second message was that he'd been forewarned and so was presumably forearmed.

"I want to say right off, Mr. Doll," Tack began animatedly, "that I never had any . . . involvement . . . with Diana. Friends! Oh, yes, we were that. A few drinks when we happened to meet every now and then. I even got her a deal on that Camaro she drives. But it never went beyond that. Never more than that. I'm sure, man to man, you understand me."

Doll dipped his chin discreetly in Tack's direction to indicate that he accepted the assurance. He also did Tack the courtesy of not replying that, from the moment he'd seen Tack, he never suspected that the circumstance might have been otherwise.

Tack, only comprehending half of the exchange, nodded back to express his gratitude for Doll's willingness to take him at his word.

"Which is not to say," he went on, "that I don't feel the pain myself for all the terrible things that girl has been put through. Diana was—is—a nice girl. She's fun to be with. That's important, more than a lot of other things that you think are all that matters when you're younger."

"You're thinking of Dabney when you say that?" Doll asked.

Tack frowned. "I was thinking generally," he said. "But Sean was certainly the furthest thing I can think of from an exception. There are times when I wonder if the good Lord doesn't put some men on this earth just to show the rest of us what not to be."

"It seems to get harder and harder," Doll acknowledged, "to find anybody who liked him."

"I wish I could say I was surprised." Calvin Tack gazed out across the field of cars. He seemed to Doll to take a comfort from their presence as he thought over what he wanted to say.

"I'll tell you this much more of Sean Dabney, and I'll let it be at that. He was what my mother—God rest her—used to call 'mean of the spirit.' He believed that the world was always out to cheat him. There's a funny thing about people who feel like that, Mr. Doll. It's my own opinion that a man who believes that believes it because, more often than not, he sees himself in others. And what he sees of himself in them is other people out to cheat the world."

Paranoid, Doll remembered, was the word that Ann Raney had used. "Let me try out another name on you," Doll proposed. "Do you know a woman called Sylvia Guillette?"

"Just another way of asking about Sean Dabney, isn't it?" Tack looked unhappy. "There are some around who'll tell you she got what she deserved for going off on her husband the way she did. And there's at least some truth in that, I suppose. Others, though, would say that she got a whole lot less than she paid for."

"And you? You're neutral? You'd rather stay in the middle of the road?"

Calvin Tack looked out at his cars again and seemed to think the matter over.

"No, I don't think I would," he replied after a time. "I know what I said. I said I wouldn't say more, and now here I am doing exactly what I said I wouldn't. But you push me on the point, Mr. Doll. The fact is, if its hip twitched twice, Sean Dabney was bound and determined to run after it. It's hard to account for a man like that, once he's had the chance to sow his wild oats. I heard it said around that he even made a pass at the sister—and that while he had whatever kind of arrangement he had with Diana."

Doll felt an ominous tug in his stomach. "Do you know when that's supposed to have happened—I mean when the pass at the sister got made?"

Tack shook his head. "I shouldn't have even said it," he retreated. "It's only rumor. I'm not even sure who I heard it from. I'm no fan of Sean Dabney's. I haven't made a secret of that. But I'm not going to turn into a backyard gossip over him either."

"Other women?" Doll asked. "I've heard there were others."

"Oh, I'm sure there were. There must have been. But none that I could say that I knew of."

"How about Valerie Albrecht?"

"Valerie?" Tack smiled, and then the smile broadened into something that was nearly a laugh. "No. Not Valerie, I think. You haven't met Valerie yet, I take it, Mr. Doll. When you do, you'll see what I'm saying. Valerie's a girl that I think of as top of the line. She's smart. She's attractive. And, more important than anything else, she's got her feet on the ground. It's that last part that wasn't true for Diana. I'm sorry to say that. If it had been, she'd never have gotten involved, much less put up, with a man like Sean Dabney."

"You know why I'm here. There's no point in my pulling punches." Doll kept his eyes fixed on Calvin Tack's face. "I'll tell you where I'm coming from because, whether I do or not, you can probably guess. The police have got Diana on a good circumstantial case. I don't believe she murdered Dabney, but there's no one around here who's going to put any credit in my opinion on that. So the only thing I can do to help her is to find the person who really did it, hold him—or her—up by the collar, and point."

"I see. What can I do?" Tack asked the question barely aloud. His voice was distant and tentative.

"I'm looking for candidates. It's as simple as that," Doll pressed. "People with reasons. There's a long line of women. I'm working on those. My question to you is, 'Who else?' You know Diana. You knew Sean Dabney. And you know the rest of the characters in the cast. What I want you to give me are new ideas. I want you to tell me what you think I could've missed."

"I don't know." Tack shook his head so vigorously that Doll

wasn't sure if the shaking was meant to deny Doll's demand or serve as its answer.

"Are you saying you think Diana did it?" Doll asked.

Tack seemed almost at the point of becoming frightened. Not an irrational response, Doll knew. The deliberate twist he'd put into the questions gave Calvin Tack an uncomfortable choice. He could start naming off his friends and neighbors as homicide suspects, or else he had to face up to the delicate job of telling Doll that the friend he'd come to help was, in Tack's opinion, very likely a murderer.

Grasping for the safest ground he could find, Tack blurted out again that he just didn't know.

"Will you think about it?" Doll asked more quietly.

Tack nodded.

Doll gave him the name of his motel and the phone number at Diana Raney's cottage.

"Anything at all," Doll said. "If I'm not there when you call, just leave the message that you want me to call back."

But even then, as he watched Tack's eyes, Doll had no hope that Calvin Tack was going to make that first call.

Willard Giesler leaned back in his high-backed swivel chair. His foot was propped up on a half-open bottom desk drawer. His hair was dark and of a medium length, his face an almost cherubic pink. He was slightly on the short side of average and built like an athlete whose time had gone just a bit by. A toothpick stuck out at an upward angle from the corner of his mouth.

Apparently Giesler had caught Doll's notice of it.

"Goddamn pacifier," he said. "Tobacco substitute. I quit my pipe eight years ago, now. Hell, there was hardly anyplace I could smoke the damn thing anymore. Eight years, and I still miss it. Addictive bastards! Can you believe that, Mr. Doll?"

Doll sensed the lawyer's antennae gathering in their first impressions, but then, Doll conceded, his own antennae were doing exactly the same.

"I want to thank you for your help," he said, "in getting me in to see Diana this morning. I take it from the way things worked that you've got a few friends over there."

"Some people that I make sure not to forget at Christmas," Giesler answered lightly. Then he let the airiness fall away.

"I'll tell you, Mr. Doll, I've had clients like Diana before, clients who won't lift a finger to help themselves. The law isn't built to handle that. It's an adversary system. It assumes the accused is going to put his best face forward. When he doesn't, he gets screwed. That's the way the process works."

"If that's a way of asking if I got any more out of her than you or her sister," Doll replied, "the answer is that she told me to forget the whole thing and go home."

"Damn woman!" Giesler swore and slammed the flat of his hand on the desk. "She won't talk to you. She won't talk to me. She won't talk to her sister. Who will she talk to? She talks to Eldwin Rush. She talks to the state's attorney. They're not fools. They're not amateurs, Mr. Doll. They know what questions to ask, and with every one she answers she digs her own hole just that much deeper. How the hell do I justify sending her a bill? There isn't a goddamn thing I can do that's going to help her."

"I've been talking to some people about other angles," Doll said. "You probably already know what I'm going to say. Dabney seems to have had a fairly large appetite for women. One affair he had with a woman named Sylvia Guillette ended up with Dabney dumping her and the woman going through a divorce."

"Motive, motive, who's got the motive?" Willard Giesler traced an endless circle in the air with his finger. "You find any two people who know one another, and you can probably come up with a plausible motive for murder. Any motive you find for Dabney's other women works as well against Diana as it does against them. I don't say it applies necessarily, mind you. But the state can sure make the case that it does."

Still, Giesler made a note on the yellow legal pad at his elbow. "Other people you've been talking to . . . ?" he asked.

Specifics, live bodies you can get to talk in a courtroom, Doll thought—that was what you had to produce to make a case under the law. Willard Giesler was covering the bases.

"The building superintendent at Dabney's condo. He can tell you about the number of visitors Dabney had," Doll answered. "Diana could tell you about Sylvia Guillette. But, if you don't want to use her, you can use Calvin Tack."

" 'Yours-For-Less-Than-One-Percent-Down'?" The trace of a sense of humor spread across Giesler's face. He grinned and leaned back in his chair again. "So you did get out to see him. What did you wind up driving away in? Did he offer to throw in tinted glass and air?"

"He doesn't fit," Doll replied obliquely. "Not with Dabney. Not with Diana. That's what makes my mind keep going back to him. He's not part of any satin sheets crowd. I try to put him together with the others—Dabney, Diana, this Sylvia Guillette— and there just isn't any way that he fits."

"Wait till you get to Doc Truitt," Giesler said. "Doc's got another ten or fifteen years on Calvin. He's a dentist who retired down here from someplace up north. He got a Florida license and does fillings for extra pocket money. Lace curtains, railed front porch, and a wife who's a perfect match for her husband."

"You're saying that he was tied up with Diana too?"

"Somehow," Giesler said and shrugged. "Doc Truitt. Calvin Tack. Valerie Albrecht, who you asked about this morning. Perry Wellman, who I gather you haven't run across yet, but you will. Dabney and Diana. Sylvia Guillette, along with her former husband. They pal around together. That's all I know. Don't ask me how it fits. But as sure as God made cloudy days there's something out there that ties them together."

"You said this morning something about the Piña Colada club," Doll recalled. "Diana's sister talked about the same place."

"Mickey Zale's spot." Giesler nodded. "But that's a where, not a why. You ought to try it once—if only for the experience. The Treasure Coast in its comic book version. A theme park that got itself made into a bar."

"If that doesn't mean flamingos and palm trees, I don't understand it," Doll said.

"Flamingos." Giesler rolled the toothpick between his fingers and then replaced it in his mouth. "No. Actually, you don't get those for a little farther south yet. Up here it's more the Spanish Main motif. In the case of the Piña Colada, it's a cannon here and there. A few muskets and swords hung on the wall. A fish tank behind the bar with a painted, ceramic diver opening a treasure chest and bubbling away. The waitresses wear skull and crossbones bandannas, black boots, short skirts with sashes at the waist."

"Sounds colorful," Doll said because he couldn't think of anything inoffensive that seemed more appropriate to say.

"Why, you're just not a party animal, are you, Mr. Doll?" The expression on Willard Giesler's face suggested a collusion in cynicism. "The best you can say about it, I suppose, is that at least the history behind the hype is real. The treasure fleets really did sail the coast. With the Bahama shoals to the east and the northerly current, the passage was the best route they had back to Spain."

"It doesn't help very much, does it?" Doll said to get Giesler back on the track. "I don't mean the history. I mean any of the rest."

Doll's question seemed to collapse what remained of Giesler's upbeat mood and prompted him to do some active poking at his cuspids with the toothpick while he thought.

"It helps less than that," he replied when he decided that the dentistry was done. "It helps so little that it doesn't help at all. Everything goes back to questions that Diana has to answer, and that, from what happened again today, leaves us nowhere at all."

"So, what happens next?" Doll asked, though he knew that Giesler could offer no optimistic—or perhaps not even any—answer.

Another moment went by before Giesler replied.

"You do, I suppose," the lawyer said. "For right now, there doesn't seem to be a whole lot of anything that I can do. You find something somewhere out there. I don't know what it is, only the kind of thing it has to be—and you know that as well as I do. If you don't find anything, then we are where we are. I can go to court. I can call in expert witnesses and throw stones at the state's case. I can open up a closet full of hypothetical alternatives and not be able to offer so much as a thread of support for even one. I can put Dabney on trial and show he was a bastard. And none of that is going to change anything."

"Then they'll convict her," Doll concluded.

Willard Giesler made a point of meeting Doll's eye. "Maybe not on murder. With the intoxication, I can probably get it down to manslaughter. But convict? You can bet your ass they will. They'll convict her sure as the goddamn 'gators crap out there in the swamp."

6

The sign inside the gate said that the parking was by valet only. Doll followed the graveled semicircle and stopped at its apex where an imitation gangway rose at a modest incline from the driveway to the entrance to the club.

In the deep blue and purple sky, the first stars were barely visible. The air had lost the warmth and humidity of the day. It was the time of the magic cusp that, in tropical climates, exists in the few moments that come between the twilight and the night.

A young man dressed in black—shirt, pants, shoes, and a bandanna—held open the Camaro's door to let Ann out of the car. Doll, meanwhile, got out on his own, leaving the keys in the ignition.

The man in black came around to the car's left side. In the bright, white flood of the club's halogen lamps, his eyes looked glazed and his stare seemed vacant. The odor of his breath was bad, but with no trace of alcohol Doll could detect. His chin, near the point, had a long, horizontal scar of a type that admitted of only one likely cause. He might very well have been dead, Doll thought, if the blade of the knife had, instead, sliced his neck, only an inch or so lower.

*   *   *

The outfit of the hostess who showed them to their table in the dining room included a plumed black hat and a blue and white vertically striped pair of skintight pedal pushers. Willard Giesler, Doll thought, had left that out. Otherwise, as Doll looked around, he conceded to himself that the lawyer's description had been accurate both in detail and in spirit.

A costumed waitress came to the table, presented them with menus, and took their orders for drinks.

"I wish I could say I felt a whole lot like eating," Ann said as the two of them were once again alone.

"Willard Giesler?" Doll asked. "Because of what I told you he said?" Doll asked.

She nodded without looking up from the tablecloth. "How little he says he can do. That's the worst part of it. It's much worse than he ever admitted to me. And those names he came up with, what are they supposed to mean? I don't see what good they can possibly do."

"Certainly nothing that's obvious right off," Doll agreed. "What Giesler's done is probably all he could have done. He's feeling the frustrations, and he's thrown the problem back at us. That makes the stakes on finding something that much higher. That's another way of saying that it makes it more important that we don't keep secrets from each other."

"Keep secrets!" Ann looked across at Doll. Her eyes flashed, but she held herself in check, still not certain she ought to be angry. "Well, that's full of possibilities, isn't it? This from a man whose FBI record makes him sound like a cross between Rambo and the goddamn CIA. Not to mention a dead man you left somewhere up in Delaware. Oh, I'm sorry. I forgot. That's all right because it doesn't count. That one was only self-defense."

It had to come, Doll told himself. The half questions, half accusations had been in the cards since Eldwin Rush's office the afternoon before—almost guaranteed to burst out in the first, inevitable moment of tension.

"We can talk about the dark parts of my checkered past," Doll said evenly. "It's not nearly as exciting or sinister as you might like to think, and it won't do a damn thing to help Diana, but we can dredge up the details if that's what you want. Or you can tell me the truth for a change, and maybe—just maybe—that *will* get us somewhere. It's your choice. I can't make you do what you won't do. How you want to spend our time is at least half up to you."

"Get us where? What the hell are you fishing for, Doll? Am I supposed to guess what 'secret' you think you've found and pour out my soul for you to get off on?"

"I'm not going to play that game either," Doll replied. "One of the reasons we're here tonight is that I'm still trying to figure out where this whole thing is going. I need to know the mix if I'm going to find out what happened. If you want it crisp, I can handle that too. One thing Calvin Tack said that I didn't tell you because I wanted to see if you'd tell me yourself—he says that Dabney tried to hit on you. Is it true?"

"Where did he . . . ?" Ann stopped, then blushed and looked away. "All right, he did. So what?" She turned defiantly back to face Doll. "I'm sorry about that. I'm not usually so modest. First the back door, then the slap in the face. You'll forgive me if you caught me off my guard."

"Do you want to tell me about it now?" Doll invited.

"No, I damn well don't," Ann snapped. "In fact, it's very nearly the last thing I want to do."

She gazed out across the room. Doll said nothing. He knew he had no need to. He let her take her time to get used to the new circumstance, to see the implications, and to understand that the rest would have to come out.

"What a bastard," Ann said under her breath. Her voice was tired. Her defenses had been breached and to that extent, she'd suffered a defeat. She shook her head.

"It happened that same day he died," she began, making the

obviously difficult struggle to meet Doll's eyes. "The night that he and Diana came here. I was supposed to go with them. All three of us together. Now you know why I didn't go."

"Is that what the two of them were arguing about?"

Ann shook her head, more assertively this time. "It couldn't have been. Diana didn't know."

Doll asked how it happened.

Ann drew in a breath. "Sean came by that day in the afternoon. Just a casual drop-in was what he said. Diana was out doing some shopping. He kept to small talk for maybe five minutes before he made his intentions clear. I told him that if he so much as came near me, before I was done with him, he'd be able to look for a new job guarding harems."

"And?"

A thin, droll smile appeared on Ann's face. "That seemed to discourage him. That was the first time he'd tried anything, and, even if he hadn't died, it would've been the last. He started pleading with me not to tell Diana. Not that I ever would have. I wouldn't have hurt her, even though the man she was with was a lecherous creep. Instead I came down with a convenient case of cramps. It's amazing how often the menstrual cycle comes in handy."

"Why didn't you tell me this before?" Doll asked.

"Because I was embarrassed. And because I'm not a fool, Doll." She stared at Doll for long enough to amplify the point. "I can add things together as quickly as you can. You said just the beginning of this afternoon that you didn't think Diana murdered Sean because you couldn't find a motive. Eldwin Rush, from what he tried to ask me, is obviously having problems with the motive angle too. So what was I supposed to do—make everybody's search a little easier? Just come right out and say that Diana might have killed Dabney—not because she thought he was cheating on her, but because she thought she was protecting me?"

"Well, well." She let the two words hang dramatically until she seemed satisfied that she'd captured Doll's undivided attention. "Proof that persistence pays off, I suppose. You dragged me here tonight against my will. In part to set me up, I see that now. But also, you said, to lure some of the other names on your list out of the woodwork. No, don't turn your head or you'll spoil the surprise."

"Our host, making his rounds?" Doll guessed.

"Oh, now you did spoil it." Ann frowned in a farce of disappointment. "Mickey Zale. You'll know when the pale pink jacket arrives. Pink jacket, black slacks, black or pink or gray bow tie. That's the extent of the variations. The man has a superb sense of fashion."

Zale stopped when he reached the side of the table. He glanced at Doll and nodded briefly, then ignored him while he turned his attention to Ann. He was short and heavyset. His head was round. He reminded Doll of a fireplug. His choice for the evening's tie was gray. The lapel of Zale's pink dinner jacket sported a fresh, white carnation, the edge of which was dip-dyed a brilliant blood red.

"And how are you this evening, Miss Raney? Always so nice to have you honor us." Zale's voice was a raspy baritone. His cologne and mouthspray let him down. He still smelled of tobacco smoke.

"Mr. Zale, this is . . . Doll. Doll, this is Mr. Zale. Mr. Zale owns the Piña Colada. Doll is a very good friend of Diana. He knows her from years ago when they both lived in Tampa."

Zale nodded again in Doll's direction.

"You came to try to help her, then? I only hope you can. The lady shouldn't be in jail. That much I can tell you. The police here, they're like everywhere else—it's like they got to keep their ratings up. A man gets killed, they got to find someone to convict. There's nothing that says the one who killed him and who gets convicted have got to be the same."

"But she didn't know about Dabney. You just told me that,"
Doll objected. "So she didn't have that motive. She couldn'
have been acting to protect you if she had no way of knowin
you needed protecting."

"But who'd believe she didn't know?" Ann demanded. "Onc
the story got out, who'd believe me? They'd just say that I tol
her and that now I was lying by saying I didn't in order
protect her. You can't use that, Doll. You can't let it g
around."

"It's a long time too late for that." Doll tried to say it as tl
indifferent fact that it was, not in any kind of condemnatio
"Tack knows, and the somebody else he got it from knows. I
only a question of time before the sheriff finds out. We might
well take out ads in the paper. You said you didn't tell Diar
Did you tell anyone else?"

"Of course not," Ann answered. "Not even you, remembe

"And we can pretty much assume that Dabney didn't eithe
Doll speculated, "since he doesn't sound like the kind of n
who liked to brag about his failures. So the big money quest
comes down to how whoever told Calvin Tack knew."

The buccaneer waitress came back with their drinks:
Coconut Flip that Ann had ordered and a gin on the rocks
Doll. Doll said that they hadn't yet decided on dinner.

"How could anyone have known?" Ann asked.

Doll swirled the gin around the ice in his glass, then lift
in a tacit toast which admitted that he had no adequate re

Ann met the toast and put her drink back down on the t
"I never realized how tricky it gets when you start trying t
different stories together. The little things, the throwaway:
say—or even don't say. You fit things together, and sud
they stand out like they're all wrapped up in neon."

She looked beyond Doll's shoulder, out across the
searching, it seemed, in the wider space for somethin;
would give her an answer.

Zale turned back to Ann. "I won't ask about Diana. Only 'cause I can see where it's, maybe, something you don't want to talk about. So just leave it that, at any other time, I would've asked. How's that, okay?"

"Thank you," Ann replied. "All I could tell you anyway is that she's holding up just about the same as she has been. No changes. Not for the better or the worse."

Mickey Zale nodded soberly. He took a step in anticipation of taking his leave.

"Before you go, I just wanted to ask you . . . ," Doll said, stopping him. "What you were saying just now about the police . . . It makes it sound—if I understand what you said—that you think Diana's innocent, that you don't think that it was she who killed Dabney?"

"Killed Dabney? Hell, no, I don't think she killed him. I *know* she didn't kill him. It's not in her to kill anybody. You're her friend. You oughta know that too. It's rubbish, garbage— this whole thing they're trying to pin on her."

"You knew both of them—Dabney and Diana—well, I gather from what I've been hearing around. From what I understand, they came here fairly often. If you knew Dabney and you don't think Diana killed him, maybe you've got somebody else in mind who might have."

"You think so, eh?" Zale studied Doll closely again before he went on. "And what would make you think a thing like that?"

"I just thought maybe you'd want to help Diana," Doll said.

"Want t' help? Hey, what d'y'think? Sure I want t' help." Zale glanced back toward Ann, trying to plead his own case in the face of what he took to be Doll's deprecation. "All the *want* in the world doesn't make me a psychic. Doesn't mean I go around accusing other people—making trouble for them when I don't know."

"Then something you do know?" Doll suggested. "Diana and

Dabney, they came here on the night he was murdered. They had a fight."

"Did they?" Zale moved on to a new form of defense. His face showed nothing beyond the belligerent protest of innocence reflected in the roundness of his eyes. The message in them seemed to Doll to be, "If you don't like what I've told you, see my lawyer."

"Diana says so." Doll kept up the attack. More an interpretation than a fact, he admitted to himself, but then Zale couldn't know what Diana had or hadn't told him.

"All right, so they maybe had some words when they were here. If that's what Diana says, who is Mickey Zale to say no?"

"Do you know what they argued about?"

"Diana didn't tell you that?" Zale asked with a slender grin. "Funny thing, if Diana didn't tell you, I must've forgot. Or maybe it was something I never knew. Maybe something nobody ever told me."

"How about their other friends?" Doll ran through a part of the list that he'd only that afternoon acquired. "Doc Truitt, Calvin Tack, Perry Wellman? Were any of them in here that night—any of them likely to have a better memory than you?"

The grin that Zale had let himself show broadened into something full of teeth and savage. "Let me tell you something about the bar business, Mr. Doll." The tone of condescension was rich in his voice. "Bars are public you think, but they're kind of private too. That way they're a little like people's houses. Folks who come regular start to make up a sort of family. What they do is between themselves. A smart guy respects that. You run a bar, you mind the bar business. You make sure the drinks get served and paid for, and you keep your nose as far as you can from the rest."

Zale offered a nod and a rewarmed smile in Ann's direction, then shot a last, curt stare at Doll.

"Now, if you'll excuse me, there are other guests I've got here tonight—who maybe don't have so many questions," he said, and moved off in the direction of the bar.

Ann arched an eyebrow as she took the last swallow of the Coconut Flip and nodded when Doll asked if she wanted another.

"Nice work." She put down her glass. "You made quite an impression on Mickey. I could tell. Is it just your nature to go through life bringing out the best in people?"

"Who is he, do you know?" Doll asked. "I mean aside from owning this place."

Ann shook her head. "I've only seen him here the three or four times I came with Diana. You know what I know—more than what I know. I'll tell you this: I never saw anybody else get under his skin like that before."

Doll flagged the waitress and ordered the second drink for Ann. His own gin was less than half finished.

"I'd really like to know where he fits in all this." Doll peered across the room in the direction Mickey Zale had gone as though some kind of trail that Zale had left might somehow tell him something more. "If this place is a key, then so is he. The trick is in finding the lock that he opens."

Ann traced the rim of her empty glass with the tip of her finger until something caused her to look up at Doll. "What is it? What are you looking at?" she asked.

The threesome moved through the dining room like an approaching squall line.

Doll had seen them first as Ann was talking, an impression of movement that, after a second, resolved itself into two men and a woman emerging from the bar. They huddled together like self-involved adolescents, bumping into one another and laughing as though something they shared was tremendously funny.

In those early seconds, their path seemed uncertain, but,

again, like an advancing storm, the farther they moved, the more their track betrayed their impending direction.

An instant later, what remained of the charade fell apart. As the trio neared the center of the room, the younger of the two escorting males made the mistake of meeting Doll's eye. Involuntarily, the man's stare locked. From that moment on, the pretense of a chance encounter was over.

When they reached the table, the woman, between the two men, smiled down at Doll.

"Well, Mr. Doll, I think it's high time that we met in the flesh, so to speak. I understand you've been asking about me. My name is Valerie Albrecht."

Doll stood.

Her face was tanned, her eyes a brilliant emerald green. Her ash-blond hair was medium-short, cut to a length she could get wet without a lot of trouble if she wanted. The way she moved and carried herself implied a body not only trim, but fit. She wore a sleeveless cotton jumpsuit, the color of straw.

The man to her right was taller than she and conservatively dressed in a summer-weight jacket and a solid-colored tie. The second man, the younger one, looked to be in his early to middle thirties. His tan was dark, deeper even than Valerie's. His shirt was a knit pullover in a shade of peach, his slacks khaki, and his shoes a pair of moccasin-styled Topsiders.

Valerie turned to Ann. "I don't know if you remember— Diana introduced us. I promise you we won't impose ourselves on the two of you—at least not for very long. How about a drink's time? Is that all right? With these two, that comes down to hardly any time at all."

"You're not imposing," Ann invited. "We haven't even ordered yet."

The man in the knit shirt pulled up a chair for Valerie.

"Oh, and these two," Valerie said as though the arrival of the chair had only then made her aware of the omission. "The polite one here is Perry Wellman. The other is Clayton Rivers. Clayton, as you might have guessed from his attentiveness, is my date."

The two men found chairs for themselves, and everyone sat.

"How's Diana holding up?" Valerie looked to Ann for the answer to her question. "Those Neanderthals haven't come to their senses yet? I know they haven't, the imbeciles! It's hard, but sometimes you just have to wait and trust. I know things don't look awfully great, but Willard'll make them work out."

"Does that mean it was you who suggested Willard Giesler to Diana?" Doll asked.

"You don't approve?" Valerie turned her attention toward Doll.

"The opposite. I do approve," Doll replied. "I don't know what the other choices were, but whatever they were, I don't think Diana could have done any better."

"Thank you, Mr. Doll." Valerie Albrecht nodded and smiled to accept the compliment. "I'll take that as high praise coming from you. You see, I don't mind your asking questions about me. I understand you're a long way from home and that you're down here to help Diana. I'm glad about that."

The buccaneer waitress brought Ann's fresh drink. Valerie ordered refills all around.

"Everybody, this is our round." She addressed the waitress. "Clayton's is a Scotch and soda. Perry'll have a bourbon on the rocks. And I'll have another of those sunrise things—but, for God's sake, this time leave out the half peach. Tell Enrico he can add some extra peach liqueur to it instead."

The waitress looked toward Ann, who glanced at her just delivered drink, then nodded to say she'd take yet another. Doll acquiesced, making the order complete.

"So this is your grand opportunity, Mr. Doll. If you want answers, the best place to go is the source. I'm here and utterly at your disposal." In a burlesque of the obedient schoolgirl, Valerie folded her hands on the table before her.

"Wrong night. I'm off duty." Doll smiled back. "No questions. Maybe I'll have some for you later. If I do, you'll be the first to know. Right now I don't even know what they'd be."

"Oh." Valerie's voice and exuberance wilted together. "I guess I wasn't ready for that. I think I'm disappointed. I heard out in the bar you were in here with Ann, and I got myself all worked up for this. Now it's all kind of a letdown. It's got the same kind of empty feeling as bad sex."

Smart, Doll remembered, was the word that Calvin Tack had used. *Clever,* he thought, was maybe even better. It included the *smart,* but also gave credit for knowing how to apply the intelligence. Valerie Albrecht had come to the table prepared.

The game, in the circumstances in which she offered it, was stacked against Doll and vastly in her favor. She had her advisers and moral supporters on either side of her, and the chance to withdraw from the field if the questions got hard. Besides that, the battle was on her turf; the party was hers as long as her side bought the liquor.

Doll, instead, chose to attack the flank, shifting his focus from Valerie to Perry Wellman. Keep it all relaxed, light and breezy: that was the flavor for the night.

"Your name came up, too." Doll turned toward the younger of the two men. "I don't remember where exactly. I think the context was that you were also a friend of Diana."

"I was. Valerie was. It's true. We all were—are." Wellman stumbled on his vacillating tenses. "Hell, I suppose the way you say it depends on which of the two of them you mean. We were all friends of Sean. We were—and are still—friends of Diana, Mr. Doll."

"What made *you* her friend? What made any of you friends?" Doll asked.

"Me? Well, I guess I can only answer for me." Wellman

shrugged with his eyes toward the tablecloth, at the same time shifting his position in the chair. "You said you heard my name? Was it from Diana?"

"I don't remember where I heard it," Doll said in what was an outright lie. "Jog my memory. Was there something special that Diana should have told me?"

The waitress brought the new round of drinks, setting Ann's third beside her barely started second one. Valerie explained that all would go on Clayton's tab.

Perry Wellman, meanwhile, looked from Rivers to Valerie. Having gotten no apparent response, he entrusted his thoughts to a swallow of his bourbon.

Doll waited for Wellman to continue. But before he did, Valerie intervened.

"Perry's a wonderful believer in friendship—unique in our jaundiced little circle, I'm afraid." She smiled gently across at Wellman, ostensibly with the purpose of taking whatever sting there might be out of her words. "He knows that's a joke—a little on him, but probably a lot more on us. Perry lives with his dreams. He's never grown up. The rest of us have all succumbed to reality. We gave up our dreaming years ago."

Valerie Albrecht drank a sip of the thing without the half peach.

"Diana," she asked, "never told you about that?"

"Are you talking about dreams? I'm not even sure what 'that' is," Doll replied.

"Not dreams. Well, Perry's dream. Perry's gold," Valerie said and laughed.

"It's not a secret anymore. I've been at it too long." Wellman looked from Ann to Doll, then back down at the tablecloth again. "I've even gotten used to people making jokes about it. I've spent the last four years down here trying to find a treasure wreck worth filing a claim on. That ocean out there is probably the richest source of gold and silver in the world—all refined and waiting to be picked up. The only problem is it's so big. I used to tell Diana about it. Maybe because nobody else would listen anymore. There are hundreds of thousands—millions—of dollars out there. All of it just waiting. Time and faith and luck are all you need. If the faith—or the money—doesn't run out."

The last part was Wellman's sermon. The label seemed to Doll to fit. Spoken like some overly zealous preacher, as though conviction alone were enough to turn the statements into fact.

"Diana didn't tell me," Doll said. He glanced at Ann, who seemed to take a moment to think before she shook her head to give her answer.

Perry Wellman nodded with an apparent fatalism, then moved on to looking disheartened.

On Valerie Albrecht's opposite side, Clayton Rivers consulted the face of his watch.

"I'm afraid that I mistook the hour before." He looked back and forth between Doll and Ann with an expression that didn't quite rise to an apology.

"But we only just sat down. We were going to stay for one round of drinks," Valerie objected.

Rivers, in what he seemed to feel was an indisputable reply, regarded his own already empty glass.

"There's no point in arguing with him," Valerie said with a sigh as she pushed her chair back from the table. "All he gets, when he's like this and you fight with him, is surly. Mr. Doll . . ." She smiled and extended her hand.

Doll took it. The skin was smooth. Her grip was strong and, at the same time, sensual.

"I'm sure I'll be seeing you again," she said. "And Ann." She turned her attention from Doll. "Please, when you see Diana, give her my best. That sounds so overdone, but it really isn't meant to be. Tell her there's a day coming up when all of this mess will be through."

Rivers, who seemed to prefer to keep his good-byes to the

minimum, was already moving away from the table. Valerie Albrecht caught hold of his arm, and, like a phantom in a wisp of air, the two of them were gone.

"Clayton Rivers." Doll repeated the name into the vacuum that followed the exit.

"You know him, too?" Perry Wellman asked and looked surprised.

"You sound as though there's some reason I shouldn't," Doll replied—disingenuously to the point of not correcting Wellman's obvious assumption that Doll's knowledge of Rivers went beyond Valerie Albrecht's introduction.

"No, no. No reason at all," Wellman tried ineffectively to recover. "But you knew Valerie and me—and now him. We all think we have our private little worlds where we have control over who gets in and who doesn't. It's a little scary when you realize how easy it is for someone or something to come in from the outside without there being any way for you to stop it."

Then Wellman recalled he too had a watch.

"Actually Clayton was right," he said and, as suddenly, stood. "It's long past what I thought it was. I'd really like to stay. I'm sorry, though. I can't; I have to go."

In the speed of his departure, Doll decided, Perry Wellman conceded nothing to Valerie and Rivers. The only quicker exit that Doll could remember seeing had come in a magician's puff of smoke.

"Why is it," Ann asked, "that I feel like I ought to be checking my teeth to make sure the fillings are still in place?"

Doll shook his head. "That wasn't an accident. That pack didn't just happen by. They had it planned. They wanted something. Then they left. I'm not sure if they left because they got it or decided that they weren't going to. How about you? Any guesses as to what?"

"Nothing I'd want to commit myself to," Ann replied. "But that question that Perry Wellman asked—about if Diana had said anything about any gold . . . I didn't know what to say, so I just went deadpan and said no. Which is true, by the way. Diana never did say anything. Can we settle the check and get out of here? I still haven't got any appetite for dinner. Besides, there's something back at the cabin that I think you'd better see."

7

The object fit easily into the palm of Doll's hand. It was flat, thin, and irregularly round. Metallic. Doll estimated the weight at something like half the weight of an equal volume of lead. The color was a drab speckled gray and black. Except that the analog that came to Doll's mind was too large, what he held in his hand looked like nothing so much as an Oreo cookie slid slightly off center, with the roundness of the edges chipped away.

"I found it in the bottom of a drawer in the dresser," Ann said. "Beneath the paper liner. I wasn't being snoopy. I moved some clothes that Diana had in it so I'd have someplace to put my own while I was here. I got everything out and looked to see what was causing the lump under the paper, and there it was."

"What did Diana say about it?" Doll asked.

"She didn't say anything. I never told her I found it," Ann replied. "I was curious at first, but then that passed. And the time just never seemed right to bring it up the few times that I had to talk to her. Everything else that was going on seemed more important."

"Until Perry Wellman's story tonight," Doll said.

"That's why I thought I had to show it to you. I know it looks old and like what you might expect. But what I think doesn't count for very much. Anything I know about the subject comes from parts of a couple of TV programs that I tuned into strictly by accident. On the other hand, I keep telling myself you don't hide something worth nothing under the paper in the bottom of a drawer."

"If you're smart, you don't hide something that's worth anything there either," Doll replied.

"No lectures, please! Not right now. You know what I'm asking. What about it, Doll? Is it real? Is it gold? Is it what Wellman was talking about?"

Doll shook his head. "I don't know enough to tell very much. It isn't gold. I can tell you that." He turned the object over between his thumb and forefinger. "Gold doesn't corrode, not even after a couple of centuries in seawater. Besides that, the weight's wrong. It's too light for gold by almost half."

Ann curled her lip into a morbid smile and glanced toward the ceiling as though she were crediting God for His dark sense of humor.

"Silver. That's a better bet, even a good one," Doll said. "Two coins." He held them edge on to examine them more closely. "Fused together by the years and the water. I've seen it before. Not in anything I've ever found myself, but in what others have. In one case, enough coins bonded together to make up one solid piece the size of a serving plate."

"Then it is real? It's part of a real treasure?"

"At a guess, it's silver," Doll repeated. "I suppose it could be French or something else, but the overwhelming likelihood is that it's Spanish. A treasure, though? That's another thing again. Two coins don't quite add up to any kind of treasure."

"Don't dangle me. Not about money," Ann said impatiently. "It's not that I'm particularly greedy, but I haven't seen so much in my life that I find it a subject that's easy to joke about."

Doll turned the two coins over again, then handed them back to Ann. "What do you figure it weighs, two ounces give or take? Did you get the market quote this morning? I didn't, but silver usually goes for somewhere between five and six dollars an ounce."

"Six dollars?"

"If you take the high end." Doll nodded. "Twelve for the piece. You've got about two ounces there. But it's worth something more than that. The coins—if we're right about what they are—have the intrinsic value of their metal, but they also have a lot more value as a historical artifact. How much that is depends on what you find when you get the crust off."

"Make a guess."

Doll explained that he couldn't make a fair one. "You need an expert, one who can read whatever markings there are and who knows the collecting market. A couple of hundred dollars? That's very, very rough."

"That's all." Ann's voice reflected her disappointment, but with no suggestion of protest or doubt. "More of the luck of the Raneys," she said. "Like the loser's prize on a game show, I guess. In all the world, only Diana could turn up a treasure worth a lousy couple of hundred dollars. Is that what Perry Wellman finds? Why in the world does he bother?"

"Because he doesn't plan on bringing up two coins," Doll answered. "You heard him—what he said himself tonight. He was talking about finding a wreck site. That means a place he can dig around and bring up some reasonable percentage of a cargo."

"And that could be worth what he said? A hundred thousand dollars—even a million?"

"Those kinds of discoveries have been made," Doll said. "But the odds against making one are long enough that the smart money people don't even try."

"I suppose the odds have to be long," Ann reflected. "Otherwise we'd all buy boats and be millionaires."

Doll didn't answer. Ann's words reached his ear, but Doll's mind never heard them. His thoughts were caught up in a loop of the evening's making—Valerie Albrecht, Perry Wellman's gold, and the coins that Diana had hidden in the drawer.

"Something I want to do . . ." he said, not realizing that nearly a minute had passed since the last time he'd spoken. "I don't know if you'll agree, but I want you to let me take the coins tonight. You'll be better off if you don't ask questions."

"But I am asking. I have to. There are only two reasons you can have for not telling me. The first is that you think I wouldn't approve. The second is that you're trying to shield me from the responsibility for something. If it's the first case, I'm certainly not going to agree. And, if it's the second, there's no way I'm going to let myself be patronized."

Doll nodded. "Somehow, I knew you'd come up with something like that. I want to have them cleaned—get that crust taken off and see what's underneath. I don't want to ask Diana's permission because I don't want to give her the chance to say no."

"Are you saying they could have something to do with what happened to Sean Dabney? Is seeing what's on them somehow going to help her?"

"I doubt it. I don't see how it could. But I don't want to just let it go on the probability that it won't. It won't hurt the value. Knowing what they say will even improve it a little. And I'll set it up so it can't hurt Diana. At least I can promise you that."

Ann held out the coins for Doll to take. "You told me what you wanted to do before I gave them to you—and I agreed," she said to make the terms of their compact clear. "I'll tell you this, though: When Diana gets out, we'd both better be a long ways out of town."

"You think so?"

"I know so," Ann said with a conspiratorial smile. "We're twelve years apart she and I, but we're sisters. I only have to think what I'd do if the situation was the other way around."

When Doll left Ann at Diana's cottage, the time was twenty minutes to midnight. But, despite the lateness of the hour, he felt in no mood for sleep.

He drove, aimlessly at first, keeping deliberately to the back roads but otherwise with no more thought to where he was heading than the effort it took him to follow his headlamps. He had the VW's side window down. The night was clear. The cool air played gently against the side of his face and tousled his hair. He drove like that with no attention to the minutes that passed, letting the physical sensation of the night and the driving relax him. He left his mind to wander as freely as the car, working the loop, then moving free of it—until finally car and mind came to settle on a common direction.

The brilliant antitheft lights around the condominium blotted out all but the brightest of the stars. Closer to earth, bugs swerved and dove in the glare and smashed themselves into the glass of the lamps in their destructive attempts to reach the luring, transcendent arc within.

Doll parked the VW and crossed the planted strip. His shoes were silent on the dew-laden blades of the grass. The night around him was quiet enough so that he was able to hear the almost silent waves that broke and hissed in their rush onto the beach.

There were no other people that Doll could see. Only the witness of the apartment windows, where the dim yellow light filtered out from around the borders of the draperies, betrayed the presence of life within. Doll came to a coconut palm. He stopped and breathed and leaned his back against its trunk.

The truth, he admitted, was that he had no real idea of why he'd come here. The closest he could get to rationalizing the process that had brought him was that it was something like going to the site where a miracle was supposed to have happened in the vague hope that one might happen to you. He stood there, with his back against the palm, staring at the steel and glass condominium and waiting for the moment when his inspiration would arrive.

What arrived was nothing like what he'd expected.

"Don't move from where you are, and raise your hands above your head."

The accented voice was steady, without a trace of strain or excitement. There was a message in that. The speaker anticipated his instructions would be followed. He was neither eager to shoot nor reluctant to fire if he felt that response more appropriate.

Doll stayed where he was and raised his hands exactly as he'd been told.

"Now turn toward me slowly," the flat voice ordered.

Doll turned. Halfway through the turn, the beam from a flashlight caught him in the eyes. He saw white. Nothing more. Otherwise he might just as well have been blind.

Seconds passed. The light was too bright for Doll's eyes to adjust.

"Señor Doll? Is that you?" the voice from behind the light said.

"Emilio?"

The light switched off. Doll was blind again, except that this time everything was black.

"I'm very sorry, Señor Doll," Emilio Secassa said in Spanish now. "You shouldn't stand around out here. I could have shot you for a burglar. If you're coming out, especially at night, you have to let me know."

"My fault," Doll said as he lowered his hands.

"No one's fault. Thanks to God, nothing happened. Is there something you're looking for? Perhaps I could help you?"

"You want the truth? I was hoping for an inspiration." His eyes, Doll noticed gratefully, had begun to adjust to the darkness again. "That's how bad it is. I'm out here looking in the middle of the night, and I don't even know what it is that I'm looking for."

"For inspiration, I think, I sometimes know where to go."

Secassa's voice had a mischievous quality that Doll hadn't heard in it before.

"*Cerveza?*"

"*Si, una poca de cerveza,*" Secassa answered and laughed. He came up to Doll and clapped him on the shoulder. His other hand, Doll could see, held the barrel of his flashlight. The butt of the pistol stuck out from the waistband of his trousers.

"My house, it is your house, Señor Doll," the superintendent of the condominium said.

Emilio Secassa's apartment was in the basement of the building. It couldn't be said that there weren't any windows, but the ones there were were up so high in the wall that any normal-sized human being would have needed to stand on a chair to look out. The unit had three rooms, which gave it one up on Diana's cottage: a living room and bedroom and a separate kitchen with a modest dinette off the back.

Secassa pointed to a chair on one side of a gray-topped Formica table and snatched two beers from the refrigerator while Doll sat. He served them in cans without taking the trouble to offer glasses that later would have to be washed.

Tilting his own can toward Doll, Secassa took a pair of lavish swallows. Doll did the same but held the number of swallows down to one.

"So, we get the chance to meet for a second time, eh, Señor Doll? I have to admit that this pleases me. Even setting the matter of your Spanish aside, there are ways in which you're not very like the run of your countrymen—at least those of my experience. Your appreciation of people as individuals, I think, is broader. You're far less quick to stand aside and judge."

"I think that you flatter me," Doll replied.

"I think I do not. Besides, I have no reason." Secassa laughed, showing a line of straight, white teeth. "Americans, like peoples the world over, have their good points and their bad. On the bad side, they are racists and xenophobes, and yet they claim in the same voice they are a nation of immigrants. They are avaricious, and in another contradiction, they are also lazy.

"Please understand that is not a complaint. It only means that, in America, a man with no special skills can nevertheless earn a decent living doing what Americans won't do for themselves. I cite myself as an example. I spoke before of having a position with low status—which still remains true. But, as you see, my living quarters are supplied, and the money I make is still enough to feed and clothe myself—even to afford occasional amenities."

Smiling down at his can of beer, Secassa tipped his head to suggest one example.

"And you, Señor Doll? What is it you do?"

"Like you—a job with no status, and, in my case, surely better pay than I deserve."

"But specifically. It seems only fair," Secassa argued with a smile. "Otherwise you have the advantage of me."

"I'm a diver—tanks, not hard hat—when I work." Doll watched an expression he couldn't read begin to etch itself into Secassa's face. "I hire on for assignments with different companies that do underwater construction or demolition projects."

"A trade you learned in the service. Puerto Rico and the Philippines, if I recall, was what you said?"

Doll nodded to confirm Secassa's conclusion.

"But hardly unskilled." The superintendent raised an eyebrow. "And hardly of no status. I don't doubt you're well paid. That is dangerous work, Señor Doll. People down here do it as a sport. But I understand that is altogether a different case. To work below the water—to perform what must sometimes be difficult tasks—is more than just swimming around where you please."

"Routine," Doll replied. "That's what keeps you safe and alive. Like any other job, most of it comes down to boredom."

"Not to me." Emilio Secassa shook his head adamantly. "Being down there with only the air on my back and I can only guess which of God's creatures around me . . . I keep a small boat. You may regard it as one of those amenities I spoke of. That, and to swim now and then along the beach, is as close as I want to get to the sea."

As Secassa looked across the table, his expression seemed to turn suddenly solemn.

"This thing of yours saddens me," he continued with no explanation of the shift in topic. "It's the Latino in me, maybe, but I hate to see a woman in trouble. Mind you, I feel worse when the woman is beautiful, as your friend and her sister most certainly are. What will become of her? Will you be able to help, Señor Doll?"

Doll shook his head and answered that he didn't know. "I can only hope so," he said.

"I know only what there is from the television and the local papers. So, in that sense, you could say I know nothing." Secassa inclined his head in a small bow that added yet a further level of humility. "But from those places, I would say that things look very bad. I tell you that, for your sake, I want to believe your friend is innocent. And I, as an honest man, must tell you I have trouble even saying that. Had I been one of the bastard's women, and known what he was doing, I tell you this, though it does me no credit: If I could have found a way, I would have killed the prick myself."

"In your heart, then, you think that she's guilty?" Doll asked.

"If you ask my opinion, the best I could say is that I don't know. One thing I do know, though it won't be very helpful, is that what we pass off as justice is very often not that. A court will look always at what the accused person did and, if they find that he did certain things, they then must determine he is guilty. The system, though, is very weak when it tries to ask why a thing was done."

"You say 'why' as though you're talking about something more than motive."

"Motive—and, at the same time, more than motive," Secassa agreed. He paused, perhaps to compose his thoughts, but also to consume another portion of his beer before going on. "Take you and me. Two friends. We go to a bar—an all-Latino one that I know down in Miami. A gringo black—that is to say a North Americano black—comes in. Or turn it around. Make it the other way. It doesn't matter. The man who is where he shouldn't be goes on from there to use some names he should have not used and to make some ill-advised remarks. A fight breaks out. He is stabbed. He dies. I ask you, now, who caused this crime to happen?"

Secassa shrugged and then went on to begin the formulation of an answer to his question. "The catchphrase that everyone cries in the United States today, Señor Doll, is 'Law and Order.' " He spoke the last three words in English, then returned to Spanish. "I think, perhaps, that mine may be a not very popular position."

"All of this works its way around back to Sean Dabney," Doll inferred.

"At the root, Señor Dabney's story is the same as the one of the man in the bar," Secassa answered. "It isn't, you must understand, that I'm saying the person who thrusts home the knife is totally guiltless. What I am suggesting is that Señor Dabney played as big, or, perhaps, even bigger, a part in bringing about his own death as the person who actually killed him. It's a good line of argument, and true, I think." Secassa smiled. "I doubt, however, that it is one which will carry very much weight with the authorities."

The smile broadened into a laugh, which Secassa drowned with a succession of swallows that drained the rest of his beer. Reaching across the table, he swished Doll's half-full can and frowned his disappointment. Then, stretching toward the refrigerator, he reached in and got himself another.

* * *

The luminous dial of Doll's wristwatch on the table by the bed put the time at past three in the morning. And sleep seemed as though it would take yet a long time to come. The restless thoughts that moved through his head seemed intent on playing a compulsive game of hopscotch with themselves—running, vaulting, and being vaulted in turn.

The bar was a catalyst. In some way, he knew, it had to be. Under the umbrella of its costumes and Treasure Coast glitz, the Piña Colada somehow brought people together—people who, as Willard Giesler had explained, seemed otherwise to have no other observable circumstance in common.

Again from the bar—Valerie Albrecht and her two friends. What had that tempest been about? They'd clearly wanted something. What?

A release from anxiety? Doll could dress the theme so it looked appealing. Valerie had been in the bar with Clayton Rivers—with Wellman too, or he'd simply been there on his own and Valerie had gathered him up for added support.

She'd heard during the day from—from Calvin Tack?—that Doll had been asking about her. Then she'd heard the same thing again from Zale, who'd also told her that Doll and Ann were, at that moment, only a fraction of the width of the dining room away. So fine, she'd decided. She'd get the whole thing over with—go to Doll instead of having to wait for him to get around to her. And she'd do it while she had some protection along. Let the bastard ask his impertinent questions. Let's see if he likes what he gets back!

And then it had all collapsed because Doll declined to play. He'd turned his attention, instead, to Wellman, who'd told of how Diana had listened to his stories. And Clayton Rivers had gotten quickly bored and said to hell with this; it's time to go.

Plausible. Nearly satisfyingly so—until Ann Raney tied Perry

Wellman's stories in with the coins she'd found in Diana's bureau drawer.

The coins. In them, there were only guesses and questions. The guesses Doll was mostly comfortable with. So far as they went, it seemed to him still, they were good. But what more was there that might be important? What would the cleaning reveal? How precise could anyone be on where they were found? Or, more to the point, where Diana had gotten them? Why had she kept them hidden in the bottom of a drawer? And what, if anything at all, did they have to do with Sean Dabney's murder? There were answers that Doll could provide by guessing. Lots of answers, some very logical. Every one was absolute speculation.

And Emilio Secassa with his argument for the victim as a contributor to his own murder? Doll had read or heard the theory somewhere before. It had been, as he recalled it, accompanied by a lot of psychoanalytic mumbo jumbo about Oedipus complexes and unfulfilling relationships with parents of one or the other sex. But the idea beneath it had an appeal—and more than appeal, it had value in that it offered at least another way to approach the circumstances of Sean Dabney's death. Victims weren't simply passive. They did things—sometimes anyway—consciously or unconsciously, that played some greater or lesser role in making them victims.

Which brought Doll back to the murder itself once again. Recalling the arrangement of Dabney's apartment, he tried in his mind to construct a picture of the crime. He began with Diana's story as she'd told it to the police and as Ann had related it, but with the added assumption that it wasn't Diana who'd killed Dabney.

That assumption placed her in the bedroom, oblivious of anything going on around her. Dabney was in the living room. So was whoever killed him. Had the police found any evidence implying that someone else had been there? Where in the living room was he when he was hit? Near the sofa where he'd fallen? where the body and bloodstains were found? The blow was struck to the back of his head. Did it hit on the left-hand side or the right? Go back to the basics! What was he hit with? Doll couldn't even answer that.

In that moment of realization, Doll reached a single, over-powering conclusion. What was appalling—almost inconceivable —about the circumstances of Sean Dabney's murder was how much he didn't know.

The awareness, paradoxically, seemed at last to open the path for him to sleep. As the adage went, Doll recalled with mild and increasingly distant amusement, knowledge can only begin when the inquirer understands that he knows nothing.

But that wasn't totally right. Doll yawned as his mind slipped from the darkness of the room into a quiet gray of its own making.

At least, in the hours ahead when the next morning came, he knew now where he wanted to start.

8

"Silver," Willard Giesler said. He produced a small postal scale from a drawer in his desk, dropped the lump of metal in the tray, and adjusted the mechanism until it balanced. "Two eight *reale* coins. To use the term Robert Louis Stevenson liked, 'pieces of eight.' "

He made a show of consulting his watch. "You got me out of bed at six in the morning for this? If I'd wanted to keep an obstetrician's hours, Mr. Doll, I'd have been one and made better money at it."

"I thought they might be more impressive than you seem to find them," Doll said.

"Maybe two hundred dollars, if that's what you're asking. You lose two faces. The value goes down, not up, when they're fused together like this." Willard Giesler leaned back in his swivel chair and sighed. "Sorry, I find no special joy in raining on anybody's parade. As I told you, though, I'm something of an addict about the local history. I could take you back to my house and show you a trophy case with a dozen of those. Single coins. Cleaned. Readable strikes, both front and back."

"What about these? Suppose they were cleaned. What else could they tell us?"

Giesler picked up the disk-shaped piece and examined it with a critic's eye. "Depends. Does either side have a legible mint mark? Not that many do. Is it dated so you can read it? The odds on that are less than one percent."

"But, if we are lucky, and those things were there, then you could make a reasonable guess as to where the piece came from."

"Not even close," Giesler answered. "You might just as well get a chart of the Gulf of Mexico and the Caribbean and start throwing darts. You're talking about pocket change here. Even if there's a mint mark—let's say it's Potosi—and a date, the coin might have been in circulation for a hundred years before it wound up in the water. In that time, it could have been to Cartegena, Havana, Portobelo, Mexico City, and back again. Chance could have dropped it anywhere along the way."

"Or along the coast along here?"

"On its way to the king's accountants in Seville? The likelihood is as good as anyplace else," Giesler said.

"For the coast here, you'd be talking about the 1715 fleet. Somewhere between ten and twelve ships went down in one night in a late July storm. That's not absolute, of course. There were other sinkings in these waters. But for something found here, the 1715 disaster is by far the most likely source. This is one of those unusual circumstances where proving the negative is easier. If either of the coins has a date past 1715, the odds are good that the piece wasn't found around here. With an earlier date, there's a much better chance. If you had a lot of coins and the dates tended toward 1715 with none after, then the probability gets even higher. That's because the older coins tend to drop out somewhere else along the way."

"What about the crust? Is there someone around who cleans these things?"

Giesler nodded and said he could get it done. "If it needs to be said, you've piqued my interest, Mr. Doll. I gather these coins somehow loop back to Diana. That means you think they may have some relationship to what happened to Dabney?"

"Not because I have any reason to think it," Doll replied. "The murder certainly doesn't have to do with theft. Whoever killed him could have walked out of that apartment with ten times what you say those coins are worth. Diana's sister found them in one of the dresser drawers."

"And?"

"And not very much," Doll admitted. "It's only that yesterday, when we talked, you mentioned Perry Wellman. Then I ran into him last night at Mickey Zale's. It almost seemed he went out of his way to make the point that he'd talked with Diana about his looking for treasure."

"And you think maybe Diana got the coins from him?" For a second, Giesler appeared to consider the proposition. "Not impossible. If she did, it's only an isolated find. In the first place, the prevailing wisdom is that all the lucrative sites have already been found and exploited. In the second, to salvage a wreck you need an exclusive site permit and then a second permission to excavate. Those documents are all public information. If Wellman had filed for those, I'd know it. He hasn't filed for a site, much less the right to dredge it."

"And even on a piece, as I understand the law," Doll said, "he'd have to have reported the recovery and paid the salvage duty."

"Assuming that the law in such matters is always obeyed. You can see, when the scale gets small, how it gets to be hard to enforce."

"What about another man by the name of Clayton Rivers? Has he ever filed for any of those permits?"

"Clayton Rivers? Hunting treasure? Then giving even a piece of it to Diana Raney!" Giesler broke out into a flash flood of laughter. "I don't know which is funnier, the thought of him risking his money and time on anything with that small a chance of paying him back or the idea of him giving away anything he found to anybody. How'd you come up with Clayton's name anyway?"

"The Piña Colada." The club seemed to Doll to recur so often that he felt mildly embarrassed repeating the name. "He was there with Valerie Albrecht and Wellman last night—when Wellman was talking about his treasure stories and Diana."

"Not surprising. Predictable even that they'd be together." Giesler searched through his pockets, found a toothpick, and intruded it between a space in his teeth. "Not Rivers and Wellman directly. There's no tie there that I know about. But Valerie and Wellman. We talked about that connection yesterday. And Valerie and Clayton Rivers. They're a kind of an on-again, off-again item. Rivers has the money to make him attractive. A lot of money, actually. Old money along with a very old name.

"You keep brushing up against the history, Mr. Doll. Seems almost as though it's becoming a kind of a destiny."

Giesler pushed himself up from his chair and went to the floor-to-ceiling bookcase that covered one of the walls of his office. He ran his hand along the shelf and appeared to scan the titles.

"Vosterman's *History of Florida*," he announced, selecting a dark brown volume from among the row of books. "You're not one of those people who borrow and then don't return 'em, are you, Mr. Doll? I'm really kind of partial to this one. It's like an old friend, and I'd like to be sure I get it back when you're done."

Doll took the book and promised to return it. He was careful not to promise to read it, but then realized that the reading might be hard to avoid. Willard Giesler was already handing out assignments—very likely, Doll guessed, with the anticipation of springing pop quizzes later on.

"Take a close look at the part about the ranchers," Giesler

said. "The Rivers name isn't there specifically, but you won't be off the mark to read it in."

"What about Perry Wellman?"

"A contemporary vagabond. Hardly of a standard for inclusion in Vosterman."

"What I was really asking was where I could find him," Doll said, declining to pick up on Giesler's attempt at humor. "I assume he's got a boat somewhere that he does his treasure hunting from."

"The *Fair Wind*." Giesler nodded. "Try the causeway to the north island, on your right just before you get to the bridge. At the south end of the marina, near the fuel dock and restaurant. If you get lost, ask. Anyone there will be able to tell you."

Doll stood, taking the book of Florida history in hand. "The police reports from the night of the murder. Eldwin Rush said you had copies of those."

"For what they say, I've got them. You're welcome to read them. But those things are sanitized like a surgery, Mr. Doll. They're good for times, places, people present, and the professional jargon. Code words like 'blunt trauma'—that's a hit on the head to you or me. If you want more than that . . ."

Giesler looked at Doll and frowned, then scribbled something down on a piece of paper.

"Here. You want all my secrets! If you're looking for the details, he's your best source. Tell him I sent you. He can call me to make sure if he likes. The press, m'boy, can get away with things that would get a lawyer disbarred in a minute. I've already talked to him myself, but you'll probably think of questions I didn't ask. Every once in a while, when circumstances allow, I throw him a scoop. It makes for a nice symbiotic relationship."

Doll took the slip of paper, then hesitated. "One last thing. I saved it for the last because, up to this second, I've been trying to decide if I should tell you at all. What you know as Diana's attorney—there's no way for the state to get that information from you and use it against her?"

Giesler shook his head. "I can't stand by and watch her lie on the stand. But as far as I know . . . Even if you gave me absolute proof she killed Dabney, she has a right to representation. The state has to prove its case, and there's the question of what charge she's guilty of. Through all of that, she remains my client, and there's no legal way for anybody to force information regarding a client out of me."

"Did you know that, on the day that Dabney died, he also made a play for Diana's sister?"

"Crotch artist!" Giesler twisted his mouth and exhaled his frustration. "Then that's what they argued about in the apartment, I suppose, and maybe out at Zale's place, too? That means the whole world probably knows about it. It's not what I wanted to hear, Mr. Doll—not what I wanted to hear at all. But it's the kind of surprise, if I'm going to get it, that I'd rather get now from you—and not later on from the state."

"If it helps," Doll offered, "according to the sister, Diana never knew. I think Ann believes that. I can't tell you whether or not it's true."

Willard Giesler looked down at his watch for a second time. "Three-thirty this afternoon I'll be leaving from here to go out to the Pods to talk with Diana. I didn't think I had any reason to do that. Now I think maybe I do. I'm telling you because I thought you might want to come with me."

"She won't want me there."

"The hell with what she wants. She's my client, and she's going to get the best defense her goddamn money can afford—notwithstanding the accounts receivable portion, for getting talked into which I include myself among the profession's more credulous saps."

*   *   *

The dock where Willard Giesler had said that the *Fair Wind* was berthed was one of several that stretched out for nearly a hundred yards over the quiet water of the marina. On both sides, vessels rode in their slips, tied off by common custom in a pattern of a fishbone with their sterns toward the dock and their bows facing into the channels.

Two-thirds of the way along the spine, Doll found the boat and no one aboard. If Giesler had told Doll to try the *Fair Wind*, it was because he'd thought of the boat as the most likely place for Wellman to be. On the other hand, Doll reasoned as he inspected the vessel, men who spent their lives looking for treasure were rarely the sort who kept regular hours—especially if they'd had a late night the evening before. But then, if Doll was willing to wait, aboard *Fair Wind* seemed at least as good a place as the next to pass the time.

Fair Wind had been built as a sports fisherman, a twin diesel, V-hulled, thirty-eight-foot Bertram. But, as Wellman kept her, the gear that made her a fisherman was mostly gone. The fighting chair had been sacrificed to gain the extra deck space. Only its recessed mount remained. Gone, too, were the distinctively backward raked outrigger poles. Seemingly alone from the original outfitting was the chromium tuna tower that provided the added height from which a man could look down into the sea. As though kept as token of deference to a more glamorous past, the tower remained to join the more esoteric equipment that *Fair Wind* now carried aboard.

Secured against the roll of the sea, to the port and starboard sides of the cockpit deck, were a pair of gray, cylindrical objects, tapered and finned at the end like slender aerial bombs. Marine magnetometers. Doll recognized them as such without a second look. Towed astern, they detected submerged concentrations of metal, from lost outboard motors to nuclear submarines—as well as anything else metallic in between.

Doll moved to the forward end of the cockpit. From the

sliding door in the after bulkhead, he was able to see into the cabin beyond. The helm station included the standard pairings of throttles. clutches, and dials which controlled and monitored the Bertram's twin engines. The array of navigation equipment mounted around helm, however, was anything but the routine.

Besides the compass and pelorus of maritime tradition, *Fair Wind* possessed a formidable collection of electronic boxes and screens. Doll recognized the systems: radar, loran, and Satnav components which, either individually or redundantly, were capable of fixing a position at sea within a very few yards of error, as well as a recording fathometer able to plot the contour of the seabottom to a sophistication measured in inches.

Whatever Perry Wellman had found or hadn't, he had aboard *Fair Wind* all the equipment any captain could ask to find his way around at sea.

Doll took the next step. He leaned on the door. It moved. He pushed harder until it slid open.

The cabin, except for the claustrophobia-producing excess of electronics, was Spartan. The creature comforts of the land were held to a minimum—no carpets, no curtains, no nautical-theme glasses, no built-in tape deck with quadraphonic speakers for producing the illusion of all-around sound.

The first locker Doll looked in repeated the pattern of the cockpit and cabin. It held a pair of handheld, submersible metal detectors, strapped for seaworthiness against the ribs of the hull. Scuba tanks and other diving equipment were likewise mounted to either side.

Doll tried the chart drawer. Among its inventory, he found a NOAA offshore chart for the Florida coast between Jupiter Inlet and Bethel Shoal. The chart, by its publication date, was current or very close to it, but ancient judged by any standard of use. Its stained and creased surface had holes in the shape of four-pointed stars at the intersections where the paper had been worn through by repeated foldings. In other places, Doll found the original data made nearly illegible by a spider web of hand-drawn triangulation vectors, each vector line painstakingly described by its compass bearing to an anchored navigation marker or else to a landmark somewhere on the shore. Loran coordinates supplemented the triangulations to fix precisely more than a hundred index numbered positions spread out across the featureless surface of the sea.

To interpret the information recorded on the chart, Doll made the assumption that the numerical indexing corresponded to the chronological order in which the positions had been plotted. A few minutes of interpretation and testing seemed to imply the hypothesis was true—or at least was true to the extent that it provided a framework that yielded up a consistent and plausible story.

Fair Wind's work, it seemed, hadn't been a single search, so much as it had been a succession of searches. Each had begun with a scattering of more or less geometrically distributed positions within the boundaries of an area outlined on the chart. Gradually, the data suggested, as the electronic exploration of the bottom progressed, a second and more randomly configured category of positions emerged to identify those actual sites which might warrant more elaborate—most likely subsurface—investigation.

Not that the actual numbers on the chart ever disclosed a pattern quite so simple, but at the level of generalization, Doll concluded, that was the way the operation had worked. The process was one of progressive elimination. The search continued until the time when the last site thought to have potential was discarded, and the area was abandoned in favor of what was felt to be the next most promising locale.

Doll skimmed through the charted histories that remained, finding each, in turn, essentially the same. The final search recorded seemed fundamentally no different from the first, except, of course, for its obvious lack of a successor. Beyond being past the date of issue of the chart, there was no way for Doll to tell how long ago that had been.

What more did he know than he'd known when he'd come aboard *Fair Wind*? No more than that her considerable and exotic gear, together with what the chart recorded, made a reasonable case supporting what Doll had already been told. His eyes drifted mechanically over the last of the marks and triangulation angles, but his concentration already was elsewhere. As far as Sean Dabney's murder was concerned, Doll admitted to himself, his visit aboard *Fair Wind* that morning had told him absolutely nothing that was new.

The sole of *Fair Wind*'s cabin dipped, then as quickly rebounded under Doll's feet. Doll instinctively looked toward the stern and saw the man who'd come aboard in the same precise instant the other man saw him.

His eyes fixed on Doll. He made no exclamation of surprise or outrage at having found an intruder on board. Neither did he issue any challenge.

He simple drew from behind his back a filleting knife with a long, thin, curving blade. Advancing in a semicrouch, he kept his arm bent, held short of full extension, still allowing for a lunge and thrust of the blade. And all the while, as he inched in closer, his eyes never once strayed from Doll's face.

Doll grabbed a cushion from one of the seats, the only thing he could find close enough at hand to use as any kind of defense. He held it out with both hands before him, watching the approaching body and eyes for any sign foretelling movement.

At the same time, Doll realized, he recognized the man. The black pirate outfit was gone—so too the hazy stare from the night before—but the horizontal scar that cleaved the chin left no chance for a mistake.

"Easy," Doll said. "I'm a friend of Perry Wellman." Not

exactly precise, Doll conceded to himself. But verbal precision could wait until later—if there was going to be a later, and if the precision mattered to anyone by then.

The distance between them closed to a final few feet. The man was at the bulkhead door. Passing through it restricted his lateral movement.

Doll chose that moment to lunge with the center of the pillow toward the knife. The plan was that the man would have to move forward or back; either way would be unexpected and afford the chance of catching him off balance.

But the man did neither. Instead, he slashed the blade of the knife across the face of the pillow, nearly halving it in the process and catching the knuckle of one of Doll's fingers. The honed steel cut to the bone. Not as deep as you think it is, Doll told himself. The bone beneath a stretched knuckle is very, very shallow. But the swelling would begin, and, in a very short time, that hand, as a weapon of any kind, was going to be useless.

It was time, Doll decided, that things got ended as quickly as the situation would allow.

He tossed the severed cushion toward the man's face. He needed only a second of distracted attention, but the deteriorated foam rubber stuffing gave him more than that. A cloud of dust-fine powder sprayed out. The man's free hand reached up too late to shield his blinded eyes.

Doll, meanwhile, grabbed the knife arm—one hand on the wrist, the other on the biceps—and slammed the man's elbow, the opposite way from the way that it bent, against the frame of the cabin door.

The scream was guttural; the curse that followed came out in Spanish. Above it, Doll heard the knife hit the floor.

There was no way on earth for the man to have held it. His arm was very likely broken, and that was the best news he was going to get. The tendons and cartilage, ripped at the joint, were going to take a lot longer to heal.

A sharp punch from the man's free hand slammed into Doll's side. Doll grunted and took it and worked at absorbing the pain.

"Hey . . . what the hell! Stop that. What's going on here?" The voice came from above *Fair Wind*'s stern, somewhere up on the deck.

Doll ignored it. He hauled the man who had had the knife toward him.

The man's eyes were still squinted closed against the dust, and his right arm hung limp at his side. At the same time, he drew his left hand back to strike again.

Not smart, Doll thought. Persistence was one thing, stupidity another.

Grasping the man by the sides of his shirt, Doll snapped his featherweight body from one side to the other and back again. The already disoriented head responded like the clapper of a bell, striking the doorjamb to Doll's right, then left, then right again. Doll had only to let the man go. The body dropped backward from the open doorway, falling onto the cockpit deck in a heap.

Looking up toward the *Fair Wind*'s stern, Doll saw that the voice had come from Perry Wellman.

"Mr. Doll! Is that you? What the hell's going on? What are you doing here? What the hell have you done to him?" Wellman demanded all at once.

Doll bent down, picked up the knife with his right hand, then flexed the fingers of his left to keep them working. He held the knife up for Wellman to see.

"Do I look like the day's catch to you? Your friend was pretty stoned in the car lot last night, so maybe he had trouble telling the difference." Doll tossed the knife toward the portside gunwale. It landed with a quiet *splop* in the water between *Fair*

Wind and the boat abeam. "What's Mickey Zale's car boy doing on board your boat, anyway?"

"He's a . . . Hey, wait a minute," Wellman said catching himself. "What the hell am I explaining myself to you for?" He hopped down from the dock into *Fair Wind*'s cockpit and walked over to where the still inert body was lying. He looked down, which turned out to be a mistake. His eyes went wide at what he saw.

The sides of the ersatz pirate's forehead were scraped near the temples where the abrasions showed as thin streaks of red. More dramatic, though, was the discoloration from the forming bruise which imparted to the surrounding skin a sickly tint of gray. A small trickle of blood had seeped from the mouth where, Doll guessed, the teeth had cut the inside of the cheek. And finally, as though to enhance the overall effect, the angle at which the right arm lay was preposterous.

"My God, is he dead?" Wellman dropped to a knee and felt at the neck for a pulse.

"He's not dead," Doll said. "But he's probably going to be a little nauseous when he wakes up. The arm, I'm afraid, is going to need some X rays and a cast."

"What did you do to him?" Wellman asked with scarcely masked horror.

"I took his knife away from him," Doll said.

The man's leg moved as though in sleep, the first sign of consciousness beginning to return.

Wellman stood, stepped meticulously over the prostrate figure, and went on into the cabin. There, he moistened a small supply of paper towels in the galley sink and disregarded Doll's advice that he also bring a bucket.

Bending over the injured man again, he began to pat with the towels at the blood at the sides of the head and mouth.

"Carlos?" he asked doubtfully. "Can you hear me? This is Perry Wellman. Are you all right?"

Carlos revived slowly, shaking his head tenderly to rid it of what Doll knew would be a blurry fog and wincing as he tried to move his arm. After a moment of that—too soon—he tried to stand. His face went white. His pupils began to dilate.

Doll caught him as his knees began to collapse. He swung the top half of Carlos's body over the rail and held him there while he was sick.

It was all enough—and too much—for Wellman. When Carlos recovered enough to stand by himself, Wellman gave him money for a taxi, then told him to see a doctor and get himself home.

By then, the pain in Carlos's arm was such that he needed his left arm to carry the right. Having made it onto the dock again, he stopped to turn toward Doll.

"You're a dead man," he whispered at Doll in Spanish.

"After enough years," Doll replied in the same tongue, "I'm sure what you say will be true."

9

"Goddamn it to hell, Doll, what the hell do you do for a living—goon squad duty for the goddamn Mafia? Where the hell do you get off coming aboard somebody's boat—snooping around to your heart's content—then beating up on somebody who's got a perfect right to be here?"

Wellman's face was flushed with anger. Doll could see the color even beneath the deep tan.

"It wasn't me who brought out the knife," Doll said flatly. "You'll forgive me if I overreact and take that kind of thing seriously. Did you miss that scar across his chin? Today isn't the first day he's handled a knife as a weapon. Your friend, Carlos— does he have a last name to go with the first?"

"Bandalos," Wellman answered. "I saw that scar." With his attention distracted from the issue of Doll's trespass, Wellman's temper seemed to wane. "I saw it, but I never really thought about it. Is that what it's from? And you took him on with your bare hands? That doesn't sound very smart to me, Doll. You're lucky you didn't get yourself killed."

The tentativeness in Wellman's attack led Doll to pursue the momentary advantage.

"Last night he was Mickey Zale's parking valet. Now, this morning, I find him with you. What was he doing here? Does he work for you too?"

"Who, Carlos? Work for me? No, not exactly. Sometimes

he . . . Goddamn it, Doll!" Wellman suddenly swore. "I don't believe I goddamn almost let you get away with that. It's you, not me, who's got some explaining to do. What are *you* doing here? How did you even know about *Fair Wind*? What were you snooping around for?"

"I didn't feel particularly like I was snooping," Doll replied, in what he privately conceded was at the least a generous stretching of the truth. "I didn't think there was anything you were trying to hide. Last night, if you'll remember, you said there wasn't any secret about what you were doing. You even made a point of complaining about how you couldn't get anybody but Diana to listen to you. Now I show up, and suddenly you decide it's time to lock up the store and run away and hide."

"I didn't mean that. Not exactly," Wellman fumbled. "Stories . . . I mean . . . well, they're one thing. I can talk about what I do and keep it to the general. I don't have to say it happened here or there. It's the details that get sensitive. What gets found under the water out there belongs to who finds it. I've spent a long time surveying that bottom. It doesn't seem fair from my point of view if you come along and find out where I've been, then use that to decide where you want to look next."

"Is that what you think? You figure I'm down here to undercut you? No boat. No equipment. Just put on my swim fins and jump off the end of the pier?"

"You make it sound ridiculous." Wellman stared out across the water, avoiding Doll's eyes. "It isn't." He seemed to protest to himself as much as to Doll. "It wouldn't be the first time it happened. Maybe not you. I'm not saying that. But it just doesn't pay to take chances."

"What do you look for? What's out there?" Doll asked. "I don't see how it can hurt a whole lot to talk about that. If I go to the library, I'm sure they can find me a book with some pictures."

"Yeah, I suppose," Wellman acknowledged reluctantly. "You're right about the books. They've got plenty of them. Making the comparisons is one way you identify a wreck."

He hesitated, then seemed to shrug.

"You don't get the same kind of thing everywhere. Fact is, what you find depends a lot on where you look. Around here, there's a Spanish fleet that went down in 1715. According to the records, it was carrying both bars and coins. Some of it royal tax; other, cargo that passengers held. Probably more than the manifests show because the gold and silver—especially the gold— were always being smuggled. You could also expect to find jewelry—crosses and rings and things like that. Chains—they were fond of those, too."

"Still out there?" Doll said dubiously. "I heard that every- thing that went down around here has long since been recovered."

"Some say that. I don't believe it for a second." Wellman looked back and forth now between Doll and the sea. "The Spanish got some of it back themselves. So have other salvors since. Some recent ones, it's true enough, have done pretty well off the wrecks. But you can't tell me they got all of it. Nobody'll ever convince me of that. Hell, how would they know? That was damn near three hundred years ago. The real truth is they're not even sure of exactly how many ships went down."

"You said last night you've already been at this four years."

"I know. That's the funny part of it. What Valerie said was right. I'm a fool, and then I'm not a fool. I understand how it has to look." Wellman walked to *Fair Wind*'s rail. "But what nobody realizes, Mr. Doll, is how close it all is to being over. Ten, twenty years, and everything that's out there'll be gone. We don't have the know-how yet to do it right. But I can tell you what's going to happen: Some bright-ass boy from MIT or someplace else, who likes to tinker, is going to find some trick that lets him look down through the water and sand and pick the gold right out. And then it'll all be a grocery shopping trip. In another five years—that quick—he'll be richer than Croesus.

One way or another, the thing he comes up with will get around. And then there won't be anything left for anybody to find."

Doll nodded toward *Fair Wind's* cabin. "What you have in there maybe won't pick out the gold, but it has to come close to being the next best thing."

"What, all the nav gear?" Wellman glanced over his shoulder at the array of electronics. "It's good equipment. I'm sure not saying it doesn't help."

"Hell of an investment, isn't it though, when you start to figure the odds against a payback? That kind of gadgetry doesn't come cheap. You've probably got more tied up in that than you do in the rest of the boat."

"Maybe. What if I do?" Wellman's voice took on an edge again. Something new seemed to be working to close him down.

"I didn't mean to touch a nerve," Doll apologized. "If you've got yourself in hock over that, it isn't any of my business."

"No, it damn well isn't." Wellman's reply wasn't hotly contentious, but strong enough to insure that the message lost nothing in coming across.

"Do you ever find anything, or is it always just looking?"

"You're pushing me. I can feel it, Doll," Wellman said, backing farther away.

"Sorry, it's not a part of the plan." Which didn't mean, Doll thought, that other things weren't. He felt a small twinge of conscience about the maneuver, then thought of Diana out in the Pods and set the twinge behind him.

"I was only remembering again what you said last night—the part about Diana being special because she listened to your stories."

The bait was in the water. The only question now was one of whether Wellman would take the hook.

"What about it—about her being special?" Wellman asked. His tone seemed cautious and his manner uncertain.

"Well, I don't know. This could all sound silly. But it's one of the reasons I came by this morning. Something her sister found in Diana's place. It doesn't look like much—like a small puddle of solder, if anything. But Diana kept it hidden, which, I suppose, means she put some value on it. Then you started talking about the gold last night, and I got to thinking. . . . What I wondered was if it was something that you found and gave her. Maybe like a reward for all that listening?"

"Me?"

Wellman's effort to keep his face controlled was visible—and, so, utterly self-defeating. Behind his eyes, Doll could almost see the ghost trails of his thoughts as they raced by.

Bait taken. Hook set. Now ease off on the drag.

"Just a thought," Doll said, seeming to dismiss the idea. "I'm going with Diana's lawyer to see her this afternoon. I suppose the easiest thing to do is just to ask her about it then."

"If you want to, go ahead." Wellman tried to pass the whole thing off. "I gave it to Diana. It's not gold. Gold looks like gold—even after a couple hundred years in the ocean. It's a scrap of old silver I found. That's all."

"Seems like a lot to give away to a girl who only listens."

"A lot?" Wellman smiled—or made himself smile. "How much do you think is there? Maybe an ounce, maybe a little more. Five, maybe ten dollars, Mr. Doll. I like knowing Diana thought it was worth something more. But the fact is it would cost more than the silver is worth just to get it cleaned up."

Doll said nothing.

"I didn't tell Diana that last part," Wellman went on, his words still seeming indifferent. "I guess you'd do me a favor if you didn't either. But you do what you have to do. It's not a favor important enough that I'm gonna ask it of you."

Don't we all do what we have to, Doll thought. Or what we think we have to. The fish sees the bait. It studies it awhile, decides it's food, and then it thinks it has to eat. Fish catch themselves. It's only human conceit that makes people think otherwise.

The air-conditioning was on so high that the temperature inside the bar felt cold. The only windows, looking out onto the street, were curtained with an opaque fabric to keep out the heat and the glaring light and the stares of the inquisitive, as well. A background twang of country music competed with a baseball game on the television. Incongruously, a night game, Doll noticed, taped and played back on a VCR. The team at bat was the Mets out of Shea.

The bar didn't have a lot of customers. A few businessmen remaining at tables from the noon meal lingered over their coffees and side drinks, postponing their return to the office under the pretense of tidying up odds and ends that they'd failed to resolve over the lunch.

At the far end of the bar, a group of three men sat spread out across the space of five stools for the slack business hours of the early afternoon. Their talk rambled on through a series of segmented thoughts and twisting interlocutions. Even they seemed to lack any interest in the content. Talk as a further way of passing time, but more than that, Doll thought—talk as a way of asserting communion.

Also at the bar, by himself, near the center, was the man who had to be Harvey Archer. No one else in the place had the combination of a 1950's crew cut and a dazzlingly bright Hawaiian shirt, which were the characterizing features the girl from the newspaper's office had used to describe him.

With a half-empty glass of beer and a partly finished chili dog on the bar before him, he sat with a preoccupied expression on his face and all of his attention seemingly focused on the game.

Doll took the seat beside him and the chance of addressing him by name.

Turning with evident reluctance from the television, Archer took his time inspecting Doll before he replied.

"Business," he announced, when it seemed that he was done. "Has to be business. You're nobody I know. And I've got a memory for names and faces. You here to get back at your boss for shafting you? You think there's something that you've got to tell?"

"I'm a friend of Diana Raney. My name is Doll. I'm here because Willard Giesler suggested that I talk to you."

"Willard! He give you one of his toothpicks, did he?" Archer said and grinned.

The grin, Doll thought, made Harvey Archer look like an idiot and, in consequence, nearly hid the fox behind the mask.

"It didn't seem like it'd be the sanitary thing to do," Doll answered. "He said you could call him if you wanted to confirm that—the part about him sending me to see you."

Archer dropped the pretense of the grin. "What kind of friend—of Ms. Raney's, I mean?"

"One who'd like to see her get out of the trouble she's in."

"Then I take it you think that she didn't kill Sean Dabney. Or do you? Maybe you're saying that you don't care either way."

"And it would matter to you?" Doll asked in turn. "You'd talk to me if it were the one way and not if it were the other?"

"Hot damn! What the hell. Well, I've got a weakness for impudence." Harvey Archer smiled, and then went back to his serious face again. "Yes. It'd matter a lot, as a matter of fact, if I thought you were here to knock justice on its ear. But you're not, Mr. Doll. Because you already answered the question. The answer is you made a choice. You choose to believe she's not guilty. If you thought she was, you wouldn't be here digging around for facts that might prove it—and Willard wouldn't have sent you to see me in the first place. For the rest—if you really believed she was guilty, I mean—I can see where you mightn't've wanted to face up to what you'd do. Hell, why put yourself through a cleaver like that when it's still a choice that you don't have to make?"

"Seems like you've been in the business a long time."

The bartender came by. Doll ordered a beer for himself and a new one for Archer.

Archer took a swallow from the glass he had and tipped the lip toward Doll. "I've been in it long enough," he said, "so I know a little bit about people."

"Do *you* have an opinion?"

"On Diana Raney? You mean if she killed Dabney or not?" A surging roar from the crowd on the television set took Archer's attention momentarily away. "I'll tell you the truth, Doll. I try not to have 'em," he said turning back. "I try to limit myself to the facts, and, that way, I don't fool myself or my readers. No better way I know to lose an audience than to call the tune early and call it wrong."

"That's twice you mentioned facts. That's what I came for," Doll said.

"Well, then . . ." Archer paused while the bartender returned with the beers and poured half the new bottle into Archer's fresh glass. "You're here. You bought the beer, and you said the right grease words. I don't know what you expect to get, but where'd you want me to start?"

"With the murder," Doll answered. "I've read the police reports and I've been to the apartment, so I know what the place looks like. But how exactly did he die, and what do we know about when?"

"Bludgeoned. Struck twice on the head," Archer stated authoritatively. "Coroner'll say on the stand that either blow was sufficient to cause death. The instrument was a statuette. Naked lady, they tell me. Seems appropriate—since Dabney, by accounts, had quite an eye for the gals. Clotting, temperature, and other factors understood by men of medicine, 'to whose vast minds ours are but those of insects,' put the time at between three and three-thirty Sunday morning. Since the coroner examined the body less than three hours after death, they're pretty precise about that."

"Struck where on the head?"

"Right parietal region." Archer pointed to a spot on his head above and behind the right ear. "Which, yes, means he didn't see it coming. You're going to ask me next if the assailant was left- or right-handed. I'm supposed to say right, but the truth is I don't know. A forehand blow would mean he—or she—was right-handed. But the blow could have been backhand, and that would mean the opposite. On the other hand—no pun intended— the unlikelihood of two successive backhand blows tends to favor the right-hand version. Your friend in the Pods is right-handed, as I understand."

"Fingerprints?"

"Interesting point." Archer nodded his approval. "The statuette is clean as far as prints go. Wiped clean, obviously. That, as far as you're concerned, is the good news. The bad news is that it was your friend's handkerchief that wiped it. Keep that close. It's not supposed to be out. Positive ID. Minute traces of Dabney's blood on the handkerchief. Traces of handkerchief fabric on the statuette. The handkerchief was found stuffed down inside her purse."

"What about evidence of anybody else who might've been there?"

"Nobody thoughtful enough to leave his wallet behind. The sheriff's investigators might have turned up other prints. Probably they did. But if they did or didn't, nobody's leaked it to me. No one's come forward to say that they saw anybody. But that doesn't cut a lot of ice either way, given the notorious shyness of witnesses combined with the time of the morning."

"Pictures. The police must have taken pictures."

"They most always do," Archer said evenly, though his face seemed to take on a cautious expression, different from any Doll had seen on it before. "Why bring it up? Willard Giesler tell you to ask me that?"

"No. It wasn't even a question," Doll replied. "Only me thinking aloud. I was trying to figure out some way I could get a look at them."

"And you thought maybe I could get hold of them for you."

"I didn't think it, but could you?" Doll asked.

Archer grinned again and laughed. "Forget it, Doll. You know what a thing like that could cost? If I had a contact inside the sheriff's office who could get me anything like that and it got out, not only would I lose the source, it'd be the end of the man's career. Pass it back to Willard Giesler that nobody who was in his right mind on the inside would ever take a risk like that."

Archer nodded and turned back to his cold lunch and the TV set. Doll gathered from that that he meant for the interview to be over.

"Just remember where you found me," Harvey Archer added as though the idea was an afterthought. "Just in case you do come up with something. I figure Willard already told you that sharing information works two ways. One thing more—for what it's worth: From all I've seen and heard—the Sean Dabney thing aside—I think your friend's a decent girl. I hope for both your sakes you're fighting this one on the side of the angels, Mr. Doll. And, if it turns out to be that you are, I hope you win."

Doll had an hour until his three-thirty appointment with Willard Giesler. Not time for what he really wanted—not the swim he would have liked to have, not even, given the traveling time to his motel and back, enough for a modest cold shower. Instead, he settled for a palm tree–shaded bench in a park that overlooked the river.

The small park was quiet and, from a human standpoint,

empty in the midafternoon heat. Its only other observable occupants were two stern-faced pelicans who studied Doll with mistrustful glances, then waddled off a few additional yards to give themselves the wider margin of safety.

A soft breeze blew in off the water. It wasn't, perhaps, as good as the swim or the shower, but, after awhile, it began to drain the worst of the steambath heat away.

Doll found himself, some uncertain time later, staring down at the unopened copy of Vosterman's *History*.

When Giesler had taken the book from the shelf, it had been in the context of describing Clayton Rivers. From a family of ranchers or something like that. If that wasn't exact, it was close to what Giesler had said.

Doll had thought the association strange at the time, but not enough so to have said so to Giesler. Florida and ranchers didn't seem to Doll to be a natural mix.

He began scanning through the history from the front, skipping quickly through the sections on the explorers and the Spanish years except for the two paragraphs that added nothing to what he already knew of the ill-fated 1715 fleet. What little of the rest he read had a school-days familiarity that, perhaps unfairly, succeeded only in making it seem dull.

The nineteenth-century Indian wars, when he came to them, mildly surprised him. Doll had thought of the Seminole, quite wrongly as he discovered, as a reluctant, basket- and canoe-making people, without ever recognizing their capacity for carrying out what, from their point of view, were two wholly justified wars of survival.

Florida's "Fort" towns—Myers, Lauderdale, Pierce, and the others—all came from that period. They had gotten their names from being exactly what the idea of a fort suggested, strongholds from which the Army ventured forth to keep the Native American population under thumb. Identical in function, Doll realized, to the forts like Smith and Bridger and Laramie that had served that purpose on the far more fabled frontier of the West.

But what Doll found even more unexpected was the emergence of the Florida cowboy, who, in the years between the end of the Seminole Wars and the closing decade of the nineteenth century, dominated the flat, grassy, public land that stretched from the Everglades northward toward Georgia. Roundups, brandings, cattle drives, and camp fires all duplicated their counterparts on the Western open range.

Vosterman had included with the text a picture of one of the Florida cow towns. If the caption had said Abilene or Wichita, Doll would have had no trouble in believing it.

Then, as Vosterman continued the story, the frontier had ended. The national government sold off the land, and the open range had abruptly closed. And, with the closing of the range, had come the ranchers. Those who had been the barons of the cattle drives, now became barons both in cattle and in land.

The appearance of that first provincial nobility—that was what Willard Giesler had been leading Doll toward; the stuff of Clayton Rivers's inheritance, what being a part of Florida's old money was about.

Doll closed the book and, while he thought, looked out across the sun-flecked water. A gaff-rigged ketch with deep maroon sails slipped silently down the river. With the wind abeam and the current from behind her, she was on a broad reach and making good time.

He didn't read further on in Vosterman's *History* to learn what became of Florida's ranchers. He didn't because there were subtle ways in which, Doll realized, he already knew. Over time the cattle business had waned and virtually died off. Doll's eyes told him that. There were vestiges of it here and there to see, but nothing more. The ranchers, though, had survived. Not as ranchers, but in other roles. Some as whatever

Clayton Rivers had become. That too was a part of what Willard Giesler had implied.

The principle at work in the case of the ranchers, Doll recognized, was one of the most fundamental axioms of wealth. Wealth, no matter what it's rooted in, when it accumulates to a certain critical mass, gets hard to squander. Almost as though it had a life and a will of its own, it just goes on and on making more and more money. It moves so freely and naturally: from cattle into groves—into land speculation and land development—into stocks, bonds, and mortgages. It diversifies almost of its own accord, and, as it does, it continues to grow and, at the same time, gets harder and harder and harder to lose.

10

The graffiti etched into the tabletop was different, which was how Doll knew that the room that he was in wasn't the one where he'd met with Diana the first time. Otherwise, though—in size, in the furnishings, in the starkness of the naked walls—the two rooms were, for all intents, identical.

The strongest sensation Doll had as he sat there was one of enclosure. The space seemed crowded, even while he and Giesler were in it alone. He had the wholly irrational urge to stand and, like Samson, push the concrete walls apart—at the same time knowing in his reasoning mind that his arms couldn't even span the intervening distance.

"We won't have a guard with us for this," Giesler explained in response to nothing Doll had asked.

Doll wondered if Giesler, over what must have been his years of visits to places like this, had built a protective shell against them or if the talk was his own way of dealing with the confinement and indignity that had to be impossible for anyone who had never been inside a building filled with human cages to comprehend.

"An officer of the court has to be present," Giesler went on in his nearly mechanical lecture. "For today, the officer's me. Probably not the way the corrections folks'd like it, but the only way the system could keep the attorney/client communication privilege open and still confidential."

"I understand all that," Doll said. Whatever the intent of the talk had been, he found it succeeded, however partially, in drawing his attention away from the room. "What I understand less is why you wanted me along."

"You think I have a strategy? I do—at least a tentative one," Giesler admitted. "You have to understand that what happens today isn't the way that it usually works. Normally the clients fall all over the place trying to get their side of the story onto the burner. With Diana it's almost the opposite. The battle with her is drawing her out."

Doll asked how Giesler intended to do it.

Giesler grinned. "And that, m' boy, is the biggest part of the answer to the question of why I brought you along. Two things I know now that I didn't before: First, Dabney and the sister; and second, the coins and Wellman—what he told you this morning and what he said to you last night, before."

"You think it'll help to confront her with those?"

"No. Not directly. At least not right away." While he talked, Giesler searched the pockets of his jacket—presumably in pursuit of a toothpick. After a search of several moments, he gave up the effort, seeming to accept the temporary deprivation in stride.

"I want to try to lead her—to give her the chance to bring things up on her own. And, if she doesn't, depending on what it is, maybe that'll tell us something too. Later on, if it seems like the right thing to do, we can always make the questions direct."

"What about my pal Bandalos—" Doll asked, "whatever connection there is between him and Wellman and Zale?"

"Iffy." Giesler shook his head. "Maybe, if things start to flow—which I doubt. Otherwise, I'd say that one's too nebulous for now. It's not something—so far as we know, at least—that Diana has any direct involvement in. Too easy for her just to shrug it off and say she doesn't know.

"By the way . . ." Giesler stared down at Doll's hand. "Bandalos brings something else back to mind. I was wondering if maybe some part got left out of what you were telling me back in the car? To pin it down, I don't remember having seen that bandage there before this morning."

The question, Doll told himself, he should have realized was inevitable—which only had the effect of making the omission look foolish. At the time, as he and Giesler were on their way out to the jail and Doll had given his report, he'd limited himself to what he felt were the key points: the chart on *Fair Wind*, Bandalos's presence there, and his talks with Perry Wellman and Harvey Archer. The altercation with Bandalos had seemed a footnote, adding interest and intensity perhaps, but of no special pertinence in establishing Diana's innocence of the circumstances of Sean Dabney's death. But now Doll's silence on the scuffle took on the appearance of heroic understatement which, Doll swore to himself, hadn't been his intention.

Doll was saved from replying by a light, double knock on the door.

Diana came in. She looked first at Giesler, saying nothing, then, for a longer but equally hushed time, at Doll. The guard closed the door, this time from the outside, leaving the three of them alone.

Diana sat and raked her dark hair back from her face.

"I was talking to one of the other women," she said, not seeming to be speaking particularly to either of the two men. "Did you know there are people who serve out their time, then get out and deliberately get themselves thrown back in again? In here there's always somebody to tell you what to do. Some people just get used to it. Nobody in charge of anything gives a damn what you want, so you wind up doing what you're told. After a while you see that there isn't that much difference. Nobody on the outside gives a damn about how you feel either."

"Is that enough to get you mad?" Willard Giesler asked.

"What?" Diana looked doubtfully across the table at him.

"Simple question." Giesler shrugged. "Is people not caring about how you feel enough to make you mad? Because, if that's what it takes, then I'm all for it. I'll tell you, Diana, I'd love to see you mad. I'd love to see you stand up for yourself and start trying to knock a few heads together. Because that's what's going to have to be done. And, if you're not going to do it yourself, then you're just going to have to expect that people who *do* care about you are going to try to find ways to do that head knocking for you."

"And if I don't want them to?" Diana demanded. "Suppose I just plead guilty, Willard? Make a deal for whatever you can. I'll sign it, and then we'll both forget it."

"You can't plead to murder one—and that's what you're charged with at the moment. You want to cop to something less, you do it with another lawyer," Giesler answered. "And Doll can get himself a lawyer and maybe enter the case as a friend of the court. The system is meant to serve justice, Diana—not whatever personal need you feel to pay some self-appointed retribution."

Diana glanced toward Doll, then quickly and angrily back at Giesler. "You stop that, you bastard. You stop it," she cried out in a voice loud enough to come close to a shout. "You dot the *i*'s and cross the *t*'s and file the right papers, and stay the hell out of my head."

Doll watched as Giesler leaned back in his chair, deliberately increasing the space between himself and Diana. Consciously or otherwise, she picked up the physical cues. The initial skirmish, at least, was over. She settled down in her chair, not relaxed, but a little less rigid. With her fingers, she tried to add some shape to the limp, puckered tips of her prison shirt collar.

"All right, Diana, have it your way for now," Giesler said above an exhaled breath. "A couple questions I have from my notes from before . . ." He pulled out of his briefcase a long manila folder to which were fastened a hundred or so hand-written yellow legal sheets. "I'm going back to Dabney's apart-ment. The night that he died. This is just after you and he got back there from Zale's place."

Giesler glanced toward Diana, who only stared blankly back. Giesler went on.

"You told me—let's see here—you told me—you remem-bered being in the bedroom, and you remembered you were having some kind of an argument with Dabney. You said you didn't remember what the argument was about."

Diana shifted her weight in the chair. Doll saw the tension already returning.

"That's right? You don't remember?" Giesler prodded. "I meant that to be a question."

"That's right. I don't remember."

"How about a guess?" Giesler suggested. "What might the two of you have argued about?"

"How should I know?" Diana looked at Doll, then down at the wooden tabletop. "I told you. I was drunk. I passed out a few minutes later. I don't remember."

She pointed her finger at Doll but directed what she said next toward Giesler.

"Does he have to be here for this? Why does he? He doesn't know anything. Get him out of here, Willard. I'll answer your damn questions, but I'll do it when the two of us are alone."

"Why? What don't you want him to know?" Giesler asked. "Maybe he knows more than you think he does already. He knows, for instance, that Sean Dabney made a pass at your sister. He knows it happened on the afternoon of the night that Dabney was murdered."

"What?" Diana's glare turned from Giesler to Doll. "You leave my sister out of this. You get her involved, and I promise you, Doll, if they put me away for a hundred years, I'll find a way to make you regret it."

"It's no good, Diana," Giesler said quietly, still leaning back from the table. "Once the genie's out of the bottle, it's out. Doll knows. I know. Your sister certainly knows. And don't blame Doll. If you want to start blaming, start with Calvin Tack. He knows too. He's the one who told Doll in the first place."

"Oh, God!" Diana whispered. She looked up now pleadingly at Giesler. "Where, Willard? Where does it ever end?"

"Not here. Not yet." There wasn't any tone of conquest in Giesler's reply. His voice was gentle, sympathetic. "If Tack knows, Valerie Albrecht knows. Mickey Zale knows, and, as far as we're concerned, the world knows. What's more, you knew it too—before just now when I asked you the question. Because there's only one way all this general dispersion could have come about."

"The club," Doll said, carrying the trail of Giesler's logic forward. "Ann didn't say anything to anybody because she didn't want you to find out. And you can bet that Dabney didn't go around bragging about getting shot down. So it had to be you. Somehow—I don't know how—you found out about what happened. That's what you and Dabney were arguing about back at the apartment. It's also what you were arguing about earlier that night at Zale's."

Diana ran her hand back through her hair again, then stared down into some empty place. Finally, she closed her eyes.

"You don't have to double-team me, boys. I'm not worth the concentration of effort," she said quietly. "You can see that the best of my game is a long way behind me."

Both Doll and Giesler let the silence play itself out.

"I came home in the afternoon from doing some shopping." With her eyes closed, Diana began to explain. "I saw what I was sure was Sean's car pulling away. But when I asked Ann, she said that nobody had been there. I asked Sean that night." She looked up at that moment, meeting both men's eyes with a faint, fatalistic smile. "He said of course he'd been there. Couldn't wait until the evening to see me. I told you, Doll, that I knew what Sean was. It didn't take a mental giant to fit the contradictions together."

"You understand what it means, your knowing?" Giesler said.

"Reasons," Diana answered, almost indifferently, as though she'd relegated this, as well, to the pile with the rest of the things about her life that didn't matter. "Good ones. Two of them. Jealousy, although I can tell you here I wouldn't have killed him for that. Or else to protect my baby sister."

"All right. That's the first part. Something we can deal with; something we somehow have to answer. Now let's take the second," Giesler pressed. "I understand we have something in common—that you've started taking an interest in the local history."

Doll could see so easily what Giesler was setting up, but the question, as he'd asked it, was far too oblique for Diana to understand. She saw no possible relevance in it, and so she dropped her guard and laughed.

"The last time I even heard the word history," she said, "was back when I was still in high school. I learned enough of it then to get by with C's and D's, and I've worked real hard at forgetting all of that ever since."

Giesler raised his eyebrows and let himself look as though he'd been surprised.

"The romantic stuff? Pirates and treasure ships, too?" he asked. "Because, if you really feel like that about it, it makes it hard for me to see why you'd keep around a pair of Spanish silver coins as souvenirs."

"What coins? What are you talking about? I don't have any coins like that," Diana answered sharply.

"Ann—" Doll began, but Giesler cut him off before he got beyond the name. The lawyer was into his cross-examination, digging for what he wasn't freely being told. Doll felt the pain that was in Diana, but, for the moment, he chose to let Giesler continue.

"Your sister showed them to Doll. Doll showed them to me. They're a pair of eight *reale* coins, Diana, two one-ounce coins that got stuck together. Your sister, if it helps, said she found them underneath some paper in the bottom of a drawer."

"Then she ought to learn to keep out of where she shouldn't be and mind her own business," Diana snapped.

"None of which changes anything." Giesler's voice was temperate, but without any sacrifice in its persistence.

"No, maybe not." Diana glared at Giesler, the inquisitor. "But what changes everything is that you're wrong."

"About the coins? How am I wrong, Diana?"

"Because things aren't always what you think you see. What you just said is what it's supposed to *look* like. It's an imitation, a replica, Willard. Just a piece of junk."

"But if it's that, 'junk,' " Giesler questioned, "and you have no interest in history, then why go through the trouble of keeping it at all, much less bothering to hide it in the bottom of a drawer?"

"You may be a good lawyer, Willard," Diana said, sounding as though she were being patient with him now, "but you don't know anything at all about women. Sometimes when somebody gives a girl something, the last thing that matters to her is what it is. It's from a long time ago, all right? When I was thinking no one ever would again, I met a guy who took some interest. He took me to one of those treasure exhibits. I couldn't have cared less about what they had there, but I sure as hell pretended I cared. He bought me that thing just as something between us. I keep it around. I bet your wife keeps things, too. Old flowers and other things you forgot that you ever gave her. Men don't remember things. Women do."

Diana looked away.

Doll glanced toward Giesler, but Giesler answered only with a nearly imperceptible shake of his head.

"Okay," he said. "That's enough of my harassment for one day. You take it easy, Diana, and get what rest you can. We'll leave whatever's left alone for now. But if you want to think about something, think about what I said first off about fighting back. You've got to start helping yourself and trusting me. If we're ever going to beat this thing, that's the only way we've got a chance."

"She was lying," Giesler said with the muted authority that comes from utter conviction. "Those eight *reale* coins are the genuine article. I'd bet the family fortune on that. Which means—even discounting what Wellman said—that that phantom boyfriend of hers didn't buy them and give them to her the way she said. And that means she lied! It's just that simple."

Giesler settled back in the bamboo chair and rewarded himself with a swallow from his glass. The tumbler was filled to a generous three fingers, all of it vodka except for the solitary ice cube that Giesler had added along with a thin slice of rind from a lime.

His tie was hung over the back of the chair and his shirt open at the collar.

Doll sat nearby in the second chair, a can of beer on the floor beside him.

Ann settled onto the cottage floor, sitting cross-legged, facing the two men. She'd gone back to a light blouse and shorts, not unlike the outfit she'd worn on the day of Doll's arrival. Her aversion to shoes seemed, as well, to have returned.

The glass before her was filled to the rim with ice and a combination of vodka and lemonade. A dripping layer of condensation already clung to the side. Ann tasted some of the mixture, then drank a little more.

"Then where *did* Diana get them?" she asked.

"Perry Wellman," Doll replied. "That's what Willard meant

when he spoke about discounting Wellman just now. When I talked to him this morning, I mentioned the coins. He admitted that he gave them to Diana. I asked him if it wasn't a lot to give away, and he said they were only worth five or ten dollars."

"But you said a couple hundred." Ann glanced at Doll, then turned to Giesler, who nodded. "Then he doesn't know very much about the way he's trying to make his living."

"To a point that goes past credibility," Doll agreed. "It wasn't a mistake. It couldn't have been. Even the rankest amateur knows that old coins are worth more than the value of their silver."

"I didn't know it until you told me," Ann protested mildly.

"You also don't have a boat with enough electronic gear on board that you need an engineer's degree to operate it." Doll had the feeling of being mildly maneuvered, as though Ann's remark had been gauged to set him up to counter her own self-deprecation—like Diana had done so many years ago, Doll recalled. He forced his mind back to what he'd started saying.

"Nobody invests in that kind of equipment—and puts in the time using it—if he doesn't have a pretty accurate idea of what he's looking for. He certainly doesn't bring up a piece and miss the value of it by a factor of twenty to forty times."

"So why is everybody telling all these lies?" Ann fortified herself for the answer with another substantial swallow from her glass.

"Money. That's the only angle there is," Giesler answered simply. "He's dodging the tax."

"Then you don't think anymore," Doll asked, "that what we're dealing with is just an isolated find?"

Giesler took a pull at his vodka, then resettled himself in the chair.

"No, I'm not changing that. I'm still saying isolated—what I'm not saying is that the find is unique. There's no one site he's found that he's working to exclusion. It's a small-time operation. He's finding occasional pieces wherever he happens on them, then ducking the tax and selling them off under the counter."

"The profit from an operation like that, it's enough to make the risks worthwhile?"

Giesler shrugged at Doll as though to say that there were risks, and there were risks. "As far as the law is concerned, they're probably not that big. You might get caught after a while if your luck was bad. But as I said before, the law on a small scale is hard to police. Besides, unless you've stashed your profits badly, the only thing they're ever going to nail you for is a first-time offense involving one or maybe a couple of pieces. There's another kind of risk, of course, if what he's picking up is coming from sites already under permit.

"A few years back they found a body washed up on the beach inshore from one of those spots. He still had his tanks on, but otherwise he was pretty well chewed up by the sharks. Took the medical examiner damn near a week to figure out that he'd died from having his throat cut. If Wellman's poaching, it's not the kind of thing he'd want to let get out."

"But how does all that go back to Diana?" Ann peered into her glass as she swished the ice cubes until they chased one another around in a circle. "Are you saying that she lied to you and Doll just to cover up for Perry Wellman? I don't understand why she would."

"And herself," Giesler answered. "She's the one who has the coins now. If a prosecutor could establish that she knew what they were and knew the tax wasn't paid, she's, at the least, an accessory after the fact, and arguably a party to a conspiracy to defraud."

Ann looked toward Doll. "Then, if that's all true, why did Wellman tell you he gave the coins to Diana? Why'd he tell you anything at all?"

"He had a problem," Doll acknowledged. "He couldn't know

what Diana might tell us. The only way he could keep himself creditable was to come as close to the truth as he dared. That gave him a choice of looking like either a knave or a fool. He chose to let himself look the fool."

"The only alternative that the story didn't handle," Giesler added, "was if Diana let the whole thing out—in which case whatever he said didn't matter. The issue, as far as our finding out, would have been already lost."

"Good God, it's all like spaghetti. It just winds back and forth all over itself." Ann shook her head vaguely, seeming to fight unsuccessfully to come to terms with the analysis. "What does it all mean, Mr. Giesler? What does it all say for Diana?"

"Nothing we particularly wanted to hear." Giesler drained another inch of his drink. "All taken together, Wellman and the coins come out, as best I see it, to what the oil people call a dry hole. There could be a motive in it. That's about the best you can say for it: Dabney finds out what's going on with Wellman—blackmails him—and Wellman kills him. But Dabney can't do that unless he's willing to take the chance on having it all exposed in court, and if he does that, the odds are good it's eventually going to involve Diana. Would he do it anyway? I don't know. Maybe he would. The nearly total consensus seems to be he was a bastard. But I told Diana before that it's easy to make up hypotheticals. The problem is that they really don't help very much."

"And Dabney with me—that leaves us even worse off than before," Ann Raney said despondently. "I saw that myself. That's why, until Doll found out, I never told you or anybody else."

Giesler nodded.

"There's another wrinkle in all of this." Doll turned to Giesler. "It's one that you saw early on, but we never really took a close look at. Where does Mickey Zale fit in?"

"And Bandalos . . . ," Giesler said tentatively. "Hence the

bandage on the finger? I'm right about that, aren't I? You went aboard *Fair Wind* this morning when no one was there, with—what?—shall we call it an absence of formal permission? I don't know what it's like where you come from, Doll, but there are a lot of big money boats down here. That kind of thing gets people all kinds of touchy."

"What happened? Who's 'Ban-day-los'?" Ann suddenly asked, looking up from her glass.

Doll went back to the parking lot attendant and then through an edited version of the morning's events on Wellman's boat.

"You did well to come away with as little as you came away with." Probing his pockets, Giesler somewhere found a new supply of toothpicks. "That's a rough section where Bandalos is from, out there on the west side of the town. Knife and razor country, with an occasional shooting thrown in. I've been working the name since the first time you used it. I knew that somewhere I'd heard a connection with Zale. The kid made the papers a few months back. Cops busted him, along with four or five others, for crack possession. The four or five others got the public defender and time. Zale put up for Bandalos's lawyer, who pleaded the steady job and good work record, put on a few character witnesses, and got him off with pro."

"Which just leads us again back to Zale," Doll observed. "What does it mean? What does Mickey Zale have to do with Perry Wellman?"

Giesler took the toothpick from his mouth and used it to stir the surface of his vodka in a series of circles. Finally, he returned it to where it had come from and savored the taste of the newly flavored wood. Ann, meanwhile, seemed for the moment to have lost interest in the conversation. She tried a bit more of her fortified lemonade and stared off into some distant space.

"No change. Nothing substantive," Giesler announced after a time sufficient for his contemplations had passed. "Back to what

I said before. Wellman sold to friends or friends of friends. Zale was a friend who also had friends. If Bandalos was on board, Zale certainly knew what Wellman was doing. Probably he would have known anyway. If you want to say that he acted as a kind of a fence, maybe that's true."

Giesler finished off the last of his drink and stood in a prelude to his going.

"I'm not sure I know what we've accomplished," he said. "Maybe in a day or two the fog will clear and something will emerge. If I come up with anything, I'll call you. I'd appreciate it if you'd do the same."

Doll agreed.

Ann chose to stay in her private place. Some of what made her remain there, Doll was certain, was the alcohol. She'd already had her drink in hand when he and Giesler had gotten to the cottage. There was no way for him to know how many others she'd managed to fit in during the course of the afternoon. But another part of what she was feeling, he was equally sure, was the wearing friction that, with time, reshapes frustration into depression. If she was listening still, weighing for herself the seemingly endless questions and assertions, or if, for right now, she'd simply closed her senses to all of it, Doll couldn't know.

Willard Giesler, perhaps, had the same thoughts, too. He looked at Ann, then back at Doll, before he nodded for a final time, and turned to leave.

11

The screen door of the porch closed with the slap of wood against wood. Outside, the engine of Willard Giesler's car hummed to life. The hot afternoon had turned into a not cool, but less hot, evening. Within the cottage, the daylight had begun its slow descent into darkness, the corners already filling up with deep, empty, and bottomless shadows of the night.

"God, I hate talk," Ann Raney said. She still sat where she had been, cross-legged on the floor.

Doll said nothing. Her comment seemed to him one of those not intended to elicit a reply.

Ann took up some of her weight with her arms and uncrossed her legs. Standing again, she bent from the waist, touched the floor with her fingers, then bobbed and touched it with her knuckles, and finally with the flats of her palms.

At the refrigerator, she added more ice to her glass, then lemonade and a fresh dash of vodka—less of the latter, Doll noticed, than before.

"How does he stand it?" she asked, turning back toward Doll. "How can anybody do that for a living? Talk and talk and talk himself to death. He does it all day long. That's all the man does."

"He listens, too. He gets answers," Doll replied. "You said at the airport you thought he might be good. I think he probably is."

"He better be. I mean he's going to have to be, isn't he? God, it only seems to get worse."

"There'll be a break," Doll said. "Somewhere we'll get one. I've never seen a road so long that somewhere there wasn't a bend."

"Somewhere," Ann breathed, barely aloud. She tasted some of her drink and came toward Doll. Most of what light there was came through the window from behind her. Whatever expression she had on her face was reduced to a dim wash. What Doll saw of Ann Raney was mostly in silhouette.

"Who are you, Doll?" she asked, still softly. "You don't have a first or a middle name. You drift. You don't seem tied to anything—no place, no wife, no job."

"Perennial adolescent," Doll said, and smiled to turn the answer into a joke, which he wasn't absolutely sure that it was.

"Not right," Ann said. "Oh, it fits in a way, but only on the surface. People don't react to you on any kind of middle ground. After ten years of not having seen you—after you walked out the door on her—my sister says that there's no other man she trusts. Willard Giesler, who's known you for all of two days, treats you like the two of you were nursed together. Mickey Zale and Eldwin Rush, on the other hand—who have probably never agreed on anything else in their lives—would fight for a place in line to see you get crushed into pulp."

She was close to him now—a lot closer than Doll was comfortable having her be. Sisters were sisters, he remembered she'd said, until there was a man.

And that was the whole trouble—not that the woman tendering the offer wasn't enticing. The trouble was precisely that she *was*—almost exactly as enticing as another had been for Doll ten years before.

"Oh, and then there's yesterday. The FBI file. You remember that. And you and Señor Secassa." Ann emphasized the Spanish form of address. "The two of you talking like two old friends from Havana. Berlitz doesn't teach you Spanish like that. And what happened to your finger this morning? I know it got hurt in some kind of fight with Mickey Zale's car park boy. If I'm supposed to think it's a sprain, I'm not that dumb. Look at the dressing. It takes more than just a few drops of blood to soak through that much gauze."

"It got cut—not that badly," Doll answered on what he knew was the very weak chance the reply would suffice.

"Don't back away, Doll." Ann Raney stopped immediately before him. "I know what Diana likes to call me, but she's been wrong for a lot of years. I'm nobody's *baby* sister. I haven't been for some time now. I wouldn't come between you and Diana, not for anything if the two of you were still together. But you're not. The friendship's still there, and I'm glad. But the rest of what there was is a long time gone."

And all of it was probably true, Doll thought. True in every logical way. But the emotional baggage was heavier than the logic. When he looked down at the head on the pillow, whose hair would it be, whose face would he see there?

"I need to do a little digging around tonight," Doll said with an abruptness that made it plain that the words he used had nothing to do with the message they were meant to convey. "Part of that means going back to Mickey Zale's. Especially after what happened with Bandalos this morning, it'll probably be better if I do that by myself."

Doll sensed Ann staring up at him, though, there in the failing light, he couldn't make out the details of her face.

"And that's it? Just like that?" she asked quietly. "You just say you have to go, then walk away and leave me standing here, feeling like a total fool?"

"You want words?" Doll shook his head. "I don't have any that'll work. Everything you said is true. The only part you missed was the memories. My memories, my hang-ups.

I wouldn't even know where to begin to try to handle them. For whatever it's worth, I can tell you it's nothing in you."

"Mmmm. Can't say I very much care for rejection, but I suppose that goes some to make it better." Ann stared at Doll a moment more, then turned and walked a few steps away, cradling her glass in her hands. "No words, hmm?" She laughed softly and, to Doll's ear, a bit darkly too.

By the time Doll arrived at the Piña Colada club, the night was dark. The air was a warm, moist, flower-scented breath, almost cloying in its organic richness. The diamond chips of bright, white light that stars could be in a northern winter, in the moist density of the tropical atmosphere diffused into an uneven silver haze.

Doll pulled the VW onto the semicircular driveway and stopped at the apex, opposite the imitation gangway that led to the door.

The attendant who greeted him was taller and broader than Carlos Bandalos. His pirate's costume was meager, restricted to the black scarf that he had tied around his head. For the rest, he wore a shiny yellow shirt, the bottom of which was left hanging loose outside his jeans.

He gave Doll a half smile and revealed a pair of missing teeth, then gazed with a disconcerted expression at the gearshift.

"Hey, sorry, man," he said, adding a helpless shrug of his shoulders, "but I'm jus' fillin' in here tonight. The regular guy, he got sick or somethin'. I'm sorry, but I never driven no stick shift."

Doll answered that he'd park it himself.

The substitute pirate smiled and looked satisfied with that. "Plenty space over there on the side." He pointed.

Letting up on the clutch, Doll nodded and followed a short connecting road in the direction he'd been shown. There was, as promised, plenty of space—nearly a whole parking lot full, much more than Doll would have expected. The reason for that, Doll guessed, was the darkness. The lot, to his unadapted vision, looked as black as an abandoned coal mine. The only illumination came from the faint haze of stars and the piercing yellow white headlights of his car.

He found a place at the near end of the only row there was, a line of about a dozen other cars, each nearly as disreputable as his own. The thought that came to his mind amused him. It would be worth a look at the opposite side to find out exactly how image-conscious Mickey Zale's parking arrangements were.

Doll rolled up the window against the dew that the cooling night would precipitate, got out, and set about locking the door.

"Hey, what'sa matter, you think somebody's maybe gonna steal it, man? A piece a' shit like that, I really don' think so."

The voice, which Doll recognized at once, came from somewhere near the back of his car. Before turning toward it, he considered where he was. On a cursory inspection, he seemed confined to a narrow alley, hemmed in, on the one side, by his own VW and, on the other, by the car parked immediately to his left. Retreat around the front end, through the wall of shrubbery planted along the building's side, he evaluated as a slow and, at best, dubious option—which left only the opposite end toward the back. And that, as Doll had realized when he'd first heard the voice, was interdicted by Carlos Bandalos.

Bandalos was dressed all in black, looking almost exactly as he had the night before. Only three things were different. The first was that his black headband was gone—on short term loan, Doll understood now, to the larger replacement who didn't drive stick. The second difference was that his right arm was in a cast; the third, that now his left hand held a knife.

"I tol' you this morning you were a dead man," Bandalos said in a whisper and grinned. Doll could see his teeth, like a

Cheshire cat's smile in the darkness. "Even I didn't think, then, you would be dead so soon as this."

A noise revealed the arrival of a second man. Even in the darkness Doll could see the shiny yellow shirt. The new man, too, held a knife as he stood watching, waiting for the situation to develop, from his place at the right-hand front fender of Doll's car.

A third man came from the shadows and stood just behind and to Bandalos's right. Doll couldn't see that he had a knife, but accepted the prudent assumption that he, too, was armed.

Standing with his back to the driver's side door, Doll made himself breathe—in, out, evenly. He slipped off his jacket and held it by the collar in his left hand, then tossed it with a snap of his wrist toward Bandalos.

In the same moment, he spun around sharply to his right, using the strength of his arms and his upper body to swing himself into a feet-first vault up and over the hood of the VW. He didn't set up for a landing as a gymnast would have done. Instead, he kept his legs out for too long a time, holding a horizontal line to the ground. His knees remained slightly flexed until, at the last instant, he uncoiled, adding the power of his muscle at precisely the second his shoes hit the chest of the man on the opposite side.

It took no more than that. The man in the yellow shirt, at the least, had no air left in his lungs. If the force of the blow had also ruptured his heart or stunned its rhythm, he was dead. Doll didn't take the time to find out.

He landed awkwardly. That had been inevitable. Shaking off the effects, he rolled away from the motionless body and, in the same movement, was back on his feet.

Bandalos, who was already around to the right side rear of the car, stopped his headlong rush at Doll, deciding, it seemed, that his better chance was to regroup. The third man instinctively fanned out farther to Bandalos's right, trapping Doll in the quarter circle of arc defined by the car, the building's side, and the two men to Doll's front.

Now the new man's weapon was visible—not a knife, but a two-foot length of pipe, held in his left hand. A southpaw.

Doll moved toward him. He swung for Doll's head—all street fight and no training—left to right. Doll ducked beyond the radius of the pipe, then waited through the tenths of seconds while the momentum of the swing carried arm and pipe on toward the end of their semicircle. The distance between them was close enough so that even in the darkness, Doll saw the sudden shock of recognition flash for an instant in the man's eyes. He was caught off balance and hopelessly vulnerable with his arm still swinging helplessly farther and farther across his own chest.

The recognition and fear didn't last for long. Both vanished in the pain that followed as Doll's left fist drove deeply into the man's diaphragm. Doll felt his own pain, too, in his hand where, that morning, Bandalos's knife had slashed through to the bone of the knuckle. But the man's body doubled, arching involuntarily forward, and that was what mattered. For at least a minute, and probably longer than that, he was out of the fight.

But somewhere to the right, although he couldn't see him, Doll knew that Carlos Bandalos was coming fast with his knife.

The defense would be, necessarily, blind. A quarter turn to Doll's right was faster, but it also had the liability of interposing Bandalos's cast arm between Doll and the knife. The three-quarter turn to the left would take longer, but, once accomplished, would leave Bandalos's knife arm exposed and all defensive options available.

Doll executed the three-quarter turn and came out of it with no time to spare. His left forearm hit Bandalos's wrist barely in time to deflect the point. The blade, as it went by Doll's head, cut a short, thin slash in his cheek.

By any reasonable estimation, the bulk and weight of the cast should have made Bandalos clumsy. In the actual circumstance, it didn't. He stopped himself short in the distance of a few feet and was back facing Doll from a crouch again. He still had the knife balanced in his left hand and now held his right arm back, as if he planned to use the cast as a bludgeon.

"I think, maybe, you're all out of tricks, Mr. Doll." Bandalos made the s in the *mister* hiss.

Doll waited.

Bandalos made a provocative feint with the knife, and then a second.

The third became a lunge, almost too fast for Doll to side-step. He blocked it and took a lumbering blow from the cast to the ribs instead.

He concentrated again on his breathing.

"That hurt you maybe a little, eh?" Bandalos said and grinned, then moved at once to capitalize on the effect.

He came at Doll fast and low, the knife tip angled slightly upward, pointed toward a spot just below Doll's sternum. One thrust to the heart and the fight and everything else would be over.

Doll's right hand caught Bandalos's left on the wrist from underneath, but instead of resisting its rush Doll added to it, pulling the arm forward and upward over his shoulder. At the same time, he sat, bringing his left foot up into Bandalos's stomach.

Doll was the hub, his leg the spoke, and Bandalos, to his great misfortune, a segment of the unattached rim.

A thrust from Doll's leg added to the momentum initiated by Bandalos's rushing attack. He landed behind Doll, face first into the gravel, at a distance of about a dozen feet.

Bandalos didn't move, though he still had the knife in his hand. Doll stepped down hard on the wrist with the heel of his shoe and drew a grunt as the fingers splayed. He bent to pick up the knife and looked around.

The yellow-shirted man with the knife and his associate with the pipe were both completing the first stages of recovery.

"Okay, okay. I think maybe we've all had enough of that," a husky baritone voice said from the blackness at the back of the parking lot.

Mickey Zale stepped out of the total darkness into the little light that there was.

"You did a lot of damage today, so I figure I better call it off now," Zale said. "I think, maybe, I can't afford what you might do tomorrow."

"You just come out to see what the ruckus was about, or have you been there through the whole show?" Doll asked. His breathing began to regularize.

"I guess you could say I saw most of it," Zale answered and smiled. His pink jacket was gray beneath the starlight. The edging of his carnation looked black.

Bandalos's two friends, by then, had collected themselves enough to get to their feet. They moved closer together but kept their distance from Zale and Doll. Bandalos tried to push himself up with his hands, but couldn't manage it with the cast and newly injured wrist. He fell facedown on the gravel again, emitting a noise somewhere between an exhalation and a groan.

"So don't just stand there. Help him. Get him outta here. Take him with you," Zale called to the two. "Get cleaned up. I'll see you back at my office later. I got some things we got to discuss."

While the two men gathered up Bandalos, Doll recovered his jacket and dusted off his clothes.

"Does that mean we're going to have to go through this yet another time?" Doll asked.

"No, no. It doesn't mean that." Zale shook his head. "I said it was over. If I said it, it is. What it does mean is that, if I look back on today and tonight as a practice, those boys aren't ready to face the real thing."

"You mean," Doll said, making the same point from another perspective, "if that practice had gone as you hoped, you would have let them kill me?"

Zale shrugged. "I prefer," he replied, "to think of it more as I wouldn't have stopped them. It wasn't my idea. Successful or not, you brought that all on yourself by what you did to Carlos. If it'd been my call, and I really wanted you dead . . ."

Zale drew back his coat to reveal a small caliber pistol nestled in a holster under his armpit. "You move very quick, Doll. But faster than a bullet? No, I don't think that you're Superman."

"What happened to Carlos this morning," Doll said, "wouldn't have happened if he hadn't been on Perry Wellman's boat. What was he doing there?"

"Am I his keeper?" Zale asked indifferently.

"Maybe you are," Doll answered. "He works for you. From tonight, I take it, in more than one capacity. You bail him out when he gets into trouble. And, when he gets hurt, he runs to you. Altogether, I'd say that's a pretty good definition of a keeper."

"That means I know whatever it was he was doing for Wellman?"

"You're not going to tell me," Doll said, "you didn't even know he was there?"

"So I knew. This isn't a federal case. Look, Doll, you've been around. You know how the world is. I can tell by how you handle yourself. You saw Wellman when he was here last night, enough maybe to know he's a pretty good customer. Sometimes he needs a hand, I send him Carlos. It doesn't cost me anything. Carlos owes me so much, if I told him to go to China for me he'd have to. So if I loan him to Wellman, and

Wellman feels grateful and comes back and gives me more business, who gets hurt?"

"Do you know what Wellman does with that boat?" Doll asked.

"Of course I know." Zale threw his hands into the air for added emphasis. "It's no national security secret. You walk into the bar whenever he's here, and he'll tell you himself. If I heard right, he did just that with you last night."

"That he looks for treasure. Not how successful he is," Doll amended.

"This is my concern? Is it any of my business, as long as he pays his bar tab?"

"It's funny, but that's exactly what I was wondering—if any of it is your business," Doll replied. "For example, the rumor is that Wellman finds stuff and sells it. There's supposed to be a tax, but somehow the finds Wellman makes never get reported, and no tax ever gets paid."

Zale studied Doll for a moment, or at least that was what he seemed to be doing for as much as Doll could tell in the darkness. Then he came out with a short, raspy laugh.

"What's wrong with you, Doll? You some kind of Boy Scout or something?" he asked with a tone that sounded like deep disappointment in his voice. "You never heard before of a man who squawks at turning over what money he makes to the government? Mind you, I'm not saying for even a part of a minute that Perry Wellman is any such man. But, if he was, would it really be so hard for you to understand it?"

"And you? Would you be a part of anything like that?"

"And, if I were, I would—just like that—tell you?" The raspy laugh was back in Zale's voice. "I wouldn't even invest the effort it would take to give you an answer, since the only possible answer I could give is that certainly I never would.

"You let me go into the head doctor business, and I'll tell you what's wrong with you, Doll. You take what you think are the rules of life too serious. You gotta learn to relax. Tell you what: You're here; you come into the bar. The Piña Colada will stand you your first drink. You, for that, will forget all today's nasty business with Carlos. Do I offer a fair deal all up front, or do I not?"

"There doesn't seem to be much to do about it except forget it," Doll replied.

"Good. Then that's all there is to that." Mickey Zale reached up and patted Doll's back.

Doll couldn't be certain there in the darkness, but, as he thought about it later, he had the strong impression Zale had smiled.

The bar at the Piña Colada was big and busy enough to keep the two costumed conquistadors behind it moving at a frenetic pace. Zale gave Doll's order, then excused himself. The gin over ice, Doll noticed, was poured and on the bar before him in the minimal time that it took for Zale to accomplish his leave.

Doll asked for a glass of ice water to go with it and, when it arrived, used the water and his handkerchief to pat the thin line of blood from his cheek. The gin slid down easily after the exertion in the parking lot. The simultaneous, contrasting sensations of hot and cold helped the recollection of the immediate past to fade. Doll dabbed at his cheek with the dry part of the handkerchief. The bleeding hadn't begun again. The wound wouldn't look bad enough to make him the focus of undue attention. The effected repairs, at least for now, were as good as they were going to get.

If the bar had had a mirror, perhaps he could have seen more. But where the mirror would have been, Mickey Zale, had, instead, an enormous tank crowded with tropical fish. To enhance the scene, he'd included a large wrecked ship, modeled after the Spanish period, with flecks of gold and silver all over the bottom around it. Nearby, a helmeted, bubbling, deep sea diver was opening a bulging chest of treasure.

Doll had forgotten the tank, but now he remembered. The scene was exactly as Willard Giesler had described it.

A new image appeared like a phantasm in the semireflective glass of the aquarium—the face of a woman who'd taken the seat beside Doll's at the bar. Doll turned and found Valerie Albrecht.

"Hello, soldier," she said, and smiled at him extravagantly. "Rich American wanna buy a girl a little drink?"

Her head was sufficiently close to his that most of what Doll saw was a field of ash blond hair arranged around a pair of emerald eyes.

"I remember what they brought you last night," Doll replied. "I don't know enough from that to know what it's called."

"It doesn't matter. It changes. Just signal either of the boys behind the bar and point to me. They both know what I'm drinking tonight."

Valerie Albrecht sat back on the bar stool. She was dressed in a dark blue blouse and a medium-short white skirt. As she crossed her legs, she revealed a four-inch expanse of very tanned thigh.

Doll did as he'd been told.

"I go through a rotation. Tonight it's brandy Alexanders." She laughed. "Not too many of those. They use heavy cream and have some insane number of calories. But, if I want to, I can always switch to straight-up cognac later on."

"It must be nice to have it down to a system," Doll said because nothing else came to his mind. One of the things he wasn't good at, as he'd had other occasions before this one to admit, was making trivial yet effervescent cocktail conversation.

"It saves time," Valerie agreed with a grin that might have persuaded any man that he'd just mouthed the cleverest words ever spoken. Her brandy Alexander arrived at her elbow. "I heard," she said, "that you went to talk to Perry Wellman today."

"We talked a little," Doll replied. "Mostly about some coins that he gave to Diana."

If the fact had any meaning for Valerie Albrecht, Doll observed, she managed not to let it show in her face.

"He's a nice boy. I'd hate to see him get himself into any trouble."

"What trouble would he get himself into?" Doll asked.

"I dunno," Valerie replied. "What kind of troubles are there?"

The inquiry was an open invitation, a serious question or a straight man's line phrased to draw a witty rejoinder. Doll let both opportunities pass.

"I guess you know," he said instead, "that, the last few days, I've been talking to a lot of people. You know what I've been talking about. I've been trying to find out whatever I can that might turn out to help Diana Raney."

Valerie nodded and took a sip of her drink. "And now that you've regrouped since last night," she said, "I suppose you've decided that it's time you want to talk to me."

Doll shook his head. "No change in plans. Not unless there's something you want to tell me."

"What would that be?" Valerie asked and stared at Doll until both of them laughed. "All right, so we won't play at that game," she conceded. "I knew her, Doll. Like I knew Sean Dabney. That's all I can tell you."

"And Perry Wellman. And Calvin Tack," Doll said. "A woman named Sylvia Guillette and a semiretired dentist named Truitt. That's one of the things I've been trying to put together. Rather than being vague about it, let's just say it's a very oddly mixed group."

"Odd—and maybe not so odd." Valerie seemed to consider the matter for a moment before going further with her reply. "Calvin's Route One business and Chamber of Commerce," she explained. "Sean was, too. So was Tom Guillette in a less grand way. He used to own a sporting goods shop. That was before he and Sylvia broke up. Doc Truitt's another case—kind of a hot ticket, especially for his age. You might say his wife's more retired than he is. He comes in here when he wants to kick up his heels."

"And you?"

"And me!" Valerie smiled and took a second sip at her drink. "I used to do tax work for Tom Guillette. I'd like to have gotten Sean's account. I'd still like to get Calvin Tack's."

"And Wellman and Diana?"

Valerie responded with a slight shrug of her shoulders. "Perry Wellman just because, like Doc, he's mostly always here. Diana because she was with Sean.

"Bad subject, Doll. Sean I mean," she said, shaking her head. "Let's drop it if you're not pushing questions. There's nothing else that I can say, and it's still hard to think, much less talk, about Sean Dabney being murdered."

Looking up toward the tank, Valerie pointed. "Isn't that an incredible thing? It's the biggest aquarium I've ever seen outside of a theme park like Sea World or one of the others. Some hobby—not a cheap one either. The water has to be filtered so it's clean, then kept with the right amount of air and at the right temperature. But the only thing I have to do is look at them. I mean, it isn't my work or my money. What do you think of Mickey Zale's fish?"

Doll stared at the tank, wondering what Valerie Albrecht expected him to see. They were fish. There wasn't any question about that much. Some were broad top to bottom but almost paper thin head-on, others stockier, and others still with bulbous snouts and long whiskerlike projections. All seemed to have that graceful, dignified serenity that the peculiar properties of the marine environment allow its denizens to have. But the fish were just that, fish, and that, as far as Doll could see, was all.

"They're something to watch, I guess. Other bars have televisions," was all he could think of to say.

"But televisions are provocative. They reach out and grab at you," Valerie Albrecht explained as though it were something she herself had once been told. "The fish are supposed to be soothing—just the opposite. The essence of tranquillity. That's the theory, anyway. It's almost what they seem like, don't they?"

Her voice turned distant, becoming almost flat. The expression on her face seemed somehow abstracted.

"You see the tall, thin ones—how elegant they are? Those are angels and Oscar fish. Placid things, aren't they? Nearly godlike in their imperturbability. They're members of the same family of Chaetodontidae. Every once in a while they're exciting to watch. They have a particular fondness for picking a moment and tearing one of their kinfolk apart."

12

Middays in Florida in the summer months seemed to Doll to hold all the pleasures of time spent in a humid oven, a succession of extended and unwelcome sauna baths that, beyond the dominion of the air-conditioning systems, one had no choice but to endure. The nights, on the other hand, could be beautiful, sultry affairs, and the mornings, before the sun had had the chance to reassert its sovereignty, a fresh pleasure to awaken to.

Doll felt that way about this particular morning as he drove south through the town along the unremitting line of recessed malls, fast food restaurants, and auto dealerships that bordered Route 1. The air was beginning to warm, but a cool breeze still slipped in through the VW's open window. The traffic in both directions was heavy. The weekday world was on its way to work.

The doughnut shop, which was where Harvey Archer had called with instructions for Doll to meet him, was on the opposite, northbound side of the highway. Doll pulled to the left and waited through a duration of time that tested his patience, then made the turn when a signal light a block ahead caused the stream of oncoming vehicles to pause.

The building was a small, quick-to-fabricate affair with a too familiar franchise look about it, another testimony, Doll decided, to the sprawling homogenization of America. But for some reason or other, the original enterprise had failed. The new business that now occupied the quarters was a more modest, but independent, venture—even if a hasty paint-over of the exterior had left ridges where the earlier lettering and a former logo showed through.

Harvey Archer sat at one of the outdoor tables, paging through the morning's edition of *USA Today*. He had on a fresh Hawaiian shirt and a grayish white jacket, wrinkled enough to make Doll wonder if he'd pressed it with his mattress. Before him on the table were a half-finished orange juice, a bran muffin, and a Styrofoam cup full of black coffee hot enough for a thin cloud of steam to hover near the rim.

Archer looked up from his newspaper and breakfast with the same expression of accepted martyrdom with which he'd allowed his attention to be diverted from the baseball game the day before.

"Sort of a cafeteria system," he explained. "You go inside, pick up what you want, and bring it out. Good muffins and coffee." He frowned and shrugged. "Reconstituted orange juice. I drink it. I don't recommend it."

Doll got himself a coffee and left it at that. Returning to the table, he sat across from Archer.

With no special hurry, Archer finished the piece he'd been reading, then folded the newspaper on the bench beside him, pinning the edge under his hip so that the breeze couldn't catch the pages.

A dozen feet away, along Route 1, the unending river of traffic rumbled steadily by. The air held the acrid smell of oxidized hydrocarbons.

The hour was just after nine. The only other customers at the outdoor tables were a pair of septuagenarian gentlemen in white summer hats who looked as though they might have settled there for the day.

"I talked to Willard Giesler last night," Archer began. "As a matter of fact, I did more than just talk to him. I figured it was worth my time to drive out to his house and see him."

Doll nodded. The expenditure of effort that Archer had described implied a matter of some significance. Doll had no idea at all of what the matter might have been.

"I don't know what impression you've had the time to gather about Willard," Archer went on. "Mine comes from fifteen years, more or less. It's that he's mostly honest—which is about all you can ask of any man—but that, when he wants to be, he can be as cagey as a bullfrog catching flies."

"I guess, if that's cagey, he could be," Doll replied. He still had no idea where Harvey Archer's discourse was heading.

"We had a long talk about pictures," Archer said. "Particularly, the pictures you were asking about. I'll tell you, Doll, sometimes it's just amazing to me the way some things work themselves around."

Archer smiled as though to prolong the suspense and then, to add to it, chose the moment to take a swallow of his coffee. Finally, he returned the cup to the table.

"I guess you know," he said, still smiling, "that there are times when a man can be too smart for his own good. I really thought that Willard sent you to see me with the idea of pulling me out. I got to thinking about it more and more after you left, and, the more I thought about it, the surer I got. Then I couldn't figure out how Willard could've found out. That's guilt, boy. That's how it works. Take a lesson from that."

"You mean that you *do* have the pictures?"

Archer seemed very nearly to laugh.

"I went out to Willard's, and I put the question to him. Oh, not right off. Give me credit for being more subtle than that. I fished, and Willard came forward with nothing. I figured he was dodging, so I kept on pushing him. And all of a sudden, without even realizing that *I* was the one that I was digging the dirt up about, I found myself challenging him with what I'd

convinced myself was the overwhelming evidence. I then reduced the question to one of *how* he knew. That's called stupid,
Doll—just inexcusably stupid. There's a lesson in that for you, too."

"What did Giesler do?" Doll asked.

"What any decent lawyer would've done. He told me to shut
the hell up." Archer twisted a corner of his mouth into a sneer
of self-derision. "He said he didn't understand what he'd heard
so far and that he didn't want to hear any more. He said he
wanted nothing to do with anything that pertained to any case
he was handling if the 'anything' had been obtained by illegal or
extralegal means. Do I have to tell you twice I felt like a damn
fool!"

"So you called me instead?"

Archer smiled sardonically. "Willard went on to say that he
refused to be a party to anything seedy, and, if I was talking about
anything like that, I might do better to take it up with someone
more along the likes of you."

"Because I can afford to be seedy." Doll nodded his head to
say he understood. "I don't have any oath or ethical standard I
have to uphold."

"He can be cagey." Archer showed a trace of satisfaction at
having proved what he'd only alleged before. "And he sets me
up with an obligation. Because he stopped me just in time from
running off my mouth to a point where, maybe, I couldn't get
back from."

"So you pay that back by showing me the pictures," Doll
inferred.

Harvey Archer reached into his inside jacket pocket and
removed three folded sheets of paper. He held them out and met
Doll's eyes. Doll took them, and, by doing so, made himself a
part of the bargain.

"You can't keep them," Archer said in a low, quick voice.
"They're too hot for that. Keeping them can't be a part of any
deal. I'd also appreciate it if you made your inspection short.

While you do that, I'll keep any eye out for anyone trying to catch a glance over your shoulder."

Doll looked down at the first of the pages—and found that nothing was what he'd expected. Archer, meanwhile continued to explain.

"You'll see first off that they're photocopies of the photographs and not the actual thing. That's the way my arrangement works. The pictures themselves never leave the sheriff's office. But, these days, photocopiers have special settings that let you copy photographs. So the ones you've got there are close enough to the originals that, for any practical purpose short of further enlargement from the negative, they come down to the same thing."

As Doll gathered in the visual evidence, he realized that, in the short tour of Dabney's apartment that he'd taken with Ann and Emilio Secassa, he'd made the fundamental mistake of letting his mind create its own picture of how the murder scene must have been. He remembered the four pieces of furniture— the two matching chairs, the sofa, and the coffee table—and the half-seen and half-imagined stain from the blood.

And amid the furnishings, collapsed on the floor, Doll had envisioned Sean Dabney's corpse, stretched out and silent. The blood was there, off to the side near where the head rested—but the mental picture Doll had formed was of a man who, otherwise, might have been mistaken for someone asleep.

Very foolish, very naive, Doll thought to himself now as he stared down at the picture that Harvey Archer had provided. He knew enough of death, Doll told himself, to know it as a monster which, even to the sick, only sometimes came peacefully. And, when a death was violent, even seen from the three-fold distance of a photocopied photograph, the ultimate brutality of it couldn't help but show through.

Sean Dabney had hit the floor hard. His descent, the pictures showed, had been headlong. In its fall, his crashing body had toppled one of the chairs and, even as it had come to rest, was wedged at an awkward angle against it. An outstretched arm had flung the coffee table aside in what must have been a desperate, futile, uncontrolled thrash to get what posed itself as a dangerous object out of his way.

The side of the face Doll could see was contorted, the mouth agape, the single visible eye wide open and sightlessly staring. The fingers of the reaching hand were arched and extended to form a claw. Toward the back of the skull, the head showed an elongated depression. In the picture, both hair and blood came out black. But the collar and back of Dabney's light-colored shirt looked as though they had been splattered with large gobs of India ink. Sean Dabney, however he'd lived, had died harshly.

"Have you seen crime scene pictures before?" Archer asked.

Doll wondered if the lateness of the question had been deliberate, a small exaction of revenge for the price that Archer had had to pay.

"I've seen the real thing in service," Doll answered. "The callousness you build up doesn't stay with you. If you're not conditioned, it always takes some getting used to again."

"Yeah, I guess it does," Archer agreed. Any spirit of victory there might have been was, by then, absent from his voice. "How about it? Do they give you what you want?"

The two other photographs came down to more of the same, the death scene again shot from different angles. Neither of them revealed a picture any less ugly.

The middle one included the murder weapon. Doll wondered if it was from the photo that Archer had known what the weapon was. The figure of a nude woman stood atop a stubby pedestal. The whole piece, Doll noticed, was now slightly warped at a point somewhere around the woman's pelvis.

"He was hit with the base end?" Doll asked, trying at the same time to make out all the detail he could see. "And hard enough to bend the statue," Doll said when Archer had nodded. "A woman would have to be pretty strong . . ."

"Or pretty angry," Archer suggested before Doll had finished the thought. "Besides, even that much you don't know till you see the thing. It's one case if it's bronze, another if it's lead or something else more malleable."

Doll flipped through the photographs again, stopping this time at the one that offered the best view of the overturned coffee table. Tilting the picture, then moving it back and forth in his field of vision, he tried to bring into focus the contents of the coffee table top that, after the impact of Dabney's fall, were strewn across the floor.

"What do you make out of that assortment?" he said, pointing toward the items with his finger, then passing the photograph across to Archer.

Archer studied the image for a moment. "Keys, on a ring with one of those plastic advertisement fobs. Closer down toward the camera lens, I'd say that's one of those glass scallop-shaped ashtrays. In the mid-ground, a pair of short whiskey glasses. If you look, you can still see a little stain where the whiskey's run out onto the carpet."

"So what does that tell you?" Doll asked.

"Doesn't tell *me* anything," Archer answered. "Maybe that Dabney and the woman decided on a nightcap."

"But she told the police she went straight to the bedroom where she passed out," Doll reminded Archer. "Besides that, her tastes used to run toward long drinks when I knew her before. Maybe she's changed that. On the other hand, if she hasn't, it makes a reasonable case that somebody else was there."

"That's a long jump on a lot of *if's*," Archer said, "starting with the fact that your friend also told the police that she didn't remember whether or not she'd murdered Dabney. If she doesn't know that, she's not going to make a very creditable witness on whether or not they opted for a nightcap or what it was they decided to drink."

"Forensic work on the glasses," Doll suggested.

"If she or anyone else besides Dabney actually drank from them," Archer replied. "The fact that they were poured doesn't guarantee that. But there's no point in talking about it, is there, Doll? The only way to follow a lead is in the concrete."

He took a swallow of his coffee and contorted his face into a wince. The steam was gone from the surface of the liquid; what remained had clearly gone cold.

"What I said yesterday—it still stands," he concluded. "Those pictures are my payback to Giesler. Your debt's still out. If you get anywhere—if you break this thing open—you've got to promise me the scoop."

Doll nodded. "If I break it—and on the condition that what I find won't hurt Diana." He handed the two remaining photos back across the table to Archer.

"Not perfect, but fair enough," Archer agreed. "Because—I'll tell it like it is, Mr. Doll—if all it does is hand the lady more trouble, it isn't going to be exactly a scoop that people rush out to buy papers to read."

The sign that hung from the arm of the lamppost was done in simple black letters against a white background. The top line read DR. SAMUEL J. TRUITT; the bottom line simply said DENTIST.

Doll crossed the yard and climbed the steps to the neat white porch, where a small cardboard plaque, hung behind the glass in the door, told him to ring the doorbell and enter. Inside, the waiting room was dimly lit by a pair of vintage, wall-mounted incandescent lamps. Twin white wicker tables on opposite sides of an empty couch held tidy rows of magazines.

No receptionist was there to ask about Doll's appointment.

Only a card on the fireplace mantel, peaked like the roof of a house and set on its edges, explained what was expected.

PLEASE BE SEATED, the card announced. THE DOCTOR WILL BE WITH YOU SHORTLY.

Doll took a place on the couch and tried, with only marginal success, to immerse himself in one of the magazines and ignore the shriek of the high-speed drill.

Minutes passed. The drilling paused for a moment and then became sporadic until finally—mercifully—it stopped.

More time went by before the patient came out, a woman well past middle age with obedient tufts of blue gray hair. She had no smile of comfort or camaraderie for Doll. Her only interest at that moment seemed to be to get away from the just-ended experience and get on with whatever else was her business for the day.

Doll's eyes drifted back to the magazine again. But before he'd begun the process of reading, an impression of movement encroached on the edge of his vision. Looking up from the page, Doll found a man in a pastel tunic drying his hands on a small, white towel.

"Mr. Doll?" Samuel Truitt consigned the towel to the end of the mantel top as he crossed the room. "As I said on the phone, I expected your call. I'm only too happy to talk with you. I understand that you're here to help Diana Raney."

Truitt was short and slightly built. His gray hair showed a pair of deep receding vees, one to either side back from his forehead to a place above his temples but, otherwise, was full despite his years. Doll almost had to bow to shake the offered hand.

"We have plenty of time." Pointing for Doll to return to the couch, Truitt took his own place on the opposite end. "This is a long lunch for me. I don't have anyone else coming in until the mid-afternoon. I'm retired officially. I suppose that you know that. I've been down here for almost five years now. My practice used to be up in New England. Beautiful country. I'd have to say I miss it. But it can get god-awful cold."

Doll asked if Diana was one of Truitt's patients.

"Diana? Goodness, no. Of course, if there had been an emergency . . .

"To be frank, Mr. Doll, I'd be pushing the point to call what I have here now a practice. Replace a filling. Repair a chip. Only the most basic procedures. Anything that's a problem— even mildly out of the ordinary—I send to someone else, someone with younger and steadier hands than mine."

"But you still see patients," Doll observed.

"More as a courtesy than anything else," Truitt replied. "And to still keep my hand in a little. The patients I see these days are older—retired, like me. I meet them at house parties or on the golf course, and, to be honest, I feel sorry for them. They know they need to see someone, and they tell me that they aren't comfortable. They don't mix in with the community around, just with each other. Their old dentists, who they went to for years, are back home. They don't like going to someone new. With me, at least, I may be new, but it's somebody they know."

"You knew Diana, who certainly wasn't here to retire. I came here this morning because people I've talked to described you as one of her friends."

"It's a compliment," Truitt answered with a nod of modesty, "but to put it just that way, I think, gives credit for more of a closeness than there was. I knew Sean Dabney first—may God rest him—and, through him, I got to know Diana later. It was that way—more like a friend of a friend. You understand?"

"Then you knew Dabney well?"

"No. I wouldn't say that, either. I met him only after we moved here." Doc Truitt folded his hands in his lap. When he went on his voice was low, his manner approaching the style of confession. "There's a place I go sometimes—a bar, to give it its proper name. Sean Dabney would be there sometimes, too.

We'd sit together for the time of a few drinks, maybe tell some not-suitable-for-the-general-public stories. My wife just shakes her head at me when I go out. She thinks I'm too far over the hill for that kind of thing. Probably she's right.

"Anyway, I'd see him there on the nights when the both of us happened to stop in. This last year, most of those nights he'd have Diana with him. That was the way in which I got to know her."

"Then you saw yourself more as Sean's friend than Diana's," Doll suggested. "Not knowing him well, if you like to say it that way, but feeling closer to him than you did to Diana. That must make it hard for you, doesn't it, Doctor? Diana's in jail. The police say she killed Sean. From what you tell me and what the circumstances are, I'm not sure I see why you'd want to help her. It seems to me you'd be more in the camp of the people wanting her head on a plate."

"There comes a time in life, Mr. Doll," Truitt said and sighed, "when you understand there's very little satisfaction in having anybody's head. All our heads roll—some sooner, some later. Maybe I've gotten too soft in my dotage. I find I can't take comfort in other people's misery."

"But you do agree with what the police are saying." Doll tried to interpret the sense of the words. "You accept it as fact that Diana killed Dabney."

Truitt shook his head very slowly. "I'm not convinced that she did or that she didn't. I am convinced—and I hope this helps—that she isn't by nature a murderous woman. If she did what the police claim, then I'm sure she had some reason that compelled her. But that doesn't mean I think Sean Dabney deserved what happened to him either. I know maybe, on the face of it, that sounds a little muddled. Probably, when you come down hard on it, it is."

"That's a very provocative point," Doll said. "What reason, do you think, might have compelled her?"

Doc Truitt shook his head again. "I'm sorry, but I'm not going to guess for you, Mr. Doll—and that, in truth, is all I could do. Nor am I going to contribute to passing along the imputations about Sean that I've heard expressed by others. I'm sure you'll find other people to tell you about those if, indeed, you haven't found them already."

"Is there anything else that you *can* tell me? For example," Doll went on to specify, "I'd be particularly interested in anyone else you know who might have had something against Sean Dabney."

For several seconds Truitt said nothing while he seemed to consider what Doll had asked. "No," he said finally. "I can't think of anyone like that."

"Then I'd like to try just one more approach. That bar you talked about where you sometimes met Dabney and Diana—I take it that would be Mickey Zale's Piña Colada?" Doll watched as Truitt's answer came in a nod of agreement. "There's another man," Doll continued. "His name is Perry Wellman. I understand he also spends time at that club."

"I know him," Truitt acknowledged. "As you say, from the Piña Colada. Not as well as I knew Sean Dabney, but enough to talk to. That's certainly true."

"Well enough to have heard his stories?" Doll asked. "Well enough to have known what he was trying to do—to have heard, for instance, about anything valuable he might have been able to salvage from the ocean?"

For the briefest of moments Truitt looked doubtful, and then, almost at once, he smiled.

" 'Might have salvaged.' " Truitt beamed with satisfaction, as though he'd suddenly realized the hidden purpose behind Doll's question. "Oh, I've heard all about that. The truth is that the boy hardly talked about anything else. If he'd put half the effort that he put into the bottom of that ocean in another direction, he might today have been a neurosurgeon or an astrophysicist.

Maybe even a dentist, God help him. But I don't begrudge him any of that, Mr. Doll. I admire a man with the courage to chase dreams—perhaps because I've never had the fortitude to chase my own."

"And Sean Dabney," Doll said. "Did he know Perry Wellman, too?"

"He knew him," Truitt said with a shrug. "I wouldn't say he knew him any better than we all did. People have drinks in the same place, they're going to talk to one another. How much they talk—what they say—is something between them. If you want to know how much Perry Wellman talked to Sean, I'm sure you'd do better to ask Perry Wellman rather than me.

"I'm sorry, Mr. Doll. Honestly I am. But I don't see that what I've been able to tell you is going to be very much of a help."

13

The first reaction Doll had to his talk with Truitt was one of dissatisfaction. For all the questions he'd asked, what he'd learned came down to nothing. But as he began to set Truitt into context, he found his immediate response dissolving into a far more generalized sense of frustration which, in turn, transformed itself into anger.

He drove across the causeway bridge that connected the mainland to the south island, but not back to his motel as he'd intended. Instead he drove past it, farther along to where a graveled pull-off not much wider than a broadened shoulder opened on the right-hand side of the road. The space was enough for eight or ten cars. Along the bank, the trees and undergrowth had been cleared to expose a broad panorama of the river.

Doll parked and let the heat surround him as he stared out at the vivid patterns of blue and green that the sunlight and bottom conditions made upon the water. After a moment, he closed his eyes, slid his hips forward, and leaned as deeply into the back of the car seat as the meager padding allowed.

Doc Truitt was only the day's glaring example. Mickey Zale. Calvin Tack. Perry Wellman. Everybody! Everybody said that they wanted to help Diana. Only nobody had any answers that did.

Paranoia, Doll thought. How else did you explain the feeling that everybody he talked to was part of some kind of conspiracy of silence? Even Diana—who, herself, had hidden the truth about the coins. Willard Giesler had given his opinion that Wellman was bringing up odds and ends and selling them or giving them to friends. Was that enough to account for the reticence—a small-time, marginally illegal distribution of the proceeds among the faithful? But then, how did Sean Dabney's murder fit? If it did fit. Which brought Doll back to Giesler again because Giesler had been the first to say it: There were all kinds of theories in the offing, but not a one for which he could provide even the most elementary proof.

And Dabney himself? What was there in him? Had he, like the others, known about Wellman's unseemly little enterprise? Doc Truitt at least had had an answer to that. His answer was, "Go and ask Perry Wellman." And just maybe, Doll thought, Doc Truitt that one time had had the matter exactly right.

The only way to get at the answers was to tear through the silence and start people talking. Sometimes, if you wanted to eat the apples, the best chance you had lay in shaking the tree.

Doll waited on the dock by *Fair Wind*'s empty berth. It was just after three in the afternoon when the Bertram's deep-voiced engines burbled across the seaward end of the pier.

Perry Wellman was alone on board. He stared at Doll for the moment it took the two of them to establish eye contact, then returned his attention to handling the boat. He brought her around in a graceful arc—bow out, stern to—and backed her, holding his helm to allow for the set of wind and tide. *Fair Wind* came to a gentle rest with her bow nuzzled against a post. Wellman tied off an aft line to starboard, then a line forward to port, then secured the boat with lines to opposite quadrants.

"Mind if I come aboard?" Doll asked as Wellman shut the engines down.

Wellman threw a cutting glance at Doll before he answered.

"Today you're asking permission?" He made the sarcasm in his voice extravagantly heavy.

Doll took a long step down onto *Fair Wind's* deck.

Turning toward Doll, Wellman broke off his docking routine. "You know, you've got one hell of a nerve," he said. "You just go around with your jaw stuck out and think you can do whatever you want. I hear you had another run-in with Carlos last night. I'll tell you something, Doll. One of these days, no matter how tough you think you are, you're going to find out that there's somebody tougher."

"Kind of like a food chain," Doll replied. "Even the great whites of the world get themselves chowed down when the time comes."

"All right, laugh if you want to." Wellman turned away and twisted the master battery switch to Off. "What do you want here, Doll? I've gotten to a point where I'm not so fond of your company that I'm particularly anxious for a casual conversation."

"Then you don't have to worry. The one thing I can promise you is that this isn't going to be casual," Doll said.

Wellman offered no reply. He only stared at Doll very coldly—and very uncertainly.

"Let's start with salvaging treasure." Doll came a step closer to Wellman and kept his voice low. "The evidence on that alone makes you out a liar and a crook. Number one: You lied to me when you told me those coins that you gave to Diana were only worth a couple of dollars. I don't know anything about recovered treasure, Wellman, but even I knew better than that. What's more, I had it checked. The coins are worth a couple of hundred dollars at the least. And you knew it because you're not that dumb. You were just taking the chance that I wouldn't find out or that you could bluff me if I did."

The answer that Wellman tried to give, Doll cut off in the middle of the second word.

"Point two: You're crooked," he went on. "There's a duty

that has to be paid on salvaged artifacts. Now I'm going to be fair and tell you up front that I don't know that you didn't pay it. But if you're going to tell me you did, then I'm going to suggest that the two of us go down to the tax office together and check out your answer."

The two indictments had their effect. Perry Wellman's face was ashen.

"Who the hell are you, Doll?" Wellman managed to get out in a whisper. "What did I ever do to you? Why are you trying to do all you can to crap up my life?"

"It's this simple," Doll said evenly. "They're trying to steam-roller Diana Raney into prison on a murder charge that I don't think she's guilty of. From where I sit, it seems to me you're by far the more logical person to be standing out in the middle of that road."

"Me! It isn't my fault. What can I do? I didn't kill Sean Dabney," Wellman pleaded.

"That's not the way I see it," Doll answered. "The way that I read the cards says you did."

Wellman drew in some air in an abbreviated gasp. His reaction was a lot like that of a man who'd felt a sharp and sudden physical pain.

"I'll put it together for you nice and easy," Doll said. "You've got a little business going. You bring up a few things. You sell them to friends. Nobody worries much about the taxes. Then Dabney finds out. Which is it, Wellman: Did he just have it in for you, or did he want to cut himself in for too big a part of the action? Either way, all he's got to do is threaten you with the authorities. So you go up to see him. Maybe to try to work things out. Maybe it isn't even first degree. He gives you a short bourbon. If I recall, that's what you drink. Do you remember how the table fell over? I'll be really interested to see if one of those stains on the floor turns out to be bourbon."

"This is the South, for Chrissake," Wellman got out through

his escaping breath. "Do you know how many people down here drink bourbon?"

"I don't have the slightest idea, but I'll tell you what I do know," Doll replied. "I know what happens when the state smells a salvage scam and starts in to tighten the screws. How long do you figure it's going to take for them to come up with one of your customers? Do you know what happens when they start to threaten any of them with a charge of conspiracy to defraud—or offer immunity in return for evidence?"

"For God's sake, Doll, I swear it to you." Wellman's eyes were wide, and drops of perspiration dotted his still white forehead. "It wasn't me who murdered Sean Dabney."

"Then who was it?" Doll said and heaved himself up from the deck onto *Fair Wind's* stern. "It's all right, Wellman. Take your time with that one and think about it. You don't have to answer me now. But, as you can see, I want the truth, and I'm upping the ante to get it. And I'll keep on upping it until the game gets too rich for anybody to play."

Doll stepped across onto the dock, leaving the words to do their work, feeling neither pride nor guilt about the ghost of a man he left in the cockpit behind him.

The dinner that the waitress set before Doll was one of the basics in the *Plan Your Coronary* cookbook: two pork chops, thin and fried; mashed potatoes; a creamy, general purpose gravy; and, as an accommodation to some nutritional requirement, a token scoop of carrots and peas. With the dinner, too, came the bottle of beer that Doll had ordered. The waitress poured out the first three-quarters of a glass.

Doll had had no plans for that evening. He'd fired off his cannon shot and now could only wait to see if and where the ball landed. After his confrontation with Perry Wellman, he'd gone back to his motel. He'd showered to get the day's dirt and perspiration off, read the paper, and watched the evening TV news.

By the time that the last news was done, the bottom rim of the waning sun was closing in on the tops of the trees on the western horizon. The tall-rigged fishing boats making their return trips through the inlet trailed long but fading shadows in their wakes. Doll, by then, had felt hungry enough to go out for something to eat.

He glanced around the restaurant as he took his first swallow of the beer. The crowd was a mixture of blacks, Hispanics, and whites and almost exclusively male. The uniform of the day was work clothes. Choices ranged from coveralls to dungarees to shirts and pants in the traditional colors of blue, khaki, and green.

Business was slow. By Doll's unsystematic estimate only about a quarter of the tables were occupied. The drone of the conversation was moderate.

A tinny set of bells tinkled above the entrance door. Doll gave the sound no particular attention until his ears picked up the drop in the level of background noise.

Looking up, Doll saw Eldwin Rush in the doorway.

Rush took his time looking around the room, conducting, as it seemed to Doll, an undisguised and unashamed visual survey of the restaurant's individual customers. Finally, he let his eyes settle on Doll, then crossed the room to the table and, without comment or question, sat in the opposite chair.

He let several seconds pass, apparently for the purpose of allowing his presence to establish itself, before he decided to speak.

"That bug of yours with the out-of-state plates sticks out like a square ball at a bowling alley," he said.

The waitress who had let more than fifteen minutes pass before she'd come to take Doll's order was already at Eldwin Rush's elbow. Meanwhile, Doll suspected, somebody else's supper was languishing out in the kitchen getting cold.

"Just coffee, Mary. I'm still on duty. And make sure it gets onto my tab."

The "on duty" part and the scrupulous attention to the bill, Doll decided, had been meant for him to hear. He waited, saying nothing, to see which—or how many—shoes were going to drop.

Rush turned to Doll.

"I hear," he said, "that you've had yourself a hell of a past two days."

"I couldn't say they've been boring," Doll replied without any further elaboration.

"And you've got a big mouth and bigger set of balls," Rush shot back. "You get smart with me, Doll, I'll take you out back and close the one and leave the other somewhere up around your rib cage."

Doll said nothing. One of the things that he'd learned early on was that there was very little to be gained in life from exchanging physical threats with policemen.

"Did you really tell Perry Wellman that you thought he murdered Dabney?" Rush demanded.

"I told him that," Doll answered. "I also told him why."

"You goddamn fool." Rush shook his head as though Doll had just admitted to about the dumbest behavior that Rush had ever heard.

The waitress, meanwhile, brought Rush's coffee and placed it by his elbow on the table. He added some milk and stirred it around and made a show of letting his temper cool.

"Look, Doll," he said when he'd finished his stirring, "there are two or three things that we're gonna get straight. The first is that I don't give a good goddamn about whatever reasons you gave to Wellman. There's only one thing that motivates you, and we all know that hangs down between your legs. You need a fall guy to get your girlfriend off the hook, so why not Wellman? Well, that's not gonna happen, Doll. The lady killed a man. She's been got, and got good. And the charges against her are going to stick."

"You're that sure?" Doll made it a special point to drill the question home with his eyes.

"That sure," Rush said, matching Doll's intensity stare for stare.

"Did Wellman tell you about the treasure he's brought up?" Doll asked. "About the coins that he gave to Diana?"

"He offered to. And he told me that, if he didn't, you probably would. I told him not to bother. That's bullshit, Doll. You're just reaching for the long shots. For Chrissake, there's hardly a kid who's grown up around here who, one time or another, hasn't brought up something. And, although it may be a surprise to you, I really doubt that all of the taxes that should've got paid."

"But there's a little difference in scale, isn't there?" Doll said. "Besides which, I really doubt that all those kids also have friends with knives to keep their secrets for them."

"Ah-huh. Now that brings us to the other thing." Rush nodded as though he were satisfied by the direction in which the conversation was moving. "You and Bandalos and the other two punks—somebody gets wiped out, how can I lose? But the first time Bandalos went after you was when you were trespassing on Wellman's boat. The way people feel about their boats around here, I'm not even absolutely sure that the state would've prosecuted if he'd killed you.

"But leaving that aside, Doll, what I'm telling you is this: If you so much as go near Wellman or his boat again, if you say as much as two words to him, and he comes to me like I told him to, I'll have you booked within the hour on a harassment charge. That's no threat, no bullshit—just an out-and-out, straightforward promise."

"You're sure you don't want to tell me to get out of town by sunset?" Doll asked.

Eldwin Rush took a swallow of his coffee. "Well, now," he said, "as a matter of fact, that may be exactly what I'd like to do." Rush smiled, but not with any humor. "But if I tried to make it stick, the ACLU'd be breaking my chops the first thing come morning. All that doesn't stop me, though, from offering some free advice. You see, a whole lot of people would like to tell you that too, Mr. Doll. You'd think a guy as bright as you think you are'd start to get the message after a while. Nobody down here likes you. Nobody down here wants you here. Not even your girlfriend, from what they tell me. So why don't you do us all a favor and just pick your ass up and leave?"

Rush pushed back his chair from the table and started to stand.

"I've got the message. I'm not widely loved," Doll said. "Now how about a question from my side?"

Rush glared at Doll, almost defying him to ask it, but he stayed.

"Do you want to tell me," Doll asked, "just why it is you've made this into a personal thing about Diana?"

"You son of a bitch," Rush whispered, and let his weight settle back in the chair again. "I ought to kick your goddamn teeth out for what you're implying. But just to set the record straight, I haven't got any 'personal thing' about Diana Raney. She committed a crime. She's going to pay the price for that, like anybody else. For me, it's that simple."

"So simple that you want me out of town before there's any chance that I turn something up?"

"You know, you *are* dumb." Rush's voice was an audible sneer. "I told you once already that I haven't got anything personal against Diana. But are you so far out of things that you can't understand that maybe I do have a personal thing about you? I admit I hate even the thought of snot-nosed smart-asses like you who come down here to make my shop and my town look bad. Glory boy heroes who think that they've got the

answers. Guys like you, they get my back up, Doll. Maybe you
ought to think about that. Maybe what you ought to consider is
whether you do your girlfriend more harm than good for the time
you spend hanging around."

Eldwin Rush got up from the chair and was gone, this time
offering Doll no chance for any further questions or rebuttal.
He left behind him a vacuum that reached to every corner of
the room and, at the same time, made Doll the unwilling
center of everyone's attention.

Doll tested a forkful of his dinner. The mashed potatoes and
the gravy both were cold.

On one level, Doll found Eldwin Rush easy to dismiss. For all
the blustering and threats, Doll realized, Rush's reaction was no
more than that of a bureaucrat sensing a challenge to what he
felt was his God-given turf.

But that was only on the first level. There was a second, as
Doll only too well knew. And in that dimension the risks were
higher—just as was the likelihood that what Eldwin Rush had
said might very well be true.

Rush, in fact, had set the only important question out in the
starkest possible relief. If Doll chose to stay on in Florida, was
he doing Diana more harm or good? If he found whatever
evidence was needed to have the charges against her dropped or
else to gain an acquittal, then, of course, the answer was easy. It
was only the *if* that made it hard. If he remained and still came
up with nothing—and all his continued presence achieved was
to add to Rush's intransigence . . .

Doll played the problem like a record, over and over and over
again, without finding any satisfactory resolution. He was working at it still an hour later as he unlocked and opened the door
of his motel room.

Had it not been for the nearly total darkness inside, he might not even have noticed the message light on his telephone, which was glowing in a vibrant and insistent shade of red.

The clerk at the other end of the line took a few seconds to sort through his notes, then told Doll in a discreet deskman's voice that a woman had asked he be informed she'd be waiting for him out beside the pool.

The cement deck in the vicinity of the lounge chair where Valerie Albrecht was sitting was spotted with small, dark puddles of water. Her hair was tousled in the same haphazard arrangement where it had wound up when she'd dried it with a towel. Her swimsuit was a single piece in deep navy blue with a diagonal electric purple stripe traversing it from arm to hip and twisted near the middle to resemble a segment of a Möbius strip.

"Well, hello." She made a point of eying Doll's knit pullover shirt and slacks. "I gather that we aren't going swimming."

"You didn't say you'd be dressed for it," Doll replied.

"When you make a girl wait . . ." The implication seemed to be that, having done that, Doll should have been ready for any contingency.

"I had a couple of drinks at the bar," she explained, "but after a while I decided that, if I stayed there, by the time you got back I'd probably be stiff enough to be suitable for framing. So I changed into my suit, and here I am." She looked up at him. "Are you going to stand there, or are you going to sit down? I'm just warning you that, if we keep the present angle, I'm going to wind up with a stiff neck."

Doll sat on the adjacent lounger. The pool was abandoned for the day by all but a few of the most ardent swimmers.

"I won't ask you where you've been. I know that isn't any of my affair." She smiled at Doll as though she'd made a highly generous concession. "I assume you've had dinner. I've had mine, too, so I'm not angling for any invitations."

"Am I allowed to ask what you *are* angling for?" Doll said.

"Maybe just for the company," she replied, giving Doll a look of careful appraisal. "You're not that bad looking a specimen, all things considered. A Florida town in the off-season isn't exactly a place where a girl can take her pick of a very large litter. Of course, I could always have Mickey Zale if I wanted him. But Mickey's a lech. He's crude, and his breath smells like a two-day-old ashtray. Calvin Tack and Doc Truitt are nice, but the truth is, Doll, they're both a little old for me."

"You were with Clayton Rivers the other night."

"I was with Clayton," Valerie acknowledged. "Clayton can be interesting. He's rich, which is nice, and he knows all sorts of fascinating people. He likes me to decorate his arm every now and then. He's also the most self-centered man I've ever known."

"Perry Wellman?"

"And Perry Wellman . . ." Valerie repeated the name, apparently to emphasize it. "He's a boy, Doll, or hadn't you noticed that? You really scared the hell out of him this afternoon."

Doll nodded and sighed in resignation. "So that's where all this is leading," he said. "You could have saved yourself all the trouble. I've had the riot act read to me already tonight—by Eldwin Rush, and he's an expert."

Valerie Albrecht frowned. Doll wasn't sure at what.

"Perry told me he'd talked to Rush," she said. "That just shows how much you panicked him. If he'd called me first, I would've stopped him. It wasn't the smartest thing he could've done."

Facing away from Doll, Valerie stared out across the water of the pool. The air was warm. Above, the poolside floodlights glared. Doll had to look out over the ocean to see the black sky filled with stars.

"You got close, Doll," she said, turning back toward him again. "Closer than anybody ever thought you'd get. So close that you got half of it almost right—and the other half absolutely wrong."

"The part about Wellman salvaging treasure—that was the right part?" Doll guessed.

"Yes," Valerie answered. Her voice still held a hint of reluctance. "You don't leave a lot of choice except to tell you the rest. You go blundering around all on your own without any idea of who might get hurt.

"Yes, Perry Wellman found a wreck—or part of one. It's offshore, farther out than the others. Perry says that it probably broke up out there before it had a chance to get driven onto the beach. That's why nobody's found it before."

"And he's been salvaging from the wreck and not reporting his recoveries."

"Yes, yes. All that part is true," Valerie admitted. "I told you that you had that almost right. What you've never understood is the size of what he's found down there—and what it takes to bring it up. There's a lot of it, Doll. A fortune, Perry says, several times over. But the one thing it takes to salvage it is money—more money than Perry ever came close to having. There are investors. That's what you missed all along. Calvin Tack. Doc Truitt. Tom Guillette, before he broke up with his wife. And me. And Diana. And the one you really missed, Sean Dabney."

Doll looked sharply at Valerie Albrecht. "You're sure about that? You're telling me Dabney was in on what Wellman was doing all along?"

"That's the whole point of all this, Doll—what you told Perry Wellman. You told him you thought that he killed Dabney because Dabney found him out. Sean Dabney didn't find anyone out. He couldn't have, because he was a partner in the business. He couldn't have threatened Perry Wellman if he'd wanted to. He couldn't have blackmailed him. You were wrong— you couldn't have been more wrong—about blackmail being a reason for Perry to have killed him."

"And Diana was in on it, too?" The question was quiet and rhetorical.

"That's why she had those two coins," Valerie Albrecht replied. "They were a kind of a token, one of the first pieces that Perry brought up. That's why Perry and all of us had to find out how much you and Diana's sister knew, even if it meant that we might tip our hand in the effort. Looking back with hindsight, I guess maybe that was our mistake."

"What about Eldwin Rush," Doll asked with the sense of a new path of destruction before him. "Now that Wellman's gone and talked to him is he going to start making inquiries?"

"I don't think so. I'm not saying it couldn't happen, but it's not very likely," Valerie answered. "In the first place, it isn't technically his concern. Salvage and the taxes on it are handled by the state. They aren't local responsibilities. On the other hand, what happens to Diana is very much his concern. I don't see him looking too closely at anything that shows any chance of muddying those waters—not unless you do something that forces him to."

"And bring Diana more trouble than she already has?" Doll shook his head. "No, I'm not going to do that." He looked up and deliberately across at Valerie. "That's not a promise to keep the secret, you understand. If it comes down to exchanging it for a murder charge, I'll do it in a minute, and the chips will have to fall where they fall. But, aside from that, if the angle doesn't work for Diana, whatever anybody down here thinks, I didn't come to roust the skeletons out of any local closets."

"I don't know what 'anybody' thinks," Valerie answered and smiled, "but I never thought that you did. Diana's a lucky girl.

Luckier than I ever realized she was. I might almost be willing to trade places with her, even now the way things are."

Doll stood as Valerie Albrecht did. In her bare feet, she seemed so much shorter than she had the night before at Mickey Zale's. Her forehead of ash blond hair scarcely reached up to Doll's nose.

"Thanks for a very nice evening, Doll," she said, gazing up at him. The glint in her eyes was like the sparkle of the water in the pool. "I can handle the walk out to my car on my own. You can come around and see me some time if you like, though— now that you know how inexpensive a date I can be."

14

Tom Guillette was the obvious choice. According to what Valerie Albrecht had said, he, along with his former wife, had been the only investors in Wellman's enterprise to sell off their share in the partnership. Unlike Tack or Truitt, Doll reasoned, Guillette had a very limited involvement to hide and so was the most reliable source both for confirming Valerie Albrecht's tale and for providing, as well, a more detailed account of exactly how the salvage scheme worked.

Doll waited until half past eight the next morning before he tried the number listed in the telephone directory. He dialed it twice to be sure that he'd made no mistake, both times letting the ring persist long enough to become a nuisance to anyone reluctant to answer. Finally, though, his own patience gave out before anyone did.

Guided by a Chamber of Commerce map, he drove out to the address that the phone book had provided. The house that he found was a modest ranch design, vinyl-sided, and set on a sandy lot that was doing its unsuccessful best to support a threadbare carpet of grass.

There was neither a garage where a car might be parked, nor was there any vehicle in the driveway. Doll knocked at the door with little hope of finding anyone at home. He was on the verge of leaving when a neighbor, whose attention—or suspicion—he'd managed to arouse, supplied the name of the supermarket where Guillette now worked and even a serviceable set of directions.

But when Doll asked at the market, the cashier answered only that the day was Guillette's day off. Doll thanked her and started to leave. There were days, he told himself, there was no accounting for—when the world simply set your plans aside and told you you'd have to make other arrangements. Then, at the last moment, the checker's attitude inexplicably softened. If Doll really wanted to find Guillette, she called across the row of checkout aisles, there were no guarantees, but he might give a try at the north causeway bridge.

The north bridge, unlike its arching southern counterpart, was a drawbridge and comparatively low. The portion of the span that didn't move held a dozen or so men and a smaller number of women who used it to fish the waters below.

Doll knew only enough about Tom Guillette to know that he was a white male of some undetermined middle age, but that was sufficient to reduce the possibilities down to three or four candidates. From there it was left for Doll to make his best pick.

The man that Doll settled on had brought a lightweight folding chair in which he sat with his feet propped up against the railing of the bridge. He wore a red mesh broad-visored cap. His tackle box and a six-pack of beer rested on the walkway beside him. Three of the cans from the pack, Doll noticed, had already been opened, and two, at least presumably, had been emptied. The time by then was slightly past ten-thirty in the morning.

"Tom Guillette?" Doll asked.

The man in the red hat turned and angled his tanned face up toward Doll. His eyes were hidden behind a pair of silvered sunglass lenses. His hair was thin and wispy, long where strands stuck out from beneath the sides and back of his cap, and generously streaked with gray. Even sitting down and slouched, he looked tall. His weight was on the light side of average. He was dressed in a pair of beat-up, khaki slacks and a short-sleeved, nylon shirt.

"You somebody I'm supposed to know?" Guillette asked in reply.

"My name's Doll. I'm a friend of Diana Raney."

"Oh." Guillette's voice showed no reaction except for the neutral acceptance of the fact. He seemed to think the relationship over while he gazed out over the azure water. "Well," he said after a time, "I guess that's enough to make you a friend of mine."

"How's that?" Doll asked.

Guillette gave his pole a tug to make sure there was nothing on the line.

"Because if you're a friend of hers, I figure you don't hold with what's been happening to her. I don't either. Far as I'm concerned, if she killed Dabney, they ought to put her name up for the goddamn Congressional Medal of Honor."

"I'd like to be able to prove that she didn't kill him," Doll said.

"In that case," Guillette answered, "she oughta get the medal for putting up with him as long as she did."

"Just so there's no misunderstanding, if it wasn't Diana who killed him, that means there was someone else who did."

"What? Me? You think I killed him?" Guillette turned back to face Doll again. Doll couldn't see his eyes through the silvered lenses, but the mouth, at least, seemed to grin. "I'll tell you what I figure—what was it?—Doll, you said your name was. I figure that the night that Dabney got his the cops must've been about halfway to my door before they got called back. I guess I've got to have had a better reason for killing that bastard than just about anybody else around."

"But you're telling me you didn't," Doll inferred.

"I'll tell you the truth. I thought about it." Guillette shifted his weight in the chair and adjusted the position of his legs against the rail. "I don't mean either that it just passed through my head in an unguarded moment. No, sir. I planned it. I thought about doing it maybe ten or a dozen different ways. Shoot him. OD him. Hit him with a car. Take his body twenty miles out and drop it tied to an outboard somewhere between here and Grand Bahama.

"No balls, Doll. That was my problem. I'd always come up with some way I thought I could get caught, and every time I did I'd chicken out."

"It's the coward in all of us that keeps civilization alive," Doll replied. "It's a good story. It sounds real. The only problem with it is that it comes down to you telling me what's inside your head. There isn't any way for me or anybody else to confirm that."

"Funny." Guillette laughed. "That's just what the cops said. Oh, yeah. They came by to talk in their own good time. Closing up all the loopholes, I guess. I was down on the Keys the night it happened, Doll. Me and four other guys. We keep a boat on Marathon, but that night we were anchored off Key West. The best spring fishing around is just west of there on Smith Shoals off the Marquesas."

"Witnesses." Doll leaned his back against the railing. "Four who're willing to testify that, on the night it happened, Tom Guillette was two hundred fifty miles away."

"And at sea," Guillette added. "And one of the four is a state cop—a very creditable guy."

"What about Perry Wellman?"

Guillette looked up at Doll again. There was no humor in what Doll could see of his face now.

"What about Wellman?" Guillette replied carefully.

"I think you know what I'm asking, but I've got no trouble

spelling it out," Doll answered. "I mean about what he was salvaging and where he was getting the money to do it. I'm talking about Valerie Albrecht and Calvin Tack and Doc Truitt and maybe one or two others and, at the beginning of it, you. I already know what's been going on. I'm only asking you to confirm it."

"Why? Why should I? What business is it of yours?"

"Because I had part of the story, but only part of it," Doll admitted. "And I used that part to accuse Perry Wellman of murdering Dabney because I figured that Dabney had found out what Wellman was doing. If Wellman killed Dabney, then Diana didn't. That's the only way I care about it. But then Valerie Albrecht comes along and tells me that Dabney was part of the whole deal all along—which, if it's true, goes a long way toward taking Wellman off the hook as far as a motive for murder goes."

"You don't care about any of the rest of it?" Guillette asked, still cautiously.

"I don't give a damn about it," Doll replied. "The only way I care about it is if it works some way to get Diana off."

Guillette picked up one of the open cans from the six-pack and knocked down several swallows of beer. He wiped his mouth with the side of his hand and returned the can to the deck of the bridge.

"Like you say," Guillette said, and stifled a belch of carbon dioxide. "Dabney knew. He knew all along, from the very beginning when we all did. Besides everything else, he was a greedy son of a bitch. There's no way in the world that he'd ever have spilled the beans on the goose that was laying him golden eggs."

"Can you tell me how it got put together?"

Guillette tugged at his line again, and, finding nothing there, he nodded. "Nobody did anything special. It all just fell into place and sort of happened. We were sitting around Zale's place one night. Late. All of us pretty drunk, I guess. We all knew that Perry was bringing stuff up now and then. But never a lot. Then he started to talk—maybe brag more than anything else— about how it could be. He said that he was on to something, but that he had to have some better equipment to find the spot just right. And suddenly all of us saw a way to cut ourselves in."

"By putting up the money for Wellman to buy what he needed."

"Hell, yes. We all saw that. And it worked. Perry went out and got whatever it was that he had to have and, after a little more looking around, found what he liked to call the mother lode. He brought up a few things, but his readings showed that a lot more was down there. That was back when the thing with Dabney and Sylvia happened. After that, I guess I stopped giving a damn about the money. I said the hell with it. I sold off my shares to the others and got out. I decided that it wasn't worth getting rich if I had to do it by sitting across the goddamn table from Sean Dabney."

"This is it, Doll—the absolute last time." Diana Raney didn't meet Doll's eyes. She sat opposite him in one of the prison's, by now, too familiar consultation rooms. The guard, meanwhile, had assumed her post near the door, making the ostentatious effort to appear she wasn't listening, although she was standing less than half a dozen feet away.

"I'm going to tell Willard that he's not to let you come here anymore. I know he may not listen to me. It's pretty obvious by now that he's on your side far more than he's on mine. But that really doesn't matter, either. I've asked the guards here, and they tell me that I don't have to see any visitors that I don't want to. I don't want to see you anymore, Doll. I don't want to. I don't have to. And, if you come again, I promise you I won't."

"Maybe I wouldn't turn up so often," Doll replied, "if, on the times that I did come, you told me the truth."

Diana shook her head, still without looking up at Doll. "I don't have any idea what you're talking about," she said. "If you're going to keep on talking in riddles, I'd just as soon leave you here now to talk to yourself."

Doll remembered Willard Giesler's warning to say nothing he wanted kept confidential in the presence of the guards—then decided that the caution didn't apply. Set against a possible murder conviction, the risks to Diana from the revelation of Perry Wellman's salvage scam were nothing. Besides that, the central theme of the story was one that the authorities, in the person of Eldwin Rush at least, already knew.

"I'm talking about the coins," he said. "The ones you said the last time that an old boyfriend bought for you. Nobody bought them anywhere, Diana. You got them from Perry Wellman—who got them where he got all the rest."

"Damn you, Doll." Diana was definitely looking at him now. She glared at Doll with her eyes ablaze, then glanced in a sharp, surreptitious gesture toward the guard. "Damn you, shut up! Don't you understand what you're doing?"

"I do now," Doll answered. "I would've understood before if you'd told me the truth. Instead, I accused Perry Wellman of murdering Dabney because I'd half-convinced myself that Dabney was blackmailing him. I was half-convinced enough of that so I told the same story to Eldwin Rush. That's your fault, Diana. It wouldn't have happened if you'd been honest with me."

"Oh, God," Diana whispered under her breath. The shock and anger were gone from her voice. What replaced those emotions was a fatalism that said, in effect, that what had happened was only what she should have seen as her lot all along.

"Well, that's the end of it, then," she said aloud. "All the secrets are out, and it's finally over. There's a sign on the gates of hell, I heard once. It's supposed to say something like, 'Abandon hope, all ye who enter here.' That's a comfort, Doll—as strange as that may sound to you. When you look at it another way, if there's no more hope, it also means that there aren't going to be any more disappointments."

"C'mon, Diana." A part of him told Doll that despair was an indulgence; another part, though, said that his life, though not without its down times, compared to Diana's had been almost incomprehensibly lucky.

"You don't understand, do you? Not even yet." Diana's voice was still too tired to make the indictment in her questions harsh. "That was the only good thing left that still might have come out of all of this, Doll. You want to know why I didn't tell you or Willard? Is that what you came here to ask me today? Because I was afraid that exactly what has happened would happen. Just when you want to find something to hang on to, even the dreams get blown away."

"You're facing a murder charge," Doll reminded her because he couldn't think of any other answer that made the devastation make sense. "There isn't any time for dreams."

"Really?" Diana looked at him almost as though it was she who now felt sorry for him. "And there sits Doll," she said with the wriest of smiles. "Always the pragmatist. Logical. Good at making the hard decisions. He's got some kind of an internal scale that always lets him make the right choice. The right one for him and—so he thinks—for everybody else.

"Well, you're wrong this time, Doll. A murder charge isn't such a big thing. Not nearly so big as you're trying to make it. Who knows? If I get the right jury and flutter my eyelashes, maybe they'll even acquit me. And then, maybe, I would've had my freedom and all the rest of it too. But even if they'd convicted me and sent me away, I still would've had the rest of it. Or I would've without you. It could've waited. It could've been there for me—for when I got out in ten or twenty years—and, in the meantime, maybe it might even have been enough to send Ann to school, or maybe allow for some other dream of the kind that you say there isn't any time for."

The words came louder as her anger began to assert itself again.

"That's why I didn't tell you, Doll. What the hell is ten or twenty years to me? My life's not so great on the outside that it's really worth all that much hanging on to. If you'd listened to me instead of your own head for once, you might even have heard what I was saying. I'd've done the time gladly to keep all those little dreams alive. And you, you arrogant, intrusive bastard, you decided what was right for me, and you just tossed those dreams away.

She rested her head in her hands and cried.

Doll felt the eyes of even the emotionally hardened prison guard staring down at him in steely accusation.

And maybe all that Diana had said was true, Doll thought. He didn't understand how it could be, but maybe, somehow, in some irrational way, it was. Maybe, despite all Giesler's grim predictions, Diana could get a jury to come out on her side. Maybe even the hope of the treasure was real. Both Valerie Albrecht and Tom Guillette at least seemed to believe in it. Maybe, Doll thought, he *had* interfered—exactly, as he'd told Ann at the airport, the way he hadn't wanted to do. And maybe, as Eldwin Rush had said, all he'd done was to make things worse for his part in the bargain.

And maybe, too, he'd made the only choices he could have made. There were times—if only he could be sure when they were—when the only way to go was straight ahead.

"I'll think about what you've said," he answered, and stood.

Diana stayed seated where she was. "You do that. You think about it," she said. "But whatever you decide when you're done with your thinking, don't even waste the drive to come back out here and try to tell me about it."

It was eight o'clock that evening when Doll got to Diana Raney's cottage. He'd called Ann earlier—just after his talk with Diana—to give Ann his report on the latest encounter and to tell her he wanted to have Giesler meet with the two of them there. Then he'd taken the time to go back to his motel, where he'd showered and changed his clothes and allowed himself the much-needed chance just to think.

He arrived to find Giesler already at the cottage, settled in one of the bamboo chairs with a drink in his hand. Ann sat across the room at the table in the kitchen with the small, metallic disk on the tabletop before her. The color still wasn't a brilliant silver, but it was certainly a far more luminescent gray than it had been when Doll had first seen it.

"As predicted," Giesler announced with an obvious tone of satisfaction in his voice.

Ann took a swallow from her glass of lemonade and vodka. She picked the unspectacular object up and turned it over in her hand, inspecting the irregular edges. Her expression, if it reflected her mind, suggested she remained unimpressed.

From his pocket, Giesler extracted a magnifying glass which he gave to Doll to pass across to Ann.

"Two eight *reale* pieces," he explained. "The weight, washed as they are now: a very tiny fraction under two ounces. You get a little lucky on the markings. By no means a clean strike. Very little detail. But one side shows a date. I make it out as 1702. The other coin's undated on the side that you can see but shows a Potosi mint mark. Both impressions add to the value. The two coins together? You're looking at two hundred and fifty, maybe as much as three hundred dollars."

"Would those markings tie in with something you might find around here?" Doll asked.

"Tie in just fine." Giesler looked from Ann to Doll. "As I told you before, one or two coins by themselves are nothing to draw conclusions from. But a 1702 date mark makes it at least a reasonable candidate for the 1715 fleet."

"Let's take it a step further." Doll walked the short distance across the room and looked down at the coins from above Ann's shoulder. "I understand that most of the cargo in that fleet was lost when the ships were driven into the shallow waters just off the beach. How about a variation on that—a ship that never got that far, one that broke up at sea and sank further out?"

"You're talking about Wellman finding something like that?" Willard Giesler seemed to think a moment, then pursed his lips and inclined his head to one side. "No record of it. Not that I've ever heard. Which isn't to say that it couldn't have happened. It would also help to explain how the other salvors missed it—in the first place, because nobody had a reason to look and, in the second, because a wreck in deeper waters would be just that much harder to find."

"And to work," Doll added. "But if that were true about an off-shore wreck, then it wouldn't have to be just odds and ends that Wellman was finding."

"No. It wouldn't have to be," Giesler agreed. "It could be anything up to, and including, a major find, depending on how the ship was laden, how concentrated the wreckage is, and what the bottom conditions are like. It's enough to make a man curious, Doll. I'll admit that much at least."

"It made me curious, when Valerie Albrecht told me the story." Doll repeated for Giesler and Ann the story of Perry Wellman's discovery, as related by Valerie, and of Wellman's odd collection of patrons. "But I talked to Tom Guillette this morning, and what he said basically came down to the same thing."

"So it could all be true. All of it." Ann put the coins down on the table and looked from Doll to Willard Giesler. She seemed to forget even her lemonade. "It may really be that Diana has a share in what amounts to an underwater gold mine."

" 'The mother lode'," Doll quoted. "Exactly the words Guillette said Perry Wellman used."

"If she does, it's in an illegal gold mine." Giesler glanced across at Doll. "Diana admits to all of it now?"

"The fundamentals of it." Doll nodded. "I didn't press her for details. She knew it wasn't on the up and up. That's why she wouldn't tell us before. She didn't want the secret to get out."

"I don't wonder." Willard Giesler glanced up at the ceiling, took one of his toothpicks from his pocket, and bit down on an end with his teeth. "Money—even the prospect of it—can make people do some very strange things. But holding back something like that from your lawyer when you're looking down the barrel of a murder trial. What it says about priorities—"

"You aren't in any position to know," Ann Raney interjected, finishing Giesler's sentence for him. "Because money's something I don't imagine you've ever been without. Diana has. So don't be too fast to criticize. Don't try to make sense out of what you can't know."

"I back off. I concede the issue." Giesler held up an open palm to fend off Ann's attack. "You're right. I never had to face being anything less than what you might call upper middle class. But I'll back off on the other side, too, while I'm at it. I've also never had to face the possibility of becoming really rich."

"And you think maybe Wellman's patrons could be?" Doll asked.

Giesler shrugged in a gesture of uncertainty. "I'm supposing now that they might have gotten—or might still get—away with it. Something to think about, though. What would all of them do with it? Truitt, Tack—you have to wonder. The one I feel sorry for, though, is Tom Guillette. A one-in-a-million payoff comes in, and he's the one SOB who sold it short."

"Another kind of jealousy—another reason maybe for Guillette to want to see Dabney dead?" Doll crossed the room to the kitchen table and sat in the chair across from Ann. "Except that Guillette, by his own account at least, seems to have an alibi that's pretty close to perfect."

"You know, I'll tell you something else . . ." Giesler pointed his index finger provocatively toward the ceiling. "There's another name out there you haven't brought up. But I'll bet you a hundred dollars, right now, that it has to be in there. I'll bet you that before this is done, that name turns out to be in the middle of everything."

"Mickey Zale," Doll replied.

"You thought of that, too." Giesler sounded mildly deflated.

"It all got started at Zale's club, according to Tom Guillette," Doll reasoned. "It doesn't sound at all out of line that he'd hear about it and cut himself in. Then you put together Bandalos and Perry Wellman, and a lot of things start to fall into place."

"A lot of things," Ann said. "A lot of things about Perry Wellman's treasure." She flipped the pair of fused coins in the air. "But nothing about how Sean Dabney got murdered. Maybe out of all of this Diana gets some money. Which one of you is going to be the one to tell me what good it does her to spend it from inside a jail?"

"That's what bothers me the most about it," Doll acknowledged as he stared out the window at the nearly fallen night. "There's everything you need—gold, greed, an illegal conspiracy. It almost seems like it has to turn into a motive for Dabney's murder somehow. But every way I try to arrange it, I just can't get a handle that fits."

"Then you are still going to try?" Ann asked. "Despite all

those things you said on the phone that Diana told you? You are, aren't you, Doll?"

Ann smiled. Holding her vodka and lemonade in both hands again, she took a fresh sip and looked up into Doll's face before she went on.

"You won't walk away. I'm not sure you could. You wouldn't now if it meant that Diana and me were both going to wind up hating you for the rest of our natural lives."

"Arrogant, intrusive bastard," Doll remembered. That, perhaps, was the truest sense, he conceded, in which Diana Raney had been right.

15

Sylvia Guillette peered out at Doll through the screen door of her mobile home. From somewhere behind her in the living room, a duet by a pair of country singers played at a volume loud enough for the bass notes to shiver the metal skin of the trailer.

"So you're the one they call Doll," she said, as she took her time inspecting him.

She was short, Doll guessed no more than five-four, in marked contrast to her former husband. The thin lines around her mouth and neck implied an age somewhere in her middle thirties, but the trim figure she'd managed to keep made her look a good half dozen years younger. The rural twang in her voice matched that of the singers with whom she had to compete to make herself heard.

"You don't waste time. I'll give you that much. I suppose now you figure that I've gotta ask you to come in."

The trace of her breath that reached Doll's nose was rich with the odors of cigarette smoke and beer.

She unsnapped the lock of the trailer door, then pushed it open a couple of inches, extending Doll a tepid invitation.

As Doll opened it farther to let himself in, she turned away and crossed the room toward the stereo. On the wall above her head was a larger than lifesize portrait of Elvis Presley done in pastels and gold on a black velvet background.

A half-finished bottle of beer rested on a flamingo-colored tabletop nearby.

In the, by contrast, overwhelming silence that followed the cessation of the music, Sylvia Guillette took her place in the chair beside the beer. She lit a cigarette, inhaled deeply, then expelled an extravagant column of smoke. Propping up an ankle on her opposite knee, she further stretched her already taut jeans and directed Doll to a second chair with a motion of her finger.

"What made you think I'd be coming to see you?" Doll asked as he sat.

Sylvia took another long drag on her cigarette.

"Tom called me last night. He does that now and then. I can't say we're friends exactly, but we aren't enemies either. I'd help him if he was in trouble and I could. He'd do the same for me. Maybe that does mean we're friends in a way. Anyway, what's the difference? He told me about you, and you're here."

"Did he tell you what I've been trying to do?"

"He said you were some kind of friend of Diana's—that you've been nosing around because you want to get her out of jail. So why come to me? I don't know anything about anything. I don't know what happened to Sean, and I sure as hell can't think of any reason why I should want to help Diana Raney."

"That's not hard to understand," Doll conceded. "From your side, I can see how what happened might make you feel bitter."

Sylvia took another pull at her cigarette while she appeared to think the matter over. "I am, and then I'm not," she said. "Look, I'm not going to hide anything on you, Doll. I'll admit right off to you or anyone that I'd've liked to see Sean hurt. Hurt, but not dead. There's a difference. I'd never have wished that on the man. Sean could be a charmer when he wanted to. I still remember that charm." She curled up a corner of her mouth. "He could also be a louse. But then again, I guess, so can I. I know what they say about me, so you don't need to hold anything back out of delicacy. Nobody made me run out on Tom. They say I got what I deserved."

Doll asked if she wanted Diana hurt too.

"I wouldn't mind it," Sylvia answered indifferently. "I might not go out of my way to make it happen, but I don't mind one bit seeing her in the spot that she's in now. In some ways I blame her; in others, I don't. I made my own bed when I left Tom for Sean. I was ready to lie in it; then I got pushed out. I resent the living hell out of both of them for that."

"But not enough to have killed Sean?"

"No. I told you that." Sylvia took another draw on the nearly spent cigarette, examined what was left, then stubbed it out. "I told the cops the same thing I'll tell you: 'Hey, boys,' I said, 'you just go on and do your worst. I was right here by myself, all by my lonesome, the night that Sean died. So I've got a motive, like you say—and no alibi at all. Only I didn't kill him. So I don't see how you're ever gonna be able to prove in a court that I did.' " She laughed. "They never so much as even bothered comin' back."

"And Tom?"

"My ex? Kill Sean?" She laughed for yet a second time and, this time, shook her head. "Not likely. Back when I left him for Sean, yeah, maybe back then Tom might have had the stomach for it—except for the obvious fact that he didn't. But that's a couple of years ago now. That's the thing about passion, Doll, or didn't you know? It just doesn't last."

"Then try another motive," Doll suggested, ignoring for the time the matter of Tom Guillette's seemingly perfect alibi. "Tom gave up his stake—and yours—in that whole salvage business. From what he told me, he did it because he couldn't stand being near Dabney. Maybe after a while, as things started to happen, he came to blame Dabney for forcing him out."

"That first part, about not wanting to be around Sean, that

sounds like my old Tom," Sylvia acknowledged. "But it also isn't strictly true. Tom didn't have any more of a choice about getting out than I did. Not once the divorce was in the cards. How were we supposed to deal with our little investment? It would've been a little tricky—don't you think?—making it part of the fight in the courts. And if you believe we could have agreed between ourselves how to split it, then you don't know very much about how things get when you go through a divorce."

Doll knew one way that things got, though he didn't tell Sylvia that. Doll had told his own lawyer to make the settlement any way the lawyer thought was right. Then he'd dusted off his hands and walked away and, from that moment on, had done his best not to look back.

"So we turned it back into cash," Sylvia Guillette was saying, "which was about the only thing we could do—and let the judge do all the deciding. That steamed me at the time, I don't mind telling you—especially after I wound up losing Sean. Now, when I look back . . ." She shook her head. "I don't figure that Tom or I lost an awful lot. Out of all the mess, pulling out of that deal might have been the best thing that happened to either of us."

"Why would you say that?" Doll asked. What Sylvia Guillette was saying seemed suddenly to make no sense at all.

"We got all our money back, Tom and me," Sylvia explained with a shrug that she clearly thought made everything obvious. "Calvin and Doc were more than happy back then for the chance to buy us out. I don't know how the details worked. Tom took care of all of that. I never had the head for any kind of business."

"But now," Doll asked, still tentatively, "when you look back at it, you think that getting out then was a good thing?"

"That's two years ago." Sylvia found a fresh cigarette in the pack. After tapping it several times on the tabletop, she lit it. "All I know," she said as she exhaled the smoke, "is what I knew then and what I've heard since. Back then Perry was telling us that he'd found what he said was a wreck site worth a couple of million dollars at least. He showed us four or five or maybe half a dozen pieces—a sword, some coins, a ring, and a cross, I remember. I haven't got any idea what else—if anything—he's brought up since. All I know beyond that is that a couple of years have gone by—and nothing that I've heard or seen around here tells me that anybody I know is exactly getting rich. You talk about Tom blaming Sean for forcing him out? Not that Sean did. But, unless you know something I don't know, it seems more to me like he oughta be wanting to thank him."

Doll took the turn that Calvin Tack suggested and headed the enormous mass of the Cadillac west along Okeechobee Road. He felt as though he were driving a house—not even driving it so much as nudging it now and then with the wheel to convey a sense of the general direction in which he wanted the automobile to go.

He had taken Sylvia Guillette at her word when she'd claimed to know nothing about the details of Perry Wellman's business. He hadn't felt the need to press her as long as there were others, like Calvin Tack, who did. Unless Doll's impressions were very much wrong, he felt sure that the car dealer wouldn't have put up a dime before the apportionment of costs and benefits had been clearly and satisfactorily spelled out. But perhaps more importantly, two years had passed since the Guillettes had been a part of Wellman's clandestine venture. Sylvia could guess about what had happened since, but that was something else that Calvin Tack would know.

"You can go straight on this," Tack said from the right-hand seat as he ran a hand through his blond-white hair. "It tracks due west to Four Forty-one. Too many people back at the lot, always milling around or needing a decision on something. We won't get overheard or interrupted here. Besides—" Tack glanced across at Doll and beamed his salesman's smile "—by the time we're done, there's always the chance that I'll sell you a car."

In the pitch, though, Doll saw a trace of something almost desperate—not the sales initiative that Calvin Tack might have liked it to seem, but rather the grasping effort of a man trying to make a highly uncomfortable circumstance appear at least a little more familiar.

"Why come to me to tell you how it worked?" Tack readjusted himself in the seat. He had his seersucker jacket off and, now, threw his arm across the seat back. "Well, hell, now that you know the gist already," he rationalized, "how much more can the specifics hurt?"

"Set up like stock shares?"

"A little." Tack stared straight out through the windshield, his eyes fixed on the road ahead. "We let them out—nothing actually printed, you understand—in thousand dollar lots. Our total capitalization was eighty-five grand. Of that, I took twenty. Doc took thirty. Dabney had fifteen, and Diana twenty-five hundred. Valerie took seven thousand five of what remained, and Tom and Sylvia Guillette the last ten."

"Then the Guillettes got out," Doll anticipated.

"Yes. And right after them, so did Valerie Albrecht. Doc picked up the Guillettes' ten, and I picked up Valerie's seven-five."

"Do you know why?" Doll asked. "About Valerie, I mean. I understand about why the Guillettes had no other choice than to get out."

"I know what she said at the time," Tack answered, and shrugged as another way to imply he had no way of knowing if what she'd told him was true. "I don't know if the words are exact, but it came down to that she'd gotten herself overextended."

"That's it for the numbers, though?" Doll turned his attention back to the structure of the investment group. "Just the seven of you to start with, then down to four later on? What about Wellman? He puts up all the work. What does he get out of it?"

Out of the corner of his eye, Doll saw Calvin Tack shaking his head. Outside the car, the waves of heat rose up above the surface of the flat, green countryside. From inside the air-conditioned Cadillac, it all might just as well have been a motion picture.

"No, not just the seven—or four—of us. Of course, it was more complicated than that. Perry Wellman, as you say, put up his labor and his knowledge. He never put up money, but the way it was arranged he got a third of the value of whatever was brought up."

"Third? A third off the top for Wellman, and the remaining two-thirds divided proportionately among the rest of you?"

Tack hesitated again. "There were three thirds," he at last acknowledged. "All of us—me, Doc and the others—were one third. Perry Wellman was the second third. The last third was Mickey Zale."

Doll found a mental satisfaction in hearing it. The second—or, in an awkward analogy, the third—shoe had finally dropped.

"You see, at first it was a two-way deal—fifty/fifty—that Zale and Perry Wellman had worked out. Zale put up the first eighty-five thousand back then. When that ran out and wasn't enough, then the rest of us got in. That's why we made our investment eighty-five too, so the whole thing would divide up evenly."

"Give me a time frame for all of this. What are we talking about?" Doll asked.

"Three years for Zale, two for the rest of us." Tack seemed to think back as he answered. "It has a kind of seasonal logic to it. You can dive down here from sometime in May into roughly October. It started for us one night at Zale's place in the spring of the year after Mickey Zale had put up the first of the money, but we didn't know about that part of it then.

"Perry was into the bourbon pretty good and telling us all how close and, at the same time, how far away he was, and the next thing all of us were saying how we'd put up the cash. It all seemed like just a lark at first. Then, a few nights after that, it got serious. He told us about Mickey, then all of us—us and Perry and Mickey—got together to sit down and work the new arrangement out."

Doll came up on a slow-moving pickup. There was nothing up ahead. He hit the gas. The Cadillac bit into the road and leaped ahead. He was out and around the truck in seconds.

"Got the big engine," Tack said and tried a smile again. "Picks up like a son of a bitch when you want."

"So you, by yourself, have got in what?" Doll make a quick mental calculation. "Twenty-seven five tied up in the operation. You can afford it, can't you? If you lose it, it's not that much money to you."

"It's not something I'd line the cat's pan with, either," Tack replied with an edge of indignation in his voice. "But you're right. I can afford it no matter how it goes," he relented after a few seconds. "More than Diana can. Certainly more than Doc can afford his forty. For God's sake don't let his wife find out, but he had to mortgage the house they live in to come up with that."

"And so far, it's a dry well." Doll made the assertion flat, leaving Tack to either confirm or refute it.

"No, not dry." Tack, Doll saw in a sideways glance, showed a renewed look of discomfort. "Not dry at all," the car dealer insisted. "What would make you say something like that?"

"Take your pick. Sylvia Guillette said it. Sean Dabney thought it. And you haven't said anything yet to deny it."

"How can Sylvia know? And Sean Dabney's dead."

"But he thought it, didn't he?" Doll persisted. "You said it yourself the first time we talked. You said he was a man who thought that everyone else was out to cheat him." Doll was knitting, pulling things together, but Calvin Tack had no way to tell how much Doll was guessing. "Wellman only had a few pieces to show around by the time the Guillettes got out. Are you telling me that a whole lot more has come out since?"

"No. No, I'm not exactly saying that. I'm only saying it's not a dry hole—or, at least, that it's too early to say that it is. It's only getting to the point now where the operation's turning from pinning down the locations to actual salvage. And he's brought up a few very promising pieces now and then along the way."

"But Dabney still had his suspicions," Doll insisted.

"Yes, he had them. But that was just Dabney." Calvin Tack shook his head in his adamancy. "Believe me, I know what the rules are. I know how the game is played. I cut the cards when I get the chance. But Dabney went too far. He was neurotic on the point. He never understood that, on the bottom line, every deal you make comes down to a fundamental question of trust."

"How good a bloodhound am I?"

Harvey Archer poured the rest of the beer from the bottle into his glass. He scratched at his scalp under the crew cut and sat up straight on the bar stool.

"Don't you know this is Saturday afternoon?" He pointed toward the TV screen behind the bar. "That's real, live baseball, not just a tape up there today."

Meanwhile Archer's face told its own tale of satisfaction. "I'm damn good, Doll. At least around this county I am. But you already knew that. A damn sight more than you should, in fact. If you didn't know it, you wouldn't be here now, and I wouldn't be missing my damn ball game."

"Suppose I pay you overtime?" Doll offered.

"Overtime!" Archer looked around at Doll and sneered. "Overtime. Yeah, twice nothing is nothing. You want to talk. Okay, but not here at the bar. 'Do what you do.' Or else you don't do either thing right. Find a table, and let's get it over with. That way, it's all the sooner I can get back to the tube."

Instead of Doll finding the table, Archer led Doll to one where the air-conditioning system drowned out most of the bar's background noise. Doll bought a fresh bottle of beer for Archer and brought another bottle and glass for himself.

"Okay, I'm bribed enough," Archer said, accepting the beer. "Now what's this question that's so important that you gotta bother me with it on a Saturday afternoon?"

"Black market salvage," Doll answered.

"What? Gold, silver? Spanish stuff. Crap like that? Is that what you mean?"

"That's what I mean," Doll replied. "What do you know about how much is going down?"

"Black market? What's this all about, anyway, Doll?" Archer's eyes narrowed to dramatize his incredulity. In another place and time, Doll thought, the reporter might have made a more than passable inquisitor.

"I don't believe for a minute," Archer said, "that you're telling me you want to buy a couple of hot doubloons."

"Could I?" Doll asked.

"Doubloons? If you wanted to, sure. Probably not that much cheaper than the legal ones, though. Assuming we're talking strictly hypothetical, I could probably suggest a couple of people you could see. But then, of course, you already know about one of them yourself. I hear you had a fascinating little chat with Perry Wellman."

Archer smiled and saluted Doll with his glass. "Isn't that what you wanted to know? If I recall, you began this conversation by asking something about my pedigree as a bloodhound."

Doll saluted Archer back. "Wellman finds things and sells them on the black market without reporting them or paying the duties." Doll offered the statement not as fact but speculation.

"I've heard that he does that," Harvey Archer answered.

"How big an operation? Would you say that he's finding and selling a lot?"

Archer replied by returning a question for a question. He asked how much Doll meant by "a lot."

"To put a number on it, let's say enough to justify a one hundred and seventy thousand dollar investment."

"An investment by who?" Archer studied Doll with newfound interest. "I told you from the start, Doll," Archer pointedly reminded him, "it has to be a two-way street."

"Sean Dabney," Doll answered, admitting to himself the fairness of Archer's demand. "Calvin Tack, Tom and Sylvia Guillette—but they got out—Doc Truitt, Mickey Zale. Wellman takes a third off the top for his trouble. The rest gets split in proportion to who put up how much of the cash."

Archer swirled his beer and stared down at the glass. "A hundred and seventy grand right there," he said soberly. "How much of that is Doc Truitt in for?"

"The way I hear it, forty," Doll replied.

"Not true," Archer shot back. He had his face angled down so that his eyes stared up at Doll from just below the brow ridge. "He hasn't got forty packed away that's there to play with. It's all tied up in retirement plans. I talked to him once, and he told me about it. He couldn't come up with that kind of cash."

Doll told Archer about the mortgage on the house.

"Shit!" Harvey Archer swore. "Then Doc's a fool," he went on, as though it angered him personally to have to say it. "Tack's got most of the rest of it, then? That's the way it has to play out."

Doll shook his head. "Only a little under thirty thousand. The Papa Bear's share, half of the total, was picked up by Mickey Zale."

"No," Archer said flatly. He shook his head and drew in a

controlled stream of air. "It's wrong. All wrong. It's just not happening, Doll. At least not the way you describe it. I can give you at least two good reasons for that. The first is size. You're talking about an illegal operation carried out in what amounts to public view. That means it's got to be quiet, and quiet means the scale's got to be small. No army of divers, no heavy equipment. Two or three men. How much can they recover in a four to five month season? Twenty thousand dollars, maybe thirty, if they're lucky? Of which Wellman takes ten, leaving an optimistic twenty thousand return on an investment of a hundred and seventy? A little over ten percent a year? No way, not for that return on that kind of risk."

"I saw that too, but from a different angle," Doll admitted. "Not the economics of it, but I've done marine salvage. I understand the level of work you put in, in terms of what you get out."

"And they don't," Archer asserted with understated emphasis. "Good God, Doll, those names you tick off, they're shopkeepers, all of them except for Doc Truitt, and Doc doesn't know even as much as that. They couldn't figure the lumber and tools you need to put up a roadside vegetable stand."

"You said there were two reasons," Doll reminded Archer.

Archer nodded. "The second is what you said about Zale. Mickey Zale didn't put the Papa Bear's share into anything— and certainly not if that share is half of a hundred and seventy thousand. That place he runs is a mob money clearing house. You mean to tell me Giesler didn't know that? Mickey Zale's a third-string manager. He has trouble clearing checks to buy booze for the bar. He hasn't got his own money to put in. And the mob wouldn't lend him the five thousand dollars to pay off his car loan, much less the figure you're holding out to cover an unsecured gamble like that."

"Then what's going on?" Doll asked. "All the others put up the money. I got that independently from both of the Guillettes and Tack—all three of whom have reason to know, and none, that I can see, any reason to lie."

"About Zale I can only say what I've already said," Archer concluded. "As for the others, they're lousy investors. They got caught in somebody else's game, or else they're just another bunch of suckers who got screwed by somebody out to net a fast buck. When it's all said and done, you'll find out they're probably both.

"Now, for the keys to the kingdom, Doll, do you want to tell me what all of this salvage horse flop has to do with Diana Raney and Dabney's murder?"

"No. At least, not yet I don't." Doll thought about getting by with a smile and a thank you as he pushed himself back from the table, but that, he knew, didn't keep the bargain he'd made. "There are still parts like Mickey Zale and all of that investment money that I can't exactly fit together. But when I can, the promise stands. After Diana and Willard Giesler, you'll be the first one who gets to know."

Willard Giesler's house was north of the town, the last house on the block with nothing but a dirt road between it and the river. Its two-story framing was traditional, but the red tile roof and tan stucco sides gave the facade a Spanish colonial appearance. The yard was all green grass and clustered palms with oleander bushes along the building's side, kept lush by an underground network of sprinklers, which was in the process of doing its work as Doll and Ann arrived.

Giesler led them to a screened porch with a table and chairs that overlooked the river. He introduced his wife, who received them with more charm than was the reasonable prerogative of anyone who came to somebody's house on matters of business, then immediately absented herself to let them get on with their talk.

"Thanks, by the way, for bringing Vosterman back," Geisler began as he served the drinks: a gin for Doll, a daiquiri on the rocks for Ann, and a vodka with a dash of tonic and a twist of lime for himself. "It's the kind of book that's got to grow on you, so I don't expect you to tell me that you liked it.

"I spoke with Diana after you called me this afternoon." Geisler paused for a swallow of his drink. "As always, the conversation was a lot like trying to drag a little wisdom out of a marble bust of Socrates. What do you want to hear first today, the good news or the bad?"

"The bad news," Doll said. "We might as well start with that."

Giesler nodded. "Every dime of Zale's eighty-five was paid in full," he answered. He slapped the palm of his hand lightly down on the surface of the table to add emphasis to the point.

"Diana knows that for a fact?" Doll asked, searching for loopholes that he was sure Willard Giesler must already have seen and closed.

"You're right. That's the pivotal question," Giesler said. "So pivotal and obvious that it's exactly the same question that everybody else asked. Look at it from the viewpoint of Calvin Tack and the others. They're being asked to put up their hard-earned cash. They know that Wellman's putting up his expertise for whatever that's worth. Are they just going to take Zale's word for the cash that he tells them he's already put in and agree because of that that he ought to have a one-third interest in the partnership? Bullshit, they are—if you'll excuse me, Ms. Raney. And even if all the others would've gone along, you know absolutely that Sean Dabney wouldn't."

"And didn't," Doll inferred.

"And didn't," Giesler affirmed.

"This is all from Diana?"

Willard Giesler nodded a second time. "Dabney demanded a full accounting going in. He took the job on himself when nobody else seemed anxious to do it. He nickled and dimed it just like you'd expect he would. He got receipts for how the money had been spent and when, and inventoried the receipts against what Wellman had on board *Fair Wind*. Conclusion— mind you, Diana doesn't know the exact numbers: The vast majority of what Zale claimed to have put up could be accounted for by purchases made by Wellman for equipment actually in place on *Fair Wind*. There was some unspent cash remaining—Diana thinks around ten thousand. The remainder of the difference was expended on diesel fuel—all receipted— and in some minor living expenses which Wellman confirmed to Dabney he'd received."

"Well, that would seem to put the end to a couple of theories," Doll concluded. "First Archer's idea that Zale didn't have the cash to invest, and, second, that if in fact he had it, he never put it up."

"At the same time," Giesler said, "the question that's still around is why, even with the infusion of a second eighty-five thousand, over the next two years Wellman still came up with what seems to have been close to nothing."

"According to Tack," Doll answered, "the lucrative part of the recovery is only getting started."

"Yeah, and for whatever it's worth," Giesler agreed, "Diana said that, too. But maybe only because she wants to believe it. Dabney, according to Diana again, had plenty of doubts—enough to add up, in what he said in front of her at least, to him being openly suspicious."

"As always. But of what?" Doll asked. "Tack said it, and you did, too, when you talked about the money Zale put in. Dabney was skeptical all the way along. But if Zale saw his own money slipping down the tubes, and all the while he was watching Wellman through Bandalos, it's a little hard to see exactly what there was for Dabney to be skeptical about."

Both Doll and Giesler fell into silence.

"Don't look at me," Ann said and shrugged and took a swallow of her daiquiri.

Giesler stared out over the river.

"But maybe," Doll said half aloud, "whether Dabney knew for certain there was something going on is less important than the fact that he was looking and maybe asking around. Maybe that alone made somebody nervous."

"But who had any reason to be nervous?" Giesler asked. "If we're going to try to establish that somebody had a motive based on whatever Wellman was doing, we don't only have to come up with a person we can point to. We have to come up with a compelling connection that we can show unequivocally in court."

It seemed to Doll in that moment to have all come down to that—a single, ultimate point of impasse. He pushed himself up from his chair and walked to the opposite end of the porch, then stood peering out at the slow, steady surge of the current.

"So we get to the bottom line," he said almost to himself, "and what do we know? We know Dabney had a gut feeling that something was wrong, even though he never seemed to figure out quite what it was. And we know that, between them all, they came up with and tossed away a hundred and seventy thousand dollars."

"Not quite, if it's just what we *know*," Giesler amended. "We know that they tossed nearly all of the original eighty-five away. The second half we can only make a probable guess at. Dabney never audited that. According to Diana, after Dabney, Tack, and the others got in, the books, which had been kept by Zale, were, by everyone's agreement, turned over for keeping to Valerie Albrecht. The others looked at them now and then, but none of them, including Dabney, wanted the job on a day-to-day basis."

"And Valerie kept those books even after she sold her shares back?" Doll watched as Giesler nodded, then returned again to gazing out through the mesh of the screen. He found himself thinking again of Harvey Archer. "Which, maybe, goes a long way toward resolving one, and maybe more, of our questions," he said.

"Doll? Have you got something?" Giesler asked uncertainly.

Ann looked up from her glass and across the porch to where Doll stood.

"What happens if I come up with a couple of confessions, Willard?" The question and what followed it came out as almost an introspective thought, as though Doll were describing an unfolding chain of perceptions. "Statements given willingly to the police. Not told to me. I'm not talking about the fraud angle—or only indirectly. I'm talking about Sean Dabney's murder. Once Eldwin Rush had those statements in his hands, how long until you'd be able to have Diana out of jail?"

"Voluntary affidavits. Legal and verifiable. No tricks," Giesler said. "Something that would hold up under adversary proceedings in a court."

"They'll hold. If I get them, they'll hold," Doll answered.

"If you deliver what you're describing," Willard Giesler replied, "and Rush doesn't have her out of jail within two hours, I'll have her out on a habeas corpus before it gets to be three."

"Who are you talking about, Doll? How are you going to do that?" Ann Raney asked.

"I've only got the general idea," Doll said. His eyes still followed the progress of the river. "I haven't gotten around to the details."

"Let him alone." Giesler smiled with the part of his mouth that the toothpick didn't prevent from curving. "He's having fun being mysterious. He's got a right to that. If he pulls off what he's talking about, it's the least that he's got due."

But Doll didn't think he was being mysterious. The reply that he'd made to Ann was, to his mind, perfectly true. He knew where he had to start and saw what he thought the end had to be. But what would take place in between those two extremes would come about because of what others did. And precisely what that would be Doll couldn't know.

Suddenly he looked over at Giesler as though there were something Doll had only just remembered. "Before, you said there was good news and bad news. You told us the bad news, but never the rest."

"Oh, that!" Giesler grinned and took his own good time. "You knew that you ruined my punchline, you bastard. What the hell do you think it was? It's good news that could only be good with Diana. It's that she was willing to talk with me at all."

16

Sunday morning came quietly.

The inside door to Diana Raney's cottage was shut when Doll arrived, the time just after ten-thirty. He knocked several times at the screen door, paused, then knocked several more. Finally, convinced that he must have been heard, he settled into waiting.

The Camaro with Diana's plate was parked where Doll had found it on the first day. There was also a Jeep that Doll had seen but not considered before. It was only then, as he added his own VW in, that he realized that the number of cars parked outside the cottage came to three.

In the same moment, the inside door to the cabin opened. Ann Raney looked out at Doll and yawned. She wore, as far as he could see, only an oversized T-shirt that bore the number twenty-eight and some lettering that described it as the property of the Dallas Cowboys. It took another second or so for the man to appear beside her. His broad, tanned torso was bare down to the waistband of his slacks. He carried his shirt like a towel tossed across his shoulder.

"Well," Ann said, as she stared sleepily out at Doll, "maybe if you called before you came around, you wouldn't get so many surprises."

"Why should I be surprised?" Doll asked. "Did I ever say anything that implied I expected celibacy?"

"No," Ann conceded after a few seconds of thought. "I guess you never said in so many words that you did."

She kissed the man beside her casually on the mouth.

"Sorry, love, but this is business," Doll overheard her whisper. "You know how the phone number's listed. You can call me tomorrow—if, by then," she added, "you still feel like you want to."

The man, who'd returned the same noncommittal kiss, stepped out onto the porch. He unhooked the screen door and brushed past Doll with only the most cursory of inspections—confident, Doll supposed, in the knowledge that the man he was leaving behind was a long way too old to be regarded as any kind of competition.

Doll followed Ann into the main room of the cottage. His nostrils recognized the stale odors that hung in the air: alcohol—the remains of a beer and a half-empty glass of laced lemonade were in the middle of the floor in front of the bamboo chairs—and the sweeter scent left behind in the air, along with the too-short-to-be-smokable ends of the three joints stubbed out in an ashtray.

Ann disappeared into the bathroom. Doll heard the splash of tap water running and then the half-choking sound of an abbreviated gargle. Returning with a brush to the cabin's large room, she ran a few perfunctory strokes through her hair.

Taking one of the chairs, she tucked her legs beneath her. She was wearing underwear—bottoms, at least. Doll's sense of discomfort took a little relief from that.

She closed her eyes and worked her fingers, massaging the lids.

"I'm praying," she said just loudly enough for the words to be audible, "that you're here because you've got some absolutely tremendous news to tell me. I hope that for Diana's sake, of course. But this morning, maybe, I hope it as much for me to compensate me for the pain that you're inflicting on the inside of my head."

"We might both be better off if I opened up a couple windows," Doll suggested.

"Ah, the fresh air cure." Had Ann felt stronger, Doll thought, the observation might have reached the level of an exclamation. Instead, it came out as only a mild complaint. "From you, what else should I have expected?"

Doll opened the windows nevertheless. He also flushed away the remains of the joints and set about washing the glasses and the ashtray.

"I came over because I've been thinking since last night when we left Willard's," he said as he turned back toward Ann and away from the sink. "I told both of you then that, if we're near an end to all of this, I thought I knew where that end had to start."

As he crossed the room, Doll took a piece of paper from the pocket of his shirt. After handing it to Ann, he waited while she opened it and read it.

"What is this, Doll? It's gibberish to me." Ann stared up with no effort to veil her confusion. "It's numbers and letters. It doesn't make sense. It might as well be in Chinese."

"In a sense, it's where the end starts," Doll replied. "If I'm right, it's where the wreck that Perry Wellman's supposed to have been salvaging should be. Those are navigational coordinates. There's more than one set, but they all say the same thing in different ways. It's not important that you understand them now. What could be important is that I'm going out this afternoon to find out whatever's down there—if there's a wreck and there's treasure, if there's empty sand, or anything else in between."

"Why come and tell me? I mean, it's fine that you do. I like to know what's going on as much as anybody else. But I wouldn't say you've exactly made a point of clearing your plans with me before this."

"This time it's insurance. That's all," Doll explained. "I don't expect any trouble, but the ocean can always show off with a few surprises. Just on the very off-chance that something could happen, I figured you ought to have those. I'd give them to Willard, but I'm not sure he'd approve of exactly how I got them."

"What is this—a little added touch of drama?" Ann raised an eyebrow and her voice together. "Are you telling me now you might go out there and get yourself killed? No way, Doll! Forget it. You're no use to Diana as some goddamn martyr. If this is supposed to be so damn important, then it's important enough for me to go with you. This isn't *Ivanhoe*. I get to do more than sit home and worry. It's still my sister we're talking about, and I've got a right to be a part of any risk there is."

"That's fine. I just didn't know that you dove," Doll answered equitably.

"You know damn well I don't," Ann said and glared.

"I didn't know it, but it seemed like a reasonable guess," Doll admitted. "But if you don't dive—and if I do get into some kind of trouble—exactly what is it you're going to do to help me? As a matter of fact, if I do get into trouble, how the hell are you even going to know?"

"You could teach me. To dive, I mean."

"I could," Doll agreed. "But in how much time? How many lessons and how many dives do you think it'll take before you're not just another problem I'd have to look after? I've been at this game for twenty years, Ann. I really don't think this is my day to buy it. I just try to cover my bets where I can."

Pursing her lips, Ann Raney looked deliberately away. "You just can't stop doing things the macho way, can you?" she said hotly. "All right, Doll. You go ahead. You've got it all thought out. I can't argue with you. What am I supposed to say—that I wish you good luck because Diana needs it? All right, for Diana I do."

"Then, I'll call you tonight to tell you whatever I can." Doll took a step backward and nodded his head to say good-bye.

Staring up at him again, Ann seemed to start to stand, but then apparently thought better of the effort. Slowly she lowered herself back into the chair and looked away.

*   *   *

The sea was flat, the sun a wafer-sized platinum disk in a cloudless pale blue sky. The only breeze there seemed to be came steadily from straight off the bow of the outboard cruiser Doll had rented. It arose from no rush of the hot, still air. Its only cause was the motion of the boat across the water.

Doll held the helm over through a sweeping turn to port and came to a north-northwesterly course that paralleled the beach.

For a moment, as he looked toward the shore, the intervening water nearly succeeded in evoking in him the chronic illusion of the sea—the sense of departure and release from all the contortions and troubles endemic to lives people make for themselves on the land. But Doll had learned better over the years in which he'd watched uncounted shorelines recede. In the end, all those who survived their crossings inevitably returned to the land. And when they did, more times than not, the problems they thought they'd left behind were all but gathered on the dock and waiting, like loyal friends intent on renewing their former acquaintance.

He remembered Ann Raney and the story he'd told her that morning.

It had been the truth as far as he'd gone, but less than the truth at the same time. If Doll's logic was anywhere near the mark, Sean Dabney had died for the questions he'd asked about Perry Wellman's treasure. Doll had asked the same questions— only yesterday, openly, of Calvin Tack. And now, with his hired boat and rented diving gear, he was pursuing the answers in a far more aggressive and active way than Dabney ever had. The corollary, along with its associated danger, seemed evident to the point of being irresistible. And the act itself got progressively easier. A second murder was never as hard as the first.

The paper he'd left with Ann was insurance—but insurance against a more deliberate peril than those offered up by an indifferent sea.

He glanced down at his wrist as his hand held the wheel.

Nearly five minutes had passed since he'd made the turn. Looking over his shoulder, beyond the stern of the boat, Doll tried to gauge the distance and calculate his speed. The white streak of foam that followed on the glassy water behind him was as level and straight as a road across a prairie. The ocean, on that score, was being cooperative. Doll offered his gratitude unspecifically to whatever power might be responsible. For the task he had ahead of him, he knew, he needed any help and all the luck that he could get.

In theory, Doll had no shortage of information about where it was that he wanted to go. What perhaps was most surprising was how much he knew. He had, for example, the triangulation bearings for the last position that Wellman had charted and which Doll had committed to memory during his visit aboard the *Fair Wind*. He also knew from the same source the loran coordinates for his destination and might have established an extremely accurate position employing those alone—if the boat that he'd been able to rent had had a loran receiver aboard. Moreover, by using the triangulation and loran entries, Doll was able to plot the location precisely on his own chart and, from that, to know ocean depth and sea floor composition at the site. But the cruiser also lacked either a fathometer or lead line, and so, for the purposes of surface navigation, whatever knowledge Doll had of the bottom, without a way to read it, came out to the equivalent of none.

With the equipment on *Fair Wind*, all the theory could work its wonders. But in the more Spartan confines of the rented cruiser, the triangulation bearings were all Doll had—and to fix them, not *Fair Wind*'s radar, but only the mounted navigational compass and a smaller, sight-through, hand-held version he'd been able to pry at no additional charge from the clerk who had rented him the boat.

The process of triangulating a position at sea required the use of two fixed points and their bearings. For his first point, Perry

Wellman had chosen the four-story, end-on facade of the north island's Holiday Inn.

Doll held to his course along the beach and watched as the distinctive orange and tan-colored bricks of the hotel began to loom above the green fronds of the palm trees. Then, as the building's centerline moved to a relative angle just aft of the cruiser's beam, he brought the bow sharply around to the east, to a magnetic heading of sixty-one degrees. The reciprocal, two forty-one degrees, was the bearing that Wellman had taken from his position over the wreck site and now was the bearing directly over the cruiser's stern. Whatever there was of Perry Wellman's treasure, by Doll's navigation, it now lay at a point along a line that ran directly off the bow.

The second mark that Wellman had picked was the channel buoy at the seaward end of the ocean's inlet to the river. The mark, at first, was visible only through binoculars in the distance ahead of the cruiser's starboard bow. But as Doll kept his course with the inn astern, the buoy's position with respect to the cruiser changed, moving relatively clockwise, from southeast toward south. When it passed due south, by Doll's estimation, he was nearly three miles out from the beach. Picking up the mark's progress now with the hand-held compass, Doll followed its track through another thirty degrees to a fix of two hundred ten magnetic—the second of the bearings that Perry Wellman had entered on his chart.

Doll throttled back and shifted the cruiser's engine into neutral. The pitch of the disengaged gears hummed a few notes higher. If theory and practice corresponded, the last site that Wellman's enterprise had prospected now lay directly below.

He dropped the bow anchor, paying out by his own reckoning a little more than fifty feet when the line went slack as the weight of the metal struck the bottom. Ballpark for what it should have been by the chart, but then, he recalled, the bottom all around his intended position was sounded as pretty much level. Using the hand compass again, he rechecked the bearings on the two fixed points and nodded to express his satisfaction to no one but himself. With what he'd had to work with, he decided, he'd come about as close as he could. Whether that would prove to be close enough, he could only wait to see.

He refused to dwell on what he only too well knew—that, with no difficulty at all, he could be off Wellman's site by a thousand feet. He didn't remind himself that, in the clearest of water, it was very rare indeed that a man could see for as far as fifty.

Sitting on the deck, Doll set his attention to the task of rechecking his breathing apparatus for what would be his final opportunity. He took his time even more than he usually did because the gear wasn't his own—and because he knew from a dogma embedded too deeply to leave him that, added to all his other risks, he was breaking a cardinal rule by diving alone.

When he was done, he looked up and around at an empty sea. No other boats were near him. None seemed to have any interest in where he was or in what he was doing. With just a little more luck, he thought, he'd be able to finish his job below before any did.

The water was a clear, transparent blue that made the skin of Doll's hands look white. He could hear the evenly—almost mechanically—spaced flutter of the bubbles of air as he exhaled. But, otherwise, the world that he'd entered was silent.

For Doll, it was a familiar world and, on this occasion, even an unaccustomably hospitable one. The temperature of the water was warm. The wetsuit that he'd rented was sleeveless, and the pants went down to just above the knees. He had no heavy equipment to carry—only the diving knife strapped to the calf of his leg and a clock, compass, and depth gauge attached in a row to a small rubber pad that hung on a flexible strap from his tank frame. Besides that, the dive would be relatively shallow, enough so that the encumbrances resulting from the pressure of the water would be minor almost to the point of absence. The air supply he carried in his tanks would impose the only circumstance that limited his bottom time.

He kept his descent gentle, following the six to one scope of the anchor line down. The deeper he went, the less the sunlight penetrated, and the darker the hue of blue became. Fish approached him or he them. Some swam alone, others in schools sometimes of hundreds of individuals. The results of the encounters were rarely the same. A lethargic grouper drew near and descended with him until it seemingly lost interest. Another fish, too fast for Doll to identify, darted off with its tail fin twitching to a safer distance on the murky edge of Doll's vision. A huge school of smaller fish crossed imperturbably ahead of him, parting for him just enough to make a body-sized hole. Alice through the looking glass—and then, on an impulse or because he'd made some disturbance in the water, the mirror cut abruptly off at an angle and quickly swam away.

It wasn't, in that moment and place, an ocean that teemed with enormous numbers of fish, but neither was there an absence of them—not the weekday morning's rush hour exactly, but more like a passably busy city avenue in the middle of a summer Sunday afternoon.

On the bottom, Doll got two pieces of welcome news. The first was that his depth gauge showed there was fifty-four feet of water above him, as close as he could reasonably have come to what there should have been, based on the charted data and adjusted for the present tide. The second discovery confirmed another chart prediction. The flukes of the anchor were dug into a floor made up of a fine, gray sand. Doll's confidence rose that he'd come at least close to where he'd intended.

Establishing the anchor as his centerpoint, he began his pattern using the combination of his compass and his watch.

For thirty seconds he swam north to where he planted a small, plastic, orange pennant—then west for thirty seconds, south for a minute, east for a minute, north for a minute, and west for a final thirty seconds back to the pennant, completing the square.

The only trick was in keeping the swimming pace steady. Otherwise, the pattern could be enlarged and repeated to the limits of the diver's air and physical endurance. Taking the pennant, Doll swam another thirty seconds north and planted it again in the sand. The route that he followed paralleled the first, but now the time of each of the legs was doubled—a minute west, two minutes south, two east, two north, and a minute more back to the flag. In the third pass, the length of each leg would be three times the length of the corresponding leg in the first.

On the southward course of his fifth circuit, Doll encountered a rope.

Checking his watch, he observed the time into the leg so that, if he wanted, later, he could continue the pattern of his search where he'd left it. He then cut the rope and retied it, leaving an uncommon knot to mark his position.

The rope was thin, quarter inch manila line, strung loose and set up like a sagging fence only inches above the sandy bottom of the sea. The biotic film that clung to it suggested it had been there for a time that might have been weeks and more likely months. Doll traced the perimeter. What he'd found was a rectangle, staked at the corners, with its long sides running southeast to northwest—some two hundred feet across on the short sides and roughly twice that on the long. While the floor of the sea around the enclosed area was very nearly flat, the sand within was crested into low piles and shallow hollows. Clearly the work of man. More clearly still, the work of man moving the sand to uncover what secrets might lie beneath it.

But the telling part, Doll thought as he paddled slowly, suspended a dozen feet above the mounded floor below him, was the smallness and the fitfulness of it. The real recovery effort, Calvin Tack had said, was only now getting started. But with what? There were no stored tools for heavy dredging, nor any evidence that such tools had ever been used. The holes were empty, not marked off for further excavation. They were only that—holes—where objects had perhaps been found, or perhaps they'd simply yielded nothing. What Doll saw beneath him wasn't the beginning of any scaled-up salvage operation. What he was looking at was far more of an end than it was a beginning. The harvest, such as it might have been, had already been gathered in, and what was left behind was now no more than a picked-over field.

There was, of course, Doll realized, always the chance he was wrong. Not about the field below him. He was sure of what he saw there. But no rule said that this had to be Wellman's field. The bearings he'd taken from the compasses he had weren't anything close enough to provide for reasonable certainty. Nor was there any rule that said there couldn't be another field all marked off and ripe for exploitation—maybe no farther than fifty or a hundred feet away.

But too much else said that just wasn't so. Doll had what he accepted as the final fact before him. It was time for the pieces to come together, and time for other people to know.

Doll had waited for more than an hour, stretched out as best he could in the driver's seat of the VW. The time was dusk, going on toward night. The sun had dropped below the line of the houses and trees, blending them into a single, dark, jagged horizon. The sky had turned from purple to a deep velvet blue that, toward the east, was already fading into black.

The car that came toward him had its low beams on. As it turned onto the asphalt driveway on the opposite side of the street from Doll, an automatic garage door opened, triggering a switch that transformed the interior space into a brightly illuminated cave.

Valerie Albrecht brought the car to a stop inside and got out. Her head turned sharply at the sound of the VW's closing door. The visor brim she wore around her head kept her face in semishadow.

"Doll? Is that you?" she called, as she stared out from the lighted garage into the darkness.

Doll said that it was.

"My God, you nearly frightened the hell out of me." She seemed to start to breathe again. "Don't you know you can get arrested hanging around out there like that?"

While she waited for Doll to reach the garage, she went around to the back of the car, opened the trunk, and hoisted out a bag of golf clubs.

"Well, this is an unexpected surprise—but then, I suppose, all surprises are," she said as she set the clubs on the floor. "What brings you out here? I know what I'd like to think, but somehow I don't think that'd be right." Her red mouth smiled out at Doll from under the visor.

"I'm here because of Diana," Doll answered.

"Mmm, who'd've expected that?" Valerie replied dryly, letting herself sound only mildly crestfallen.

"I've been talking to a lot of people," Doll said, "though I don't suppose that's much of a shock to you. I've been asking questions and getting some answers."

"I hope they've been the ones you wanted," Valerie answered and smiled, but the tone in her voice was now carefully neutral.

"Not entirely." Doll hesitated for the second it took him to remind himself of what he had to do. "There are some I wish I hadn't gotten because they lead to other questions that take me off in directions I wish that I didn't have to go."

"You came all the way out here just to ask me more questions?" she said incuriously, as though she'd somehow missed the darker import of Doll's words. "If I answer them right, do I win some kind of jackpot?"

Doll could see her face, even in the visor's shadow. The pretense, he only too willingly conceded, was effective. Her smile and her tanned skin beamed confidence and a hint of mischief. The fear only showed when he looked into her eyes.

"There aren't any jackpots. Maybe that's the whole problem," Doll said.

"My, aren't we profound tonight." Valerie's smile, by then, had fallen away. "You're going to have to explain that to me, Doll. I haven't the slightest idea what it means."

"It brings us back to the question that got me out here," Doll replied. "According to what I've been able to piece together, there were basically three stages to Perry Wellman's search and salvage operation: the first, when he was totally on his own; the second, when Mickey Zale put up the backing; and the third when all the others got into the act. We can add to that a subsection of the third part: when the Guillettes got out for reasons we can all understand. But you got out, too. At least I was told that. Since then, I've been wondering why."

"As if it was any of your business," Valerie Albrecht answered stiffly. "But I don't mind telling you anyway, Doll. Aside from the part that you know already about the whole thing not being strictly legal, there's nothing else in it that I have to hide."

"You realized you couldn't afford to stay in. You needed the cash," Doll suggested.

"Not quite. But close enough." Valerie shrugged. "The fact is I know what my limits are, Doll. When I go to the track—which happens maybe three or four times a year—I take a couple of hundred dollars, and that's all I bet. If you know about my getting out, then you probably also know how much I put into the pot in the first place. It was seventy-five hundred dollars—invested in a very high risk enterprise. That was more than I could afford to lose."

"A couple of interesting points though," Doll said. "When we talked that night at the pool, when you explained about how everybody was involved, you never told me you got out or that you were keeping the books for the past two years, and you never said, that I recall, that Mickey Zale was ever in. On the other hand, though, to be fair about it, a completely honest appraisal would also allow for some doubt on that last part. There are people who say that the money that Zale put up maybe wasn't Mickey Zale's money at all."

"Who says that?" Valerie Albrecht asked caustically.

"I do, for one," Doll replied.

Valerie started to shift positions, then, in the middle of it, seemed to make herself stop. She glared up at Doll angrily.

"Just what is it you think that you're getting at?" she demanded. "Just what is it that you expect me to say?"

Doll shook his head. "There isn't any treasure out there. I looked for myself, today," he answered. "But I don't expect you to say anything, Valerie. And I don't think that I have to say any more. If what I think happened is wrong, then nothing I've said here tonight is going to make any sense. But if what I think is right, there's only one thing you can do. And that, by itself, will set some wheels in motion."

Nodding his head to say good night, Doll started to turn away.

"You know something?" Valerie Albrecht said quietly.

When Doll turned back toward her, he found her staring at him.

"You're pretty, Doll," she said, half under her breath. "But when you want to, you can be a genuine bastard."

Not entirely undeserved, Doll admitted as he parked the VW in the lot beside his motel. Nobody gets thanked for spreading pain around.

He'd driven—just driven—for a while after leaving Valerie Albrecht's, hoping that the driving would let the slightly sour feeling ebb away. This time, though, the trick hadn't worked. Doll could only guess at why.

Was Valerie Albrecht that much more to blame than Diana or Tack or Doc Truitt? She, after all, hadn't murdered Sean Dabney either. What was the scale that blame got measured by? How many traffic tickets did you have to get before they added up to enough to equal a homicide? Angels on pin heads. Games with words. Meaningless questions with meaningless answers. Except that the questions and answers mattered because they were about what happened to people. Doll wondered if maybe that was the only meaning there was.

He walked up the steps and into the lobby. Halfway across it, he was stopped by the sound of his name.

"A man dropped it off here. Less than ten minutes ago," the clerk behind the desk explained as he handed Doll a personal-sized, cream-colored envelope. "He asked that it be delivered to your room as soon as possible. I was just looking for someone to take it up."

Doll thanked the clerk for his trouble.

On the elevator ride up to his floor, he opened what turned out to be a handwritten invitation. Mid-morning coffee at Clayton Rivers's house. Not a whole lot of surprise in that. Doll recalled his last remembered image of Valerie Albrecht's face beneath the visor. Folding the stationery and envelope, he slid both into the pocket of his shirt.

17

The two-lane road, which hadn't been wide to begin with, was nearly overgrown with semitropical vegetation. Lush bushes intruded on it from the sides, and the branches of trees interlocked overhead, blocking the sun so completely at times as to turn the deeper greens into patches of black that dissolved into shadowy, sinister hollows.

Doll followed the road south from the town as it traced, to his left, the nearly straight line of the river. On that side, the high bank was too narrow and too steeply sloped for building, except in the occasional places where clinging staircases descended the face to provide access to the private boathouses and docks below.

The houses were all on the inland side of the road. Many, especially those nearest the town, were set on modest, suburban-sized lots. The homes themselves were neat but unimposing structures built within a dozen or so yards of the highway. None was cheap, Doll was sure of that—if only by virtue of the river view that each commanded. But neither could the properties be regarded as in any sense spectacular.

Farther south along the river road, all of that changed. Two-, three- and four-acre parcels of land were carpeted with golf course–like grass and sculpted with trimmed shrubs and carefully pruned trees. The houses, in their size, seemed to Doll more like manors. Architectural preferences varied from contemporary to traditional with an assortment of blends in between. One trait, though, that all of the homes had in common was that none seemed to have been built by anyone even mildly concerned about holding down the cost.

Doll braked the VW and turned in at the gate between the twin stone, moss-covered pillars he'd been told to expect. Beyond them, a curving driveway of parqueted brick ended in a wide cul-de-sac before the main entrance to the house.

A second car, which he recognized as Valerie Albrecht's, was already parked there ahead of his own.

Doll's knock at the door was answered by a Hispanic who, despite his casual clothes, bowed his head in a manner that made his position in the household clear. He led Doll through a hall to the back and into a huge, open room which seemed a combination of a living area, atrium, and porch. The total effect that the room produced was to merge the interior into the yard beyond, seemingly without any definable point of transition.

Clayton Rivers stood at the far right side before a raised hearth fireplace with a mantel that was as high as his head. A rolling, wooden cart with a complete silver coffee service and cups was set up beside him. He wore a pale yellow jacket, a patterned shirt, and a pair of dark brown slacks.

Doll took it as a given that the staging was deliberate—the lord of the keep in the person of Clayton Rivers deigning to grant an audience to one of his retainers.

"Good morning, Mr. Doll." Rivers's voice was a perfect balance. Even Doll had to admit it. It managed to be friendly without being unctuous, and yet was businesslike, all at the same time.

Rivers crossed the room with a slow, aristocratic stride and offered his outstretched hand to Doll. Doll didn't refuse it, but kept the greeting to something less than hail-fellow-well-met.

"It's time we talked. Probably past it. My guess is that you'd say that too." Rivers pointed toward the tray. "The invitation was for coffee. But there's no reason it has to be that. I keep what I like to think is a fairly well-stocked bar. It can be coffee with something in it. Or coffee with something beside it. Or just something, and forget about the coffee, if you like."

"Coffee, black," Doll replied. "I think that's about as much as I want to owe you. It won't do us any good to put a mask on this, Rivers. Neither of us is here for the pleasure of each other's company. We're here because we've got something between us that isn't going to go away."

Rivers returned to the serving cart, where he poured a cup for Doll and then another for himself. Not far away was a couch where he chose to take up his position, leaving an adjacent chair to Doll.

As Doll sat, Rivers kept his elbow on the couch's arm and balanced the full cup and saucer in his hand. If he was nervous about their meeting, Doll thought, he was doing a first-rate job of not letting it show.

"I want you to know straight off, with no flattery," Clayton Rivers began, "that I've gained a good deal of respect for you. In the first place, you've done your homework. You dug out the pieces and put them together, and you've come up with an interpretation. You could have brought it directly to me, but you didn't. Maybe I could have bluffed you. I probably would've tried, but now we're never going to know."

Rivers looked at Doll appraisingly, as though he were considering how close the contest between them might have been. "But you didn't come to me, did you?" There seemed to be in his voice a small but discernible trace of regret. "Instead, you chose to go to Valerie. Mind you, I don't hold that against you, either. You did the smart thing for someone in your position. You attacked the chain at its weakest link. You put the proposition to her, and she as much as conceded it with what she thought were her say-nothing answers. Women can't bluff. They give themselves away. Because they always have to have an emotional stake in things. You understood that, and that's how you got yourself here today."

"I got here because I put you in a box," Doll answered. "Or, more accurately, because you put yourself in one. Either way, you won't get out of it by shifting the blame onto Valerie Albrecht."

"I think, by now, we both know the essential facts of the matter. At least I'm going to assume that," Rivers continued, as though Doll's revised description of the circumstances were an insignificant distraction and not worthy of reply. "What I have to do here this morning, Mr. Doll, is in its most fundamental sense simple. I need to convince you that, at the root of it all, I'm an innocent man."

Doll didn't say what he thought to himself: that Clayton Rivers had assigned himself a very considerable task.

"My eighty-five thousand. Shall we start with that?" Rivers said flatly. "What Mickey Zale was supposed to have invested in Perry Wellman's little treasure hunt. That money, as you've guessed, was mine. It was an honest, good faith investment, Mr. Doll. Well . . . honest, anyway, if you don't mind cheating the state out of a few dollars in taxes. But that's not why you came to Florida. I don't believe that you have any more interest in quibbling over that than do I."

"Just one of those things that everybody does."

"If you want—whatever that means." Rivers shrugged indifferently. "But what you have to understand this morning is that the idea for it was all Mickey Zale's. Before he came and told me about it, I had no notion of what Wellman was up to. It was Zale who told me about it, and Zale who talked me into putting up the money."

"Your money, but not your name," Doll observed.

"I preferred not," Rivers conceded. "But I can see now that some connection may be unavoidable. My family name is a great deal more than respectable, Mr. Doll. Maybe you didn't know it, but it goes back for a hundred and fifty years around here. Maybe it does, or maybe it doesn't, make me better than the next man. And this may be a time when I made a mistake. But, as a rule, I try to be careful about what I involve it in."

"Appearance counts; reality doesn't. You can really say that with a straight face? If you put up the money in somebody else's name, you're not involved?"

"As far as appearances are concerned, obviously not. There are differences, Mr. Doll, between reality and appearance—whether you want to admit it or not. People who succeed know how to live in both worlds. Only fools believe that the two worlds are one."

The calculating coldness of the words was nearly enough to make Doll shiver, the cynicism in them sufficient to justify anything anyone wanted to do. And yet, what bothered Doll most of all about them was the knowledge that, in many ways, the essence of what Clayton Rivers had just said was true.

"It's in that sense of reality that I'm talking now," Rivers went on. "What I'm telling you is that, from my point of view, the venture was one of simple enterprise capitalism. I put up the cash, and I stood the risk. After that, it was all in the dice. I could win just as well as I could lose."

"And did you lose?" Doll asked.

Clayton Rivers stared across the intervening distance at Doll.

"No. I didn't lose." The tone in Rivers's voice was abruptly and entirely different. It was soft, apologetic, almost the tone of a confession. The only question Doll had was if Rivers's new mood was one of pretense or sincerity—except that it really wasn't very much of a question in Doll's mind. "But, again, it wasn't my idea, Doll." Rivers almost seemed to plead. "It was Mickey Zale who came to me."

He reached down and put his still full cup of coffee on the floor.

"It was almost two years ago now, a night in midsummer," he continued. "Zale called and asked if he could come around and we could talk. He had a couple of drinks once he got here and rambled on about nothing. I understood after a while there was something else on his mind he wasn't saying. Finally, he had enough liquor to let him get it out.

"He told me that the money was gone—or close to gone, to keep it accurate. Something like ninety-five hundred dollars of the original eighty-five thousand was left. Besides that, with the articles that Wellman had brought in and sold off over the past year, there was maybe seven or eight thousand more. But the worst of the news, he saved for last. According to what Zale said, Wellman had told him that the site he'd thought was so rich a year before was turning out to be a false trail. That meant it all was back to square one—the money virtually gone, and Wellman wandering around here and there poking the bottom of the ocean at random again."

"And it meant," Doll calculated, "that Clayton Rivers was something on the order of seventy thousand dollars the poorer."

"It would have . . ." Rivers stood, then began to pace, then stopped and turned to stare directly at Doll. "But," he said, "Zale told me that it didn't have to be like that. He talked about additional financing—and, when I told him what he could do with that, he said I'd misunderstood him and that he hadn't meant that the money should come from me. He said that he'd gone out on his own and had told Wellman to let it get around that he'd located a promising wreck—exactly what he'd told me the year before. He said he had at least a dozen other people who were fighting with each other for the chance of getting in."

"But there was nothing to get into anymore except for pipe dreams," Doll said. "When you put up your money, you had every reason to believe you were in on the ground floor of a pretty good deal. You called it good faith. This isn't good faith anymore."

"I know that, but what you have to understand, Mr. Doll, is what Mickey Zale was thinking. If they, all together, put up a share equal to my eighty-five thousand . . ."

"That'd be a total of a little over a hundred in the pot," Doll summed aloud.

"And my eighty-five back to me. That's what you're really thinking," Rivers acknowledged. "Break even, that was the inducement he gave me. A little to Wellman for his silence and continued cooperation. A little more to keep up the fiction of things moving forward. And the rest—somewhere between five and ten grand—goes to who else but Mickey Zale for all of his trouble. Mickey Zale, who never put up a goddamn dime, and he's the only one who comes away with a profit."

"And with Valerie keeping the books it begins to get easy. Dummy the purchases and slide over the cash."

Rivers shook his head. "I didn't know about Valerie until later," he said. "Zale never told me that she was part of his 'other people.' If he had, I would never have let her get in in the first place. I could only warn her to get out at the first chance there was. The original idea was that Zale would keep the books himself. The only problem was that nobody trusted him. It was just chance and the nature of her business that made the job fall to Valerie."

"Lucky chance for you," Doll said. "Rip-off time for everybody else. What happens then—it all drags on for two more years before Wellman starts to drop a few hints that he's oh so sorry, but the money's all gone and the find he thought he had just didn't work out? Is that the 'good faith' bargain you agreed to?"

"I watched my own tail, and I cut my losses," Rivers answered sharply. "You want to tell me that wasn't fair to the others? Okay, Doll, you're right. It wasn't. It was just what any of them with the same goddamn chance would have done if they could've done it to me."

"And they'd all have laid down and taken it. Like so many

sheep," Doll said in disgust. "Except that you made a mistake when you let Sean Dabney in. And then, among the sheep, there was a ram."

"That was the one thing that Zale completely miscounted," Rivers answered soberly. "How much heat he was going to draw from Sean Dabney. Dabney never waited for all the pieces to drop into place. He saw from Wellman's first slice of bad news where things were heading and assumed right off what was basically true—that it was Zale who somehow had managed to siphon off the cash."

"So Dabney went to Zale," Doll speculated, choosing for the moment to let Rivers continue to cast himself in a minor role.

Rivers nodded. "Dabney threatened Zale. He told him he'd let the whole thing out—to the rest of the investors and maybe even go to the police. He said he was just a little fish in the game, and that he could make some kind of deal. You have to remember that, from Dabney's point of view, it's still Zale's eighty-five thousand. Zale's the big player—right down to his boy on Wellman's boat. Anyway, Dabney winds up telling Zale that Zale's only got one way out. Dabney doesn't care where Zale gets the money, but he wants his own ten thousand dollars back. If he gets it, he shuts up. Which you have to admit, given what Zale came up with on his own in the first place, is pretty damned ironic."

"And now," Doll said, picking up on what he realized had to follow, "Mickey Zale feels pinched between a rock and a hard place."

"Worse even than Dabney knew," Rivers agreed. "Because Zale's not so clean—even leaving the salvage issue aside—that he can afford to go around stirring up trouble. But if Zale pays—which concedes the very doubtful fact that he could actually come up with the whole ten grand that Dabney was demanding—he still winds up, net, a few thousand down and with the prospect of Dabney on his back forever. That doesn't leave a man like Mickey Zale a lot of choices."

"Is that what happened?" Doll asked.

Rivers smiled and shrugged. "That's the story, Doll, all in a nice little package. You take it to the police as your own. I'll back it all the way. Your friend Diana gets out of jail. And all of us are mostly off the hook."

"Is it true?" Doll asked.

"I like to think of it more as a version of the truth." Rivers seemed to enjoy the distinction, at least to the point that he chose the moment to smile. "I don't want anyone throwing a murder charge at me, and I can see from what you said to Valerie where you might be of a mind to try to do that. I can afford—if I have to—to look like a man who made a bad and maybe even technically illegal investment. I can even afford to look like a bastard who let a bunch of other people drown so he could save his skin. I come out of it with a few scratches, but ones that I can live with. You get your friend out of jail and a story that's about as close as life ever gets to what's true."

"An' I can just guess what kinda story that is. I only wish I'd been on time for the rest of it." In his white shirt and black trousers, Mickey Zale looked like an overweight penguin standing in the hallway entrance to the room. Carlos Bandalos, his right arm encumbered by the cast, stood at his side.

"Mr. Doll." Zale nodded curtly in Doll's direction.

Doll rose from his chair as Zale and Bandalos crossed the room to within several feet of where Rivers was standing.

"What I maybe shoulda told you before," Zale said, as he got close to Rivers, "is that I like to make it a thing to do every now and then just to drive by the houses of people I know. Maybe that makes me nosy. Y'think that it does? But, I'll tell you, every once in a while I get a surprise. Take this morning, f'rinstance, when I get to your place here. I wasn't so surprised to see your girlfriend's car out front. But then I see Doll's, that I wasn't expecting. Then your man lets me in, and I hear just the end of this story you're telling. I come in on the part where a man like me doesn't have a lot of choices. And then I hear how Doll's gonna be able to get his friend outta jail, and how a man like you doesn't want to get charged with any murder. I'll tell you, Mr. Rivers, it's the kinda ending that makes me wonder just what the rest of the story mighta been about."

Rivers offered no reply.

Zale waited several seconds, letting the ominous silence hang. "Nothing to say now?" he asked with his eyebrows raised. "Lose your interest? Cat got your tongue? Mr. Doll, you can see for yourself Mr. Rivers seems like he's got himself a sudden case of lockjaw. So, I wonder, will I get the same answer from you?"

"Mr. Rivers was explaining to me why you had to kill Sean Dabney," Doll said.

Looking from Doll to Rivers, then back again at Doll, Mickey Zale let the corners of his mouth draw up to form a gargantuan grin.

"No surprise in that," he replied, still smiling broadly. "Disappointment? No, I don't even think that. Never trust a blue blood. Or trust him to do the same thing every time. Once the shit starts to hit the fan, he'll screw whoever he thinks he's got to just to cover his own royal, goddamn ass."

"You go ahead and say all you want, Zale," Rivers answered evenly. "I've got all the bases covered. Doll's got the story, and the story fits the facts. There's nothing you can say or do that's going to change any of that."

"How about that it was all your money?" Zale asked. His smile remained in place. "Did he tell you that, Doll? All the money that I was supposed to have put up for Wellman—it wasn't ever mine. I was just a front for him."

"Doll knows. I told him that myself," Rivers responded,

meeting Mickey Zale smile for smile. "He also knows how, when the arrangement went sour, you came to me and said you'd get me my money back as long as I didn't notice what you took out for yourself in the process."

"You told him *that!*" Zale stared at Rivers with a look that seemed to Doll like wide-eyed incredulity. "By God in heaven," he said, turning to Doll, "you didn't believe him, that son of a bitch!"

This time it was Doll's turn to be silent.

"Yes, it's half the truth," Zale insisted. "I came to tell him that Wellman was beginning to tell me things that were sounding bad. What choice did I have, Doll? You can see that. Come back when all of the money was gone and say, 'I'm sorry to have to tell you, pal, but you just kissed off eighty-five grand'? I was scared. You gotta understand how scared I was. Yes, I told him things had gone rotten. And he told me exactly what I knew he would—to get his money back for him. He didn't care what I had to do to get it. He said that for a lot less than eighty-five grand, he could have me floating facedown in the goddamn, fucking Everglades swamp."

"Not the way it happened," Rivers replied confidently. "You bought me off because you saw a chance to cash in for yourself. Your idea, Zale—the whole scheme. Everybody who was in on it will testify that it was you and Wellman who headed things up from the start."

"Yes, because you were the silent partner," Zale shouted back. "All I ever did was stand in for you."

Clayton Rivers shook his head and looked sadly over at Zale.

"But you're the one who made the money," Rivers explained, as though he were laying the obvious out for a child. "I broke even, but you're the one who came out ahead. The police are going to find that out. It won't even have to be me that tells them. And you're not going to be able to disguise the fact because it's true.

"And then there's Dabney, too. Granted he's not here to talk for himself, but everybody else the authorities talk to is going to say he suspected you. I'm even sympathetic, Zale. As you heard me saying to Doll before, I don't think you had a lot of choice. But with the facts the way they are, as far as helping you goes, there really isn't very much that I can do. Unless, maybe," Rivers added, as though the thought had just occurred to him, "if you didn't insist on telling lies about me—involving me beyond the money you talked me into investing—I might just be able and willing to stake you to a first-rate criminal lawyer."

"Yeah, and I take the fall, you son of a bitch, for what you told me I had to do." Zale turned to Doll. "Sean Dabney was a dead man either way," he said plaintively. "This bastard's got enough long green to call out a hit on the pope if he wants to. The only choice that I got to make was whether I wanted to die along with him."

Zale ran his hand back through his hair. "Now he brings out the carrot and the stick." His eyes flashed like a warning sign from Doll to Rivers and back again to Doll, as his mind raced in a desperate search for angles and alternatives—until, suddenly, the searching stopped and his stare settled finally on Rivers.

"You know, there's another way for all of us out of this mess," Zale said, in the muted but passionate voice of a man who had just been inspired. "We're fighting here between ourselves." He pointed back and forth between Rivers and himself. "But we're not the the only people here. Nothin' I know of says either of us has to take the fall for what happened to Dabney."

Carlos Bandalos moved his left hand toward his pocket; then suddenly the movement stopped. The muzzle of Zale's automatic pistol was already pressed into Bandalos's ribs.

"Sacrifice a pawn?" Clayton Rivers's eyes moved to Bandalos as he seemed to contemplate the contingencies.

Doll watched as the terror of realization grew in Bandalos's eyes.

"It has some merits," Rivers said academically. "It meets all the requirements I can see, including Mr. Doll's. You say you sent Carlos over to Dabney's that night with the books? Still, he'd have to have a reason—like maybe he tried lifting the silver while he thought that Dabney was looking somewhere else. Handy to have it a part of the record that he's got that nasty little habit to support.

"It has merit, Zale," Rivers repeated. "Almost airtight if our friend, Mr. Doll, goes along. The only drawback I can find is that it's unlikely Carlos will sit through it quietly. The stakes for him are going to be pretty high—with the result that he's apt to start pointing fingers. Who knows but that, if it came to trial, he might even come up with some plausible alibi? But then, of course, there's an answer to that. To point a finger or produce an alibi—even to have a trial at all—a man would have to be alive."

The swelling panic inside Bandalos's head exploded. He swung his whole body though a half circle, imparting a tremendous momentum to the arm in the plaster cast. The sudden action caught Zale off guard. Bandalos's cast struck Zale's gun hand before Zale had the chance to squeeze the trigger. The weapon discharged, but its barrel, by then, was pointed far wide of Bandalos. The pistol flew from Zale's hand, backwards and out through the room's entrance and into the hallway beyond.

Bandalos raised the cast high in the air. This time, though, the maneuver was hardly defensive. The target of the looming attack was Mickey Zale's skull.

Doll wasn't close enough to reach Bandalos, so he did the next best thing he could think of, which was to try to shove Mickey Zale out of harm's way.

Even so, the cast glanced off the side of Zale's head.

The sound of a shot, like the smack of a board struck flat against another, crashed, then echoed, even as two more concussions followed the first.

Doll's eyes flashed toward Clayton Rivers. He hadn't realized that Rivers was anywhere near to a gun.

Bandalos's spine, which was toward Rivers, bowed forward like a waxing, crescent moon. Three red, irregular blotches appeared within a four-inch circle in the center of his back, then spread across the fabric of his shirt until they merged.

The body toppled forward from the ankles, the cast arm striking first with a resounding thud as it crashed against the carpet. The rest of the corpse landed dully by comparison. It fell onto its chest and face, then lay immobile where it settled on the floor.

"Self-defense," Rivers said immediately. "You saw where he was aiming that thing. If he'd hit Zale with it, he would've killed him."

"Except," Doll said, "for the fact that you didn't shoot until after he'd missed."

"Takes time," Rivers replied and shrugged. "A man has to get to his weapon and then to take aim."

Mickey Zale, rubbing his head where the cast had struck him, began to get himself back on his feet. Looking down at Bandalos, he shook his head.

"Poor son of a bitchin' bastard," Zale said. "I almost feel a little sorry for him. In a lot of ways he was just another punk kid who never could buy himself an even break."

"Don't waste the sentiment. He just tried to kill you," Clayton Rivers reminded Zale. "And just so we all remember, it was self-defense," he repeated. His pistol was now trained at a middle point, more or less halfway between Mickey Zale and Doll. "We *do* have three clear-headed witnesses on that? Before I put this away, I just want to be sure."

"Well, well. The three men I hate most in the world, all together in one place at the same time."

Valerie Albrecht's voice came from the entrance to the room, a dozen feet from where Bandalos's body lay. Looking from

Doll to Zale to Clayton Rivers, she held Mickey Zale's automatic in her hand.

As Zale began to move toward her, Valerie let the pistol's muzzle drift toward him.

"No, I don't think so, Mickey. I've been listening out there— half listening, half thinking," she said in a voice that was tightly controlled and scarcely louder than a whisper. "I'm not really sure that you want to come any closer to me just now."

18

Valerie Albrecht wore no makeup. The skin over the cheekbone beneath her left eye, Doll saw, was discolored to a gray-tinged blue. On the right side along the line of her jaw was a slight abrasion, now scabbed over, where her head, evidently, had banged into something.

Doll remembered Clayton Rivers telling him earlier how he held Valerie responsible for giving the game away, and, with that memory, Doll promised himself that, if and when the opportunity arose, Clayton Rivers had earned a little pain.

"That's fine. Bring me the gun, Valerie," Rivers ordered from in front of the couch where he still stood.

"No, Clayton, I don't think so," she answered, slowly shaking her head. "I don't think that that's something I want to do either."

"What you want to do doesn't matter," Rivers fired back hotly. The sides of his neck near the major blood vessels were red with his fury at her show of disobedience. "I'm not asking you what you want to do. I'm telling you. You bring that pistol over here now."

"Or?" Valerie asked.

"Don't ask me 'or?' You know what 'or?' is," Rivers warned.

"Or what? You shoot me?" Valerie Albrecht shook her head again. "I don't think you're going to do that, Clayton. In the first place, I don't think you're fast enough. Not to reaim and get off the shot—especially not with a safety margin that would stop me from getting off at least one shot back at you. Remember, it was you who taught me to shoot. I suppose that may seem to you now, as you look back, not to have been such a clever idea."

"Valerie, this is your—"

"My last chance?" Valerie interrupted him. "All right, then let it be that. You've been telling me about your cowboy ancestors until there were times that I thought I was going to throw up from hearing about them. So you go ahead and try it if you think you can get away with it. But I know you a whole lot better than you think I do, and I'm betting you don't have the stomach for it. Oh, you could order somebody dead or shoot somebody in the back, but when it comes down to facing the chance of being shot, I think you're a talker. I don't think you've got the courage it takes."

"Valerie, this is silly," Mickey Zale, said doing his best to make his manner persuasive, but at the same time being careful not to move from where he stood. "With Carlos dead, we can work the rest out. With or without Mr. Doll. Whatever we have to."

"Mickey's right, we can work it out," Rivers added emphatically, endorsing the line of Zale's reasoning. "You know me, Valerie. I wouldn't've shot if I hadn't thought it through. It can all be fixed. It can be like it was. We can make it now so nothing has to change."

For a long moment, Valerie Albrecht stared at Rivers, without ever changing the direction in which she was pointing the gun.

"Tell me about it," she replied, almost in a whisper. "Tell me, Clayton. Tell me how it was and how it can be."

"Dabney's dead, so there won't be any more questions," Rivers answered, trying to coax now instead of demand. "We give them Carlos as his killer. Doll goes along with us. He has to. It's three against one, or—too bad for Doll—we could always say that he and Carlos shot each other. Mickey keeps his money. We keep ours. The rest would lose, but that was always in the cards. Everything else could stay the same. You and me, Valerie, we'd be just like we were. Once we get past this, there isn't any reason why we couldn't go on like that forever."

Valerie smiled, then shook her head as she spoke.

"That's the trouble with you, Clayton, one of them anyway. You always feel like you have to oversell things. When you made the whole thing seem over and like we were going back to a kind of normality . . . I admit it. I was tempted. You very nearly had me. It was only when you brought up you and me that I remembered you from last night." She touched the fingers of her left hand to her cheek. "And I remembered what you made me see—that the memories I used to have of us were my own made-up memories, memories of things the way they never were."

"No. That's not true," Rivers tried to protest.

"But it is true. It's the truest thing of all," Valerie answered. "You used me—the same way you used Zale and all the others. And Mickey does the same thing. And I do. And, yes, Doll, so do you. And so do the others—Perry Wellman, Sylvia, all of them. We're cannibals, and we have to understand that we're going to stay that way unless we change things. We feed on one another. We find out who the weak ones are, and then we fill ourselves up by tearing them to pieces. We have a few drinks, and then we feel and think we look so beautiful, when what we really are is vicious and deadly and ugly. It'd be funny if wasn't so sad. Don't you think so? We don't even have the dignity of the earth's grander predators. We're just like those pathetic fish in the tank behind Mickey's bar."

"Look, if this's all from last night—"

"Is that the way you'd like to make it seem, Clayton—as though last night was the first time it ever happened? Or that I'm supposed to believe it would be the last? No, it isn't just from last night. And, anyway, it doesn't matter. It's so much more than just between the two of us." Valerie glanced toward Doll, then back at Rivers, but the alignment of her pistol never changed. "I said you weren't any better, Doll, but maybe that's only halfway true. You hurt me when you used me to get to Clayton, and you would've hurt anybody else who got in the way of your helping Diana. But maybe that's your saving grace— that it wasn't for you, but for somebody else. It's not much, but maybe it's just enough to make you the least among the evils."

Valerie raised the sight line of the pistol to a level even with her eye and aimed the automatic squarely at the center of Clayton Rivers's forehead.

"Clayton," she whispered, "I think it's time you took your finger off that trigger. Do it, and hand the gun over to Doll."

"Do you know what you're doing, Valerie? You're going to land all of us in jail," Rivers shouted, desperately now.

"I know what I'm doing," Valerie answered. "I'm making it impossible for me or you or anybody else to go back to how things were. Please remember this thing has been fired. The hammer is back, and it's ready to fire again. I don't want to kill you, Clayton. But if you think for just a second about what I've been saying, you can't have any doubt that I will. Now please— this is the last time I'm asking—take your finger off the trigger and hand the gun to Doll."

Clayton Rivers looked at Valerie, then at Mickey Zale, who only shook his head to acknowledge his own state of helplessness. Finally, Rivers glanced toward Doll. Taking his finger from the trigger in a deliberately exaggerated gesture, he raised both hands into the air.

As Doll reached for the weapon in Rivers's hand, he tried to anticipate the points in the exchange where things might go wrong. In one particular sense, he found himself coming close to hoping that they would. But nothing did. The threat from the pistol in Valerie's hand was enough. Clayton Rivers surrendered the gun that he held without resistance.

Doll stepped backward with the weapon in his hand to a point where both Zale and Rivers were easily within his field of observation.

Valerie, meanwhile, lowered her weapon and slumped into a chair not far from where she'd stood.

"Are you all right?" Doll asked. "Can you call the police?"

"I can in a minute. As soon as I catch my breath and get my head together," she answered, though her voice sounded near to the edge of exhaustion. "It's strange. I don't feel much of anything right now. I thought I'd collapse into a crying jag that would last for about a year and a half. I couldn't go back to the way it was. I just couldn't, Doll. It was something that, some-how, I had to make change."

Doll replied only with some words that said that he under-stood. He didn't say what he was sure would also be true—that, once the shock had worn away, some part of the crying jag that Valerie had talked about would come. But with time, the crying too would pass. And then, even with whatever was left from the past, there would be a new chance for things to look better.

"Lead item in tomorrow morning's edition. Front page, left-hand corner, above the fold." Willard Giesler grinned at Doll approvingly. "With a great shot of Rivers, so Harvey Archer tells me—albeit from happier times. He called for you—Archer, not Rivers, obviously—just to let you know. He said he'd tried your motel and couldn't get you, so he guessed that you'd probably be coming here."

Giesler crossed the porch to a portable bar. "Why don't I make you a drink?" he said, as he poured a vodka for himself and then a gin for Doll. "After Eldwin Rush, you can probably use one. How was he? Pretty goddamn pissed off, I imagine."

Doll gazed past the screen out across Giesler's lawn toward the river. He found it hard to make himself believe that less than forty-eight hours had passed since he'd left this same house, this same porch, only two afternoons before.

"Not bad. Not half as bad as he could have been." Doll forced his mind back to Giesler's question and his own answer. "It helped a lot that he had Zale and Rivers in his pocket. From what he told me, they've been going at them pretty steady since they got there. Separately, but playing their stories off against each other. After a few hours of that, according to Rush, even their lawyers couldn't make them keep their mouths shut."

"What did he say about Diana?" Giesler handed the gin to Doll, and both men sat.

"That it had turned out that, this time, he was wrong, but that he wasn't eating any crow." Doll swirled the gin but put the glass down on the table without tasting any of the liquor. "He said that he'd gone on the facts as he saw them, and, in the same circumstances, he'd do it the same way again. He made the point a couple of times that the way it worked out didn't change anything; that, as far as he was concerned, I was still just a lucky snoop. He said he was sorry that he couldn't get Diana released until the morning. I believed him on that. I think he really was."

Giesler nodded. "I think that's probably true. Rush is stubborn and self-righteous, and I wouldn't put it past him to be vindictive. This time, though, I don't think he was.

"It's my fault, Doll, for raising your expectations the other day. There are rules and procedures and judges who aren't open around the clock for just anything—no matter how important it might be to somebody else. I made some calls. I could've pushed. But sometimes, when you push a system too hard, instead of going faster, it stalls."

"Nothing for you to blame yourself for." Doll glanced down at the gin, then looked up again and out across the river. "Maybe, if Diana had known and expected more . . . But she didn't, so the extra night doesn't matter."

"But it does to you, and I'm sorry for that," Giesler replied and took a swallow of his vodka. "What d'ya say, Doll, you going to keep me in suspense as penance? I'd sure as hell like to know how you figured it."

"There was a lot that I didn't figure," Doll said honestly. "Like I told you, all I saw ahead was the next couple moves and then what had to be the end. I certainly never saw Zale showing up at Rivers's place or anything like Carlos getting shot.

"What I did see was Rivers's money, and then the connection between Zale and Valerie and Rivers. You triggered that idea, Willard, when you said we only knew as an absolute certainty that most of the first eighty-five thousand got spent. I went back to Harvey Archer's insisting that the money hadn't come from Zale. And suddenly, it jumped out that it almost had to have come from Rivers. And then, with only Valerie watching the cash drawer, it all seemed to fit—the perfect way for Rivers to get his capital back. I went out to look at the site, just to convince myself one final time that the treasure find had gone sour. From what I saw there, I was satisfied it had."

"Sean Dabney's questions got a little too close for somebody's comfort," Giesler thought aloud. "And whoever killed him had to be one of the parties—Rivers or Zale or Valerie, or some combination of the three of them."

'More than questions. Threats," Doll acknowledged. "I didn't figure Valerie to have enough motive for murder, but I saw her as the quick way to get to Rivers. She knew it. I'm still not too proud about that. But what I felt pretty sure of was that, once the notion of some kind of conspiracy between Zale and Rivers got around, the accusations and counteraccusations had to start. And, once they got started, there wasn't going to be any way of stopping them."

"Still a clever solution. And more important than clever, basically right." In a gesture of respect, Giesler saluted Doll with his glass. "So which story is it, Doll, Rivers's or Zale's? Which of them told you the truth?"

"Both—some of it—but leaning toward Zale," Doll answered. "A best guess? The night Diana and Dabney had the fight at Zale's, Zale and Dabney had a little set-to of their own. Dabney made his threats. Zale called Rivers in a panic, and Rivers left no doubt about what had to be done. Zale went back to Dabney and said he'd get the books so that Dabney could see for himself that everything was square. Only Zale would have to get them from Valerie and drop them by Dabney's later that night. The second glass on the floor of Dabney's condo, if I'm right, was Mickey Zale's. Zale had brought something—maybe even the actual books—to occupy Dabney's attention. Then he did what Rivers had told him had to be done."

"And he deliberately set it up to make it look like Diana did it?"

Doll shrugged and shook his head. "To the extent of using her handkerchief to wipe the prints and later making the anonymous call to the police. Was she supposed to be a temporary distraction for the police or go the distance and take the fall? There's only one living witness to that, and, unless Mickey Zale decides to tell us, we're never going to know."

"It's going to be a fascinating show." Giesler sighed, then produced one of his inevitable toothpicks and inserted it into the corner of his mouth. "You'll have to be back for the Zale and Rivers trials, of course. Be a year, I'd say, maybe more, before those happen. Too bad in the meantime, though, you won't be around to watch the rest of it silt out."

"How will it end—for all of them?" Doll asked.

"Legal predictions? A very risky business. And on hearsay, from what I get from you and Harvey Archer, even worse."

Willard Giesler smiled, then turned serious.

"For Diana—which is what you mostly care about—it's over," he said. "Oh, it's possible that she has some liability if the state tax people decide they want some prosecutions out of the salvage scheme. Technically, as I said once before, I suppose they could make the case that she was a party to a conspiracy to defraud the state. There were some recoveries that never got reported, even if they never amounted to a lot, and, technically— although it's a much harder case to prove—intent to defraud can be a crime even when no actual fraud takes place. But that's not going to happen for a lot of reasons—not the least of which is that Diana's involvement was the smallest of anybody in on the plot. She also lost her twenty-five hundred dollars. What are they going to do, fine her a few hundred more? No, the worst she faces is that they'll hassle her into being a witness—and that's an absolute worst case.

"Tack and Doc Truitt, on the other hand, were the big guns—except for Rivers, of course, who's got a lot more than the tax issue to worry about. They both could wind up with fairly stiff fines. And Wellman—even though what he brought in wasn't much—it's not out of the question but that he could lose his boat and serve a little time."

"Mickey Zale and Clayton Rivers?"

Willard Giesler shifted the toothpick by several degrees. "Rivers'll have the best legal team in the state that money can buy. That's the first thing you can count on," he said, as he thought. "It won't help. The state won't even bother to charge him on Dabney; they'll charge him on Carlos Bandalos instead. He said too much in front of too many people, and he shot too late. If justice were as blind as she's supposed to be, he'd fall on a murder one, get twenty to life, and be out in maybe seventeen. But the blindfold's a lie, and he's still Clayton Rivers. I know how I'd like to call it, Doll. I wish I could tell you that's how it'll be.

"Mickey Zale—in some ways the more interesting case. 'Beyond a reasonable doubt?' I don't know. So far as we know, there aren't any witnesses or physical evidence that he was ever even in the apartment. Circumstantial evidence and inference from what he said at Rivers's place? Very, very touchy. I don't know."

"And Valerie Albrecht?"

"On what?" Giesler said and grinned. "On the tax scam? She pulled out without any profit within a couple weeks or months of getting in. Or are you telling me she was part of Zale's and Rivers's plan to defraud Tack and the rest? You can't defraud someone on the basis of their participation in an illegal enterprise. It's not adjudicable under the law."

"Tomorrow. What about tomorrow?" Doll said, returning the conversation to his greater and more immediate concern. "You're positive there won't be any trouble about Diana getting out of the jail?"

"Should be nine o'clock." The grin faded from Giesler's face. His manner turned not somber, but more serious. "I know you don't intend to be there. I'd like to talk you out of that," he said. "What I'd like to see you do is take the sister along and go out there to meet her. Strange as it sounds for me to say it, you owe her that, Doll. You got her out of some pretty bad trouble, and she knows that. It's not fair to her—however awkward you feel about it—not to give her the chance to thank you. There's a part of her life that she needs to and very much wants to close down that she can't close down without seeing you."

Doll ran his hand back through his hair and nodded back at Willard Giesler. It hadn't been so long a day as it had been a fatiguing one. Doll found himself, all at once, feeling enormously tired.

Doll set the cold six-pack down in the middle of Emilio Secassa's Formica-topped kitchen table. He pulled a can free from the plastic and slid it across to Secassa, then slipped out another can for himself and snapped open the top.

Secassa did the same and tipped the beer can toward Doll.

"A *su salud*! I'm happy for you, Señor Doll," Secassa continued in Spanish, "and for your lady friend, too. It's not an easy thing to get those in authority to say that they've made a mistake. This is especially true when the one that they must find at fault instead turns out, like Señor Rivers, to be someone important."

Doll took a long pull at his beer and wondered why it was that he felt more at ease with the beer and Secassa than he had with Willard Giesler and the gin.

He asked how Secassa had heard.

"TV news, just an hour ago," Secassa explained.

"Well, I was lucky," Doll said as he nodded. "And I had help." He gestured toward Secassa with his beer as a token of appreciation, then rewarded himself with another swallow from the can. "That's why I came by tonight—because I had to say that."

"I did nothing. I showed you an apartment," Secassa replied. "And I told you about Señor Dabney and his women, which, if it steered you anywhere, only steered you wrong."

"One way you find the right trail," Doll said, "is by eliminating the wrong ones."

"If you say that it's so, I won't argue." Secassa took a pull at his beer and shook his head. "You know, Señor Doll, you're a very unusual man—a man of so many contradictions. I don't pretend to understand you. You come here to help a woman who you describe as a friend—but in what sense a friend when the woman is with another man? You're an Anglo in your face and dress and manner when I see you. And yet, if I spoke with you in Spanish only on the phone, I would swear from your accent and the pattern of your speech and even the concepts you use that you had to be born and raised as a Hispanic. And, at the same time, you are a gentle man from every sign I've seen. But I know, too, what you did to Carlos Bandalos when you fought with him the first time on that other man's boat, and I know what you did to Bandalos and two of his friends that same night when they tried to even the score."

"Word gets around," Doll said.

"Within the Latino community, yes, señor, it does," Secassa acknowledged.

Doll looked up sharply at Secassa, then gazed down at the tabletop again. "I never thought of it. It never even occurred to me," he muttered, wondering at the same time how he could have been so myopic. "It's like a big family. An outsider comes in and breaks somebody's arm. It's a guarantee that all the other members are going to know."

"It's a very strange place, here," Secassa replied mildly, as though to exempt Doll from any criticism for the oversight. "Always, maybe, places are strange where some portion of a people live somewhere apart from their natural home. There are Latins in this town who are doctors, men of learning, Señor Doll. And others who make what livings they do by stealing the stereophonic tape decks out of cars. Normally the two would meet each other only when the one had the bad luck to get caught in the process of ripping off the other's Mercedes. That happens here too, of course, but here those thieves and doctors find they have something else besides being on opposite sides of a theft in common. They are Latins, and, by that standard alone, they are at once together and apart from everyone else."

Doll recalled from the day when he'd first driven through the town the people who'd sat on the porches beside the broken refrigerators and the rows of children who seemed content with nothing more to do than watch the traffic pass. He hadn't seen the prosperous Latins, the doctors or even the Secassas, then. He remembered the church that had marked the nearly visible line of demarcation, and the ocher bricks of the buildings in the business district beyond.

"I'm sorry for what happened to Bandalos," he said, returning his attention to Secassa. "But I'm not going to lie about it to you either. I can't apologize for what I did—that was no more than he made me do. But I never intended for him to be shot."

Secassa drank more of his beer, then rested the can softly down on the Formica. "No reason for any apology, señor. If Carlos would have killed you on the boat or in the parking lot—and I can easily believe that he would have . . ." Secassa let the thought remain unfinished. "In any case, it no longer matters. Such judgment as happens now is only between him and God."

Doll walked to his car beneath the light of the halogen lamps that illuminated the condominium's parking lot. Darkness had come to the summer night, but the hour still was early. He could hear the waves and see the ghosts of people roaming up and down like silent shadows along the line of the beach.

In the evening quiet and with the puzzle of Sean Dabney's murder behind him, Doll allowed his mind the freedom to drift. For no special reason, or at least for none that he could define, it returned him to something Secassa had said.

A strange place, Secassa had called the town, a strangeness he's set forth in terms of two rival cultures—one Anglo, the other Hispanic—forced by circumstance to live in apposition, but neither with any more desire to integrate with the other than the minimum their physical proximity required. It was, Doll conceded, the understandable, perhaps even inevitable, perception of a man who regarded himself as an exile, accurate so far as it went—but incomplete.

The town once had been as Secassa believed it still to be, a place where a commonly held white consensus prevailed. Doll thought of the 1930's houses, those first that he'd seen after leaving the interstate. The older locals, like Calvin Tack, had been children in school when they'd been built. And the younger ones—the Tom Guillettes, the Sylvias, the Valerie Albrechts—who'd seen the town only to watch it change, had heard the memories spoken by their elders and so had acquired a kind of oral memory of their own for how it once had been.

They'd also seen the resorts go up and the tourists come, and not far behind the seemingly unending waves of frost-weary retirees fleeing from the winters of the North. The Hispanics were only the most recent of the plagues, less welcome perhaps because they were even more foreign, but also because, unlike the Northern refugees, they brought to the local economy very little money of their own.

And somewhere in it all, the quiet, rural town had gotten lost—caught up beyond its own volition, and incorporated as an inconsequential part of some enormously larger American conglomerate—a world of plural and conflicting values, maybe not even man-sized anymore.

An inescapable casualty of the twenty-first century? Doll had no better answer than to wonder. The only sense he felt sure of was the one of vacuum, the absence of a quality, on the level of community, that might be likened to what, in a man, was called a soul.

19

By eight o'clock the following morning, the new day was already steamy. Ann Raney sat beside Doll in Diana's red Camaro, which Ann had insisted they take for the air. A folded newspaper with Clayton Rivers's picture lay faceup on the seat by her side. The by-line below the headline belonged to Harvey Archer.

As Doll drove, Ann checked her face in a mirror she'd found in her handbag. She was primly dressed, he noticed—very much the proper younger sister again. She wore a pair of white-strapped sandals and a modest sundress with a hem that fell decorously below her knees. Her brown hair was brushed and her makeup minimal.

"Life's hard on the dreamers, isn't it?" she said, looking not at Doll, but distantly out through the window at the countryside. "The greedy do better—unless they're unlucky enough to get caught. The ones who get hurt the rest of the time are the Dianas and the Perry Wellmans of the world. They gamble on their dreams without ever understanding how much the odds are stacked against them."

"There's never any shortage of dreams that don't get answered," Doll replied. "One of the brighter spots in human nature is that, despite the disappointments, one way or another, most people manage to muddle through."

"Do you dream, Doll? What about?" Ann asked.

"I dream about being greedy," Doll said. The answer was deliberately glib and intended to be a conversation stopper. The topic of Doll's dreams was one he set off limits, a lot of times even to himself.

Did he even have dreams, in the sense of things that he wanted? He sometimes asked himself that. When he did, the answer that usually came back to him was that he had more memories than dreams. His life seemed to him to be a rambling series of episodes. The episodes were different—some better, some worse. He wondered what he ought to dream for. Longer episodes? Some continuity? Something outside himself? Someone to share things with—a wife?—that might be nice. Hardly grand dreams, he thought. Dreams so small, in fact, that they hardly deserved the name at all. And yet, for Doll, somehow, even for their smallness, they proved so incredibly elusive.

Ann took the hint. The next few miles drifted past in silence. When she spoke again, her voice seemed to Doll to carry the tone of a complaint.

"Do you want to tell me how this whole thing is supposed to work this morning?" she asked.

"I don't know what the 'whole thing' is," Doll answered. He glanced across the car at Ann, but nothing he saw there gave him any clue.

"Why is it," Ann said, shaking her head, "that I have absolutely no trouble believing you? You've got to have the world's worst social sense. I'm talking about Diana, Doll. I mean, you do see the opportunity for a certain amount of clumsiness in all of this? Do we all stand around in a group and make small talk? Do we touch? Do we cry? Do we do it one at a time, in pairs, or all together?"

"I never thought about it," Doll answered truthfully. "I just figured it would all somehow work itself out."

"Well, it won't," Ann declared. "Not without a lot of foot shuffling and big empty spaces in between the talk. Look, I told you once before that you and Diana have things that you've got to say to each other alone. So do I—have things I need to say to her—without you being around to hear them. That's real. I mean it, Doll. I'm not talking just to make noise or sound smart."

"How do you want to do it?" Doll asked.

"The easiest way that there is," Ann Raney replied. "And all out in the open—which means we tell Diana what's happening up front. We make small talk on the way back in the car. Then you drop me at the cottage, and the two of you go for a walk on the beach or wherever you like. She and I can talk when you bring her back. I think that's the cleanest way to handle it."

Doll nodded his head to say that he agreed. Ann nodded back, and Doll was glad to have it done—except he sensed something undefined in her manner that tacitly kept on insisting there was more.

"Go ahead," he said. "Let's have the rest of it."

Still Ann hesitated. "All right," she said finally. "Maybe I don't have any right to ask this since it's part of what you're going to be saying to her, but are you going to tell Diana I came on to you?"

"Nothing happened." Doll shook his head and kept his eyes on the road. "Unless you want to tell me something did, there isn't anything for me to say to her."

"And Kendall?"

"Kendall?" Doll held the hand that he wasn't using to steer above his own head, up near the ceiling of the car. The implication of height as Kendall's outstanding characteristic was enough to cause Ann to laugh.

"Kendall," she said, smiling as she nodded. "You blow smoke in his one ear, and it comes out of the other. He called me back. I told him I'd patched things up with my husband. I don't think he's going to be calling again."

"It's a good man," Doll remarked lightly, "who knows enough to respect the sanctity of the home." But for all of the banter, he realized, Ann Raney's question—to her mind at least—still very much needed an answer.

"That's your business, Ann. What you want to tell Diana about Kendall or anybody else is up to you. It's not for me to get in the middle."

"Yuh. I had to ask, but I guess, somewhere inside, I knew you were going to say that." Leaning over from the passenger seat, Ann kissed Doll chastely on the cheek.

"I guess green suits me as a color," she said. "I was always more than a little jealous of Diana. She had the looks when I was just beginning to understand what it meant to have looks. She had, by far, the better name. And then she lucked out again when she came up with you. The only thing I don't understand is how she let herself lose you, Doll. But then, she really didn't, did she? I mean, you're here now, aren't you? You never got really totally lost."

Diana walked barefoot through the sand along the beach. She'd rolled the legs of her jeans up to her calves and tied the laces of her tennis shoes together to let her carry them over her shoulder. The sea, when it surged in, licked at her feet. Every few steps she made a low kick at the water or threw a small clump of sand with her instep. For a long time, she simply kept silent.

Doll held to a slightly higher and drier line, walking beside her only a few feet away.

"This is delicious," she said when she chose to talk, just loudly enough so that Doll was able to hear her over the tumbling, murmuring surf. "Inside there, in that awful place, you try to fool yourself. You even get good at it after a while. You convince yourself that being able to be out here—just to walk like this—doesn't matter. Because, if you let yourself believe that it mattered, being locked inside those obscene walls would drive you crazy.

"Oh, but it does matter. Oh, God, Doll, it does." Diana Raney hugged herself, closed her eyes, and held her face straight up toward the sun.

She stood like that long enough for the mood of that moment to absorb her and then went back to her walking.

"What can I say?" she continued. "There isn't anything I can say. I'd have to be a fool even to try. I lied to you. I swore at you. I said terrible things, and I sent you away. There aren't any words I could use that would even start to apologize for all of that."

"And maybe," Doll said, "you don't owe any apologies or explanations or anything to me or to anybody else. Maybe to yourself—that's the only exception I'd make. Whatever you owed, you paid off a long time back. Forget the fact that you never belonged inside there. You took it and you handled it and you made yourself adjust. You don't owe any apologies to anybody. You toughed it out, and you did whatever was needed to do to make yourself get by."

"And I'd still be there, Doll, if it wasn't for you."

"For today, maybe. Not tomorrow or the next day." Doll glanced toward Diana, who still let her gaze trace a path just ahead of her feet in the sand. "Nobody can keep secrets forever. The whole scheme and all Dabney's suspicions about it would have worked themselves out—if not before the trial, then at least in the course of it. With a little time, Willard Giesler would've made it all make sense."

"You can't know that. No one can," Diana said.

"I can," Doll replied and smiled to give the assertion conviction. "I'm a realist, Diana. Think back, and you'll know that I always was."

"I think you like to pretend you are," Diana answered. "I hate to disappoint you, Doll, but I don't remember you as being superrealistic. I've gone through a stack of memories these past weeks. I had a lot of time to think. I remembered especially the night we met at Vicarias's party. It was all set up for us. We had it all in front of us that night. We had it all in front of us for a year after that, and then it all came apart and we lost it."

Diana brushed back her hair from her face and tried, unsuccessfully, to keep Doll from seeing her brush the tear in her eye aside with her knuckle.

"I know it was my fault," she said with a sigh of capitulation. "I wanted to lock you down, and you weren't ready. My fault. If I'd had more patience or maybe better stars . . . Or maybe it was just something that was never meant to be."

"I don't know anything about stars or psychology," Doll replied. "I know there are sometimes people who don't give themselves a chance."

"Low expectations." Diana laughed weakly. "Yeah, I've heard that before, too. I've even said it to myself. It's a variation on, 'What's a nice girl like you . . . ?' 'How'd you wind up being shacked up with a bum?' The problem is the answer's reinforcing."

"Then change the question," Doll suggested.

"Just like that? I wonder," Diana said, feeling out the unfamiliar possibility. "I could do that, couldn't I? At least I could try." She looked out at the blue green ocean. "I could make a lot of changes. I'm clean. A month in the cage is great for that. Sean's out of my life—and everybody else's too."

Diana glanced across at Doll and, for the first time, really met his eyes. Her own, to his mild surprise, were mischievous, and suddenly, all at once as though out of nowhere, she laughed.

"Oh, Doll, I'll tell you this," she said, grinning. "It's going to be a long time before anything else seems like trouble anymore.

"Maybe you're right, Doll. Maybe it's time—past time—that I gave up chasing life. So I'll never be twenty-one again. Maybe thirty-two's not the worst of times to try to make a new start."

"It's one year better than thirty-three," Doll replied. He

smiled back at her, then let the smile fade. He had to make the break again, just as he'd made it a dozen years before. What he couldn't explain to himself was why, instead of getting easier, it seemed to get harder.

"You know I won't be staying around," he tried to begin. "I'll be leaving for home tomorrow in the morning. I'll be back again. If not before, at least for the trials on Bandalos's murder. I'll find you then—whether you want to see me or not—for long enough, anyway, to find out how you're doing."

Doll meant it while he said it—not questioning what the vantage of another month might bring.

"Will you?" Still walking, Diana came toward Doll and took his hand. "This isn't an opening. I promise you. I'm not raising any expectations. It's just a way of saying that I'll be looking forward to seeing you when—and if—you do."

Diana stopped and turned to Doll. Gazing up at him, she smiled again.

"See, aren't you proud of me?" she said. "I've started getting better at the patience part already."

It was midafternoon when Doll got back to his motel. Despite the fact that his breakfast that morning had been only orange juice and coffee, he still had no desire for anything substantial enough to be regarded as a lunch. He ordered an iced coffee from the waiter.

The sundeck along the side of the pool showed the effects of the off-season doldrums. Of the two dozen tables with their vibrantly colored umbrellas, only five were occupied—and one of those Doll had to himself. From where he sat, he had an unobstructed view of the beach and the ocean beyond. In the shade of the umbrella, the warm breeze off the water felt cool. The waiter returned almost at once with the coffee along with a thumbnail-sized container of cream.

There were times for Doll when the ocean seemed near to setting its own scale for man. Its immensity in size and age and all the life the sea had held in its time could make the flaws and evils, the hopes and agonies, and even the deaths of individual people seem small. And yet, Doll sensed the trap in that—the inherent falseness in the disembodiment of life. Abstraction could be comforting, even an effective means of dulling pain. It only required that a more complex understanding and maybe a little empathy be sacrificed as a part of the bargain.

The Florida Strait was emerald green on that mid-June day. A brilliant sun flashed and glinted off the mirror-bright curves of the low-cresting waves. Torpid breakers rolled over themselves and collapsed into foam as they made their run against the shore. At sea, out in the middle space between the beach and the horizon, fishing boats and sailboats rose and gracefully fell away in rhythm with the gentle swell.

Doll remembered Diana Raney from the morning as she'd stood with her eyes closed, her face turned blindly toward the sun. It was, like any other day, a very good day to be free. He raised the glass of coffee to his lips and wished her well.